Amber Waves

of

Grain

Ron Vergona

Published by:

Coeur d'Alene, Idaho

To my wife Addie, and children Jessica and Michael, for their love and support.

In memory of Robert Rathke
(1935 to 2017)

~First in, last out~

"All men are created equal, then a few
become firemen."
(unknown)

Oh, beautiful for spacious skies,
For amber waves of grain,
For purple mountain majesties
Above the fruited plain!
America! America!
God shed his grace on thee,
And crown thy good with brotherhood
From sea to shining sea

from *"America the Beautiful"*
(lyrics by Katharine Lee Bates)

Amber Waves of Grain

CHAPTER 1

Yuba City, California
September 2
9:15 pm

The man slammed the car door and pressed the button on the key fob. In the cool night air, the locking solenoids sounded like the chambering of his 9mm Sig. This made him smile as he took several steps down the rocky embankment and tossed the key into the river. Pulling off the latex gloves, he let them fall into the slow-moving currents. With the help of the full moon's glow reflecting off the surface, he watched them float away.

He no longer needed the white Ford Taurus; the fourth vehicle abandoned in the three days since he'd entered the country. Each car had been waiting in a prearranged location, starting at his point of entry at Dallas/Fort Worth Airport and leading him here to the Sacramento Valley in California. Getting through passport control and customs had felt like child's play, but that didn't mean he should leave an obvious trail.

His training taught him to stay composed under stressful situations, and after completing the convoluted route from Yemen, his forged identity as an Egyptian businessman, educated in America, remained intact. Still, with every boarding and disembarking, he expected someone to discover his true identity. He knew the American authorities had him on their watch list since escaping the country almost three years ago.

After one final gaze at the river, he turned away and walked across the clearing toward the same dirt path he'd driven while negotiating the narrow trail along the western levee. He recalled that when he'd fled the United States, the climate of political correctness and American self-hate were on the upswing. Now the federal courts had joined in on the lunacy, making his current plans easier to accomplish.

As he strode past the car, he entertained a fleeting thought about pressing his ungloved hand on the hood. Perhaps the incompetent fools working for the DHS or the FBI could use a little help.

Changing his mind, he buried his arrogance and muttered, "Screw 'em. If they can't figure out that I'm back in town after my next move…."

He wondered how they'd deal with the aftermath. Although part of a larger mission, it mattered little to him how they portrayed this next incident. His opening scene was always going to be personal.

Having spent most of his life in California, being sequestered at the training camps in Yemen for the last several years did little to change his speech patterns. Many of his fellow jihadists had distrusted his intimate grasp of the English language and American culture. But now at last he would begin to shed those infidel masks and emerge as a true follower in these final stages of the greatest of all jihads.

He'd made another stop earlier this evening where he'd tampered with the sophisticated security system and deactivated the surveillance cameras. The two large duffel bags he placed inside the enclosed grounds were hidden away from the main entrance and any prying eyes.

He climbed back up and over the levee. The moon provided ample light, allowing him to take a shortcut through the neighboring peach orchards. The cloying scents did nothing to soften his resolve. When he reached the desired street, he stopped and listened. The night was quiet except for sporadic echoes of dogs barking in the distance. He turned onto the gravel road and headed west. While he walked, the barking got louder; then faded as he approached his destination.

Before taking the final steps up the front walkway, he paused to let his eyes drink in the tranquil scene. Everything looked like he'd expected from the photos. The metallic blue Chevy Tahoe sat under the carport. Lights glowed in several windows in the front and the right side of the small, aging bungalow. He approached the front porch and listened to the TV sounds bleeding through the large picture window. With the drapes drawn, he couldn't get any glimpses of the occupants. That would soon change.

He stomped across the squeaky boards on the sagging porch before rapping his hand against the frosted glass on the door. Several moments later, the volume on the TV lowered and the porch light blinked on. When the door inched open, he watched the blood drain from the face of Faizan Ta'anari. Lingering aromas from an earlier supper escaped from inside the house and etched at the man's concentration. It caused a slight shimmer in his gut as he recalled moments of a former life. He shook off the near-forgotten memory and stared back at the older man he faced through the narrow opening. Although his features had been altered by doctors at one of the training camps, there was no question that Faizan Ta'anari recognized the man standing on his front porch—and the hate oozing from the man's dark, hooded eyes.

Faizan hesitated. Just when the man expected the door to slam in his face, Faizan blinked and took a step back while allowing the door to swing all the way open. Without speaking, he motioned for the man to enter and twisted around in a manner that appeared to drain every ounce of strength from his body. He trudged into the living room, running callused fingers through his once thick and black, but now thinned and graying, hair.

"Safura," Faizan said to his wife in a voice devoid of any emotion. "We have a guest. Go. Make us some tea."

With a furtive glance at the unexpected visitor, Safura lowered her head and disappeared into the kitchen.

The man ignored Safura.

He stared at the half-empty Coors bottle on the glass-topped coffee table. He gazed at the flashing images of a baseball game on the sixty-inch flat screen monitor on the wall above the brick fireplace. Unable to hide his scorn, he narrowed his eyes at Faizan. His hand swept across the coffee table, grabbed the Coors, and flung it. The bottle bounced off the TV, leaving rainbow-patterned lines on the ruined screen. It disintegrated after crashing against the slate hearth and spread a yeasty trail that dripped onto the carpet.

Angered even more, he grasped a heavy bronze lamp from a nearby side table. Holding it in both hands, he lifted it above his shoulders and smashed it onto the coffee table while spitting out an animalistic grunt. The glass top shattered with a deafening boom.

Safura crept back into the living room and stood next to Faizan, her sad eyes gaping at their visitor.

From outside and down the road, the distant barking the man had heard when he approached the house intensified. The front door shook from something banging against it. The incessant barking rattled the living room window. He heard a muffled voice, followed by silence.

And then the doorbell rang.

The man reached under his jacket and pulled out the Sig. He grabbed the back of Faizan's collar and pressed the 9mm handgun against his temple while pushing him into the short wall separating them from the tiny foyer.

To Safura, he whispered, "Tell them to go away. Or you'll all die." He sneered and slowly nodded. "And I'm sure you know I'd have no particular problem making that happen."

Safura stared at her husband, but his face stayed glued to the wall; his eyes diverted from her. After a final glance at the man, Safura lowered her head and receded into the foyer. She slipped the safety chain into position and inched open the door until the chrome links snapped tight.

CHAPTER 2

With the porch light blazing, Safura stared into the face of her nearest neighbor and one of the neighbor's dogs—an angry-looking black and tan German Shepherd. At the moment, the dog was sitting on its haunches next to the young woman. She held one hand through its collar while trying to clip on a heavy leather leash.

"Penelope?" Safura said. "What are you doing out so late?"

After checking that Reckless was still behaving, Penelope smiled back at Safura and swept strands of sandy blond hair from her eyes. "Everything okay, Mrs. Ta'anari?"

Safura faltered and said, "Well, of course, dear. Why?"

"Something spooked Reckless. I was heading out to the kennel to check on Ellie's new puppies when... I guess I didn't close the gate right and Reckless bolted. Then the rest of the dogs in the kennel went a little crazy." She took a breath and continued, "I'm so sorry Reckless jumped on your front door. He usually listens when I call him. Like I said, something's got him all riled up tonight."

Safura nodded. "That's okay. Reckless has good ears. He must've heard the coffee table's glass top break when I dropped a serving tray on it."

"Oh, would you like any help?"

Opening her mouth wide, Safura said, "No—no. Faizan's got it almost all cleaned up. He just ran for the vacuum to get the last bits of glass from the carpet. But thank you." About to close the door, she added, "Is Calvin home?"

Penelope's eyes narrowed, but she shook her head and said, "Nope, he's on duty tonight."

"Well, you be careful out there."

"No worries, Mrs. Ta'anari. Reckless is always close at hand. Good night."

As she turned to leave, she had to tug extra hard to get Reckless to stop growling at the bungalow. Penelope struggled to get the agitated dog down the Ta'anari's driveway and onto the gravel road back toward her house. After reaching her side yard, she headed straight to the outside kennels and pushed Reckless into the last run. He rammed against the gate and barked in protest, but Penelope ignored him. She started to head back toward the Ta'anari house. This time she stayed away from the road and worked her way up to the out-of-control jasmine hedges separating her property from the Ta'anari house. Squeezing through a sparse section of foliage, she pulled back the last leafy branch, ignoring the star-like radiance of the night-blooming petals. She crouched in the shadows and stared at her neighbor's house. The glow from the porch light still outlined the faded seafoam green wood siding.

The calming fragrances from the jasmine did little to erase the concern she'd felt when speaking to Safura. She had instantly presumed something was off.

The woman's behavior had puzzled her from the moment she'd opened the door without undoing the security chain. She appeared more stilted than usual. Penelope had almost challenged Safura's words regarding the broken table and the fact her husband was busy cleaning it up. Faizan Ta'anari would *never* perform this task—such a labor was only fitting for his wife. While the Ta'anari family had emigrated to this country many years ago and had adopted part of the American culture, Faizan would *never* elevate his wife's status by helping with such a menial chore.

But it was Safura's question about Calvin that had all but stopped Penelope in her tracks.

She recalled glancing at her husband through the kitchen window earlier in the evening while placing the dirty dinner dishes in the sink. Dressed in his sheriff's uniform, Cal had slid behind the wheel of his Dodge Ram pick-up and pulled onto the gravel road. She saw him stop for a brief chat with Mrs. Ta'anari by the mailboxes near the intersection with the county road. Every day about that same time, Safura Ta'anari hiked the several hundred yards from her house to retrieve the mail. Never once did Penelope ever see Mr. Ta'anari perform a task like that.

Since Safura had already known Cal had gone to work: *Why ask the question?*

Penelope heard loud voices coming from inside the house but couldn't make out any words. As she rose to sneak closer, the front door flew open. Faizan Ta'anari stumbled onto the porch and down the steps. He headed toward the carport. Safura followed. And then a third person appeared in the doorway, one hand hidden under the open front flap of his jacket. The Ta'anaris climbed into the front seats of their Tahoe. Penelope couldn't believe her eyes when she saw Safura get behind the wheel of the SUV. She had never seen the woman drive and assumed Safura didn't even have a driver's license.

Before Safura closed her door, the man strode to the Tahoe and barked orders. "Take us to the Islamic Center." He jumped into the rear seat, sliding over and positioning himself behind Faizan.

Safura pleaded, "Jalal—please—Jalal—why are you doing this?"

Jalal's arm stretched forward. From the soft glow of the porch light seeping into the interior of the SUV, Penelope saw a glossy reflection from the weapon held in his hand and jammed into the back of Faizan's head. Safura's door slammed shut and the Tahoe's engine rumbled to life. The SUV lurched forward and abruptly braked, but not before launching three galvanized steel trash cans through the back of the carport and scattering smelly garbage across the brick patio. This smothered any reminders of the calming jasmine perfume. The sharp echoes from the rolling cans faded as the Tahoe's back-up lights blinked on. In a more tentative measure, Safura guided the vehicle out of the carport. After several jerky attempts, she got the Tahoe turned around. The headlights belatedly flashed on, and Penelope dove for cover as the SUV inched down the driveway and spun onto the gravel lane. The heavy vehicle bucked its way to the county road, turning left and disappearing around the next bend.

Penelope ran down the driveway, back toward her house.

She reached for her cell phone, mumbling, "I'm damn sure that woman doesn't have a valid driver's license—unless the California DMV has eased up on the driving test."

CHAPTER 3

Ten minutes later, the Tahoe pulled up to the main gate at the Islamic Center of Yuba City. The fenced-in grounds presented a sharp contrast to the surrounding orchards. Viewed from the road, the wrought-iron entry gate at the end of a short bridge hinted at the seriousness with which the local Muslims regarded security. On the mosque's side of the deep moat-like drainage ditch that paralleled the county road, clear—almost invisible—bullet-resistant polycarbonate fence panels discouraged any accidental firearm discharges from interrupting prayer ceremonies. The compound's side and rear walls were of a more traditional design, with the meshed-steel fabric and barbed wire crown softened by dense stands of tall palm trees.

Jalal recited the access code. With a shaking hand Safura punched in the numbers. On the third try she got the sequence entered in the correct order and the wrought-iron gate slid sideways from the entrance lane, leaving no audible sounds as it glided over well-lubricated tracks. The late evening dew filled the SUV's interior with a hint of fruity aromas from the bountiful trees hugging the perimeter of the Islamic Center. When Jalal had earlier tampered with the mosque's security system, he left the locked gate intact. No sense making it easy for anyone else to join in on this evening's private session.

They'd driven about ten feet inside the grounds when he shouted to Safura, "Stop!"

The SUV jolted to a halt. He looked over his shoulder and watched the gate roll back across the driveway. He pointed to the stashed duffels behind the ornamental rock garden bordering the main parking area. "Get out. Grab those bags and throw them back here on the seat."

It took Safura two trips to drag the heavy duffels to the Tahoe. Jalal offered no assistance, and the handgun remained pressed against Faizan's temple.

He smirked. "If you think you can handle it without crashing into the building, I want you to park close to the mosque's front entrance."

After unlocking the ornate door, he ordered Faizan to help Safura carry the duffels. Once inside the musalla, or prayer hall, he located the lighting panel and adjusted the level to a faint glow, exposing a hint of the bright murals and the intricate patterns of the scattered rugs. He told Faizan and Safura to unzip the bags and empty out the contents in the center of the room.

Pointing to a fiberglass ladder inside an alcove near the left rear corner, Jalal motioned for Faizan to grab it and position it under one of the large ceiling fans hanging from the crossbeams. He then instructed Faizan to fasten one of the steel cables taken from the duffel bags to the fan blade and told him how to adjust the length. He had him repeat the procedure at an adjacent ceiling fan.

As directed, Safura pulled out two folding chairs from a side storage closet off the main chamber and placed them under each of the fans. Urged on by sharp commands, she secured sets of metal cuffs onto Faizan's wrists and ankles.

Jalal bellowed for Faizan to stand on the first chair and extend his arms above his head. He prodded Safura to climb the ladder and attach the clamp on the dangling end of the cable to the center links of the cuffs. With Jalal's rough assistance, Safura was soon in the same position underneath the adjacent ceiling fan: standing on a chair, her outstretched arms cuffed and fastened to the end of the second cable.

A small smile spread across Jalal's face as he stepped forward and wrenched the chair from beneath Faizan; he did the same to Safura. While he could see the fear and hate radiating from Faizan's eyes, he knew the man would never beg for mercy. Any emotion coming from Safura would only be scorned.

"Can you predict your fate?" Jalal asked while rummaging through the scattered contents from the duffels and assembling stacks of flammable articles under both figures hanging from the ceiling fans. He kept himself from getting close enough to allow Faizan to kick at his head. He had no concern that Safura would attempt such a desperate stunt.

As Jalal walked toward the electrical panel, he spoke over his shoulder, "It's a pity I can't stay to watch you die. But I'm comforted knowing neither of you will ascend to paradise. Although the consequences of your deaths could alter the definition of martyrdom."

He found the fan control switches and set them to their lowest speeds. For several seconds he gazed at the slowly rotating bodies dangling from the wide blades and the growing looks of horror on the perspiring faces of Faizan and Safura. Satisfied, he headed back to the remaining objects from the duffels strewn across the floor of the musalla. He glanced at his watch and picked up two electronic devices. After entering a series of numbers on each, he pressed the recessed red buttons. Both timers began to beep at one-second intervals, and he tucked one under each of the constructed incendiary piles.

With a last glare at Faizan and Safura, he said, "How much time do you think is left? I've given myself a few minutes lead. I won't get to witness the glow from the ignition, but there's no doubt you'll be heading on personal journeys to Hell."

Before turning, Jalal sneered at Faizan and spit out the words, "*Father*—did you know Patas is very much alive? They gave her a new name. I think it's time I pay her a little visit."

Safura screamed as her body contorted, trying to maintain eye contact with her son. Rage and sadness built from years of silence and honed from centuries of female oppression at last spewed from her lips. "Jalal! You bastard! She is your sister! Have you learned nothing from living in America? You still carry all that hatred in your heart. May Allah himself send you to Hell."

Her voice lowered but sounded stronger. "Jalal, Patas may be the only one who can save Islam—if not, we are all doomed. The paradise you and the other jihadists speak of is false."

As usual, Jalal dismissed his mother's words. Nothing of her venom registered in his brain. He gave his father a faint smile. "Patas is only another small part of my mission, but she still needs to be stopped before her betrayal poisons our holy war."

Faizan gritted his teeth and said, "Finish the job you failed to do three years ago—Patas is no longer my daughter."

As Jalal Ta'anari strode across the prayer hall and out the door, Safura's anguish filled the dimly lit musalla with a chilling portent of things to come. Not that Jalal would give it a second thought.

Chapter 4

Route 70
Sutter County, California
September 2
11:00 pm

With a fixed smile swathed across his lips, Sergeant Calvin Worthington ambled back to the patrol car after delivering a stern warning to two teenagers about parking near the shoulder of a busy state highway. His admonition had taken longer than normal since he'd waited for the couple to scramble back into their discarded clothes.

He settled behind the wheel and watched the kids in the old Ford Taurus drive away, probably looking for another place to park. As he clicked off the emergency flashers and killed the spotlight, his personal cell phone rang with the familiar chorus of barking dogs. Taking the call, he said, "Hi Penny, what's up?" In the background he heard a more realistic execution of the specified ringtone for his wife. A number of angry-sounding German Shepherds resonated through the phone's tiny speaker as Penelope's frantic voice kicked into high gear. He picked out a few key words but had trouble keeping up as her panic soared.

When she paused to take a breath, he jumped in. "Slow down, Penny. All I got was that the Ta'anaris had a visitor and they drove away in their SUV, presumably heading to the Islamic Center." He stopped talking, but still missed her next words. "What's that?" He waited for his wife to restate her last diatribe. "Well, if I repeated what you just said about a woman driver—"

He strained to listen as the pace of Penelope's rant slowed, but the background crooning barks persisted. He straightened up in the seat as one particular word hit home. "*Jalal?* You're sure Mrs. Ta'anari said *Jalal?*" He fumbled for his electronic tablet and opened up the dossier for the Ta'anari family. Scrolling through several pages, he nodded. "Got it. You're right. Jalal's the name of their son. He was last spotted just prior to the attempted assassination of Governor Blackwell in Sacramento on Halloween night. About three years ago. Then he disappeared off the face of the earth. His trail ended in Pakistan. Since then, he's been on the no-fly list. If he attempts to go anywhere near an airport he'd be picked up and held for DHS." He paused and listened. "But Penny, I don't see how Jalal could've gotten back in the country. Even after three years, the system should still have him flagged as a threat to national security—"

Penelope continued talking, and this time Calvin interrupted. "Thanks for filling me in, honey. But what the hell were you doing sneaking around their house this late at night? Okay... Okay... Of course, I know my job. My weekly report is scheduled to go out tomorrow, but I think this incident warrants an immediate phone call."

Penelope's voice sounded more relaxed, and the dogs had stopped barking; likely sensing she had calmed down. "I always take you seriously. I'm going to give the feds a heads-up." He scrolled down several more pages and stopped. "Here it is. There are two names. What? Yeah… one's a female." He shrugged. "Sure. Why not? I'm not sexist."

Calvin's finger moved to end the call when Penelope said, "Oh! Wait a second, Cal. I just thought of something else."

He settled back in his seat, trying to hide a sigh. "What's that?"

"You remember that I've got a meeting early tomorrow morning with the German Shepherd breeder from Sonoma County? Steve Casella?"

Calvin checked his watch and let out a breath. "And?"

"I read his bio again. And guess what?" She didn't give him a chance to respond. "He's not only a firefighter and a K9 handler, but he's also a consultant with the federal government. And that reminded me of the stories I read about him and his wife. A few years back, they were involved with—"

Calvin shook his head, cutting her off before she ratcheted up to a higher level. "Honey, that's not unusual for local first responders. Don't start on one of your conspiracy theories again. He undoubtedly works in a similar capacity to what I've been involved with for almost three years. Eyes and ears on individuals placed on a watch list. Speaking of which—let me do my job. I gotta go."

He glanced toward the passenger seat, and his eyes stopped on a paperback book. He'd plucked it off the coffee table a couple nights ago. Penny had been pestering him to read the political conspiracy novel for weeks. He certainly wasn't about to steer the conversation in that direction. It was written under a pen name, but Penny had told Cal that the author's real name was Steve Casella.

Penelope sounded a bit put off when she said, "Thought you didn't believe in coincidences."

"Goodnight, Penny. I love you."

"Love ya right back."

Calvin smiled, tucking the cell phone back in his pocket. He leaned over and placed his tablet on top of Casella's book. As he grabbed his department-issued phone off the center console, he felt a trickle of sweat snake its way down his back.

CHAPTER 5

Sergeant Worthington punched in the number for Agent Olivia Davenport and hit the hands-free button on the steering wheel. He swung the patrol car back on the highway. After the device rang for an extended period, a male voice in a clipped tone popped from the speaker. "Agent Davenport's line, who's calling?"

Worthington hesitated and said, "Agent *Olivia* Davenport?"

"This is Agent Mike Finley. Agent Davenport is… unavailable at the moment. Could you please identify yourself and state the reason for this call?"

Worthington recalled Mike Finley's name as the second contact person on the Ta'anari case. "Yes, Agent Finley. My name is Sergeant Calvin Worthington from the Sutter County sheriff's department in northern California. I have an additional assignment relating to the homeland security watch list. And I'm calling in regard to—"

"Sergeant. Before you go any further, let's do this according to the book. Give me a second while I open up your file."

After Finley asked a series of questions to verify Worthington's information, he said, "Sorry about that

Sergeant Worthington. Looks like you're responsible for keeping an eye on Faizan and Safura Ta'anari. Is that correct, son?"

Son? Worthington thought. *Who the hell does—?* "Yes, Agent Finley. The Ta'anaris are our neighbors, and I've been observing them since they moved next door approximately two and a half years ago."

"Right. I've got the history up on my screen now… looks like they've been well-behaved: nothing out of the ordinary in any of your previous reports. I see your next report is due tomorrow. What seems to be the problem?" Finley yawned loudly into the phone.

Worthington rubbed a hand across his face and wondered if he'd jumped the gun. "Out of curiosity, Agent Finley, where exactly am I calling?"

"That's classified, son." He laughed and added, "Just kidding. I'm outside sitting on my deck in Key West, looking out at the eastern sky, where in a few short hours the sun will be peeking up over these beautiful waters. I had planned on an early fishing trip, but…."

"Sorry, sir, maybe this could've waited—"

"Nonsense, Worthington. Let's get to it. Tell me what's going on."

For the next several minutes, Worthington outlined the events at the Ta'anari house as relayed to him by his wife. Finley appeared bored through most of the descriptions until the name, *Jalal,* was mentioned. At that point, Worthington thought he detected a subtle shift in Finley's voice, but otherwise no other indications his report corresponded to any immediate threat to national security.

Worthington had been cruising in random patterns near the northwestern border of the county during his conversation with Finley. When he glanced out the side window, he was surprised to find himself approaching a street sign that read *Tierra Buena Road*. Without thinking, he edged his foot onto the brake pedal and turned south, in the direction of the Islamic Center of Yuba City.

He shifted his attention back to what Finley was saying. "Thanks again, Worthington. I'll be sure to pass this information on to Washington."

Worthington thought Finley's voice sounded more anxious. He let his mind wander to Penelope's chiding about coincidences as his eye caught part of Casella's paperback sticking out from underneath his tablet. He blurted out, "Ever hear the name *Steve Casella*?"

After a long silence, Worthington picked up his phone from the center console and checked the screen to see if the call had disconnected. Then he heard what sounded like a faint laugh, followed by a short litany of epithets.

"Ahh… why are you asking about Casella?"

Chapter 6

While reassuring Agent Finley he'd limit his involvement to finishing up the paperwork for his next report and leave the follow up on this incident to the feds, Sergeant Worthington drove his patrol car past the Islamic Center of Yuba City. After cruising about a half mile, he shook his head and made a U-turn at the next intersection. As he approached the mosque a second time, he slowed the car and lowered the driver's side window. Staring across the fenced-in grounds, he strained to get a look at the parking lot. From this vantage point it appeared empty.

He still tried to tell himself he'd done his job—and the feds would look into it. More to the point, Finley had emphasized that once he completed his report, he should forget about the name Jalal Ta'anari.

Good job. The federal government will now take over.

Instead, he reached down to flip the switch and started to swing his spotlight around. He stared through the open window.

At first, he wasn't sure what he heard. His head twitched about, thinking a car had backfired. When he looked back toward the front of the mosque, he saw a faint reddish-orange glow flickering through the arched windows.

The next sounds to pierce his eardrums could never be confused with anything but what they were—screams—agonizing screams—human screams.

As he finished calling it in to dispatch, he backed the patrol car away from the entrance drive and turned toward the gate. He jammed his foot down on the accelerator. The car picked up speed—aimed straight at the wrought-iron obstruction. He prayed he'd have enough momentum. At the last second before impact, he swung the wheel hard and the front fender caught the gate at an angle. The sounds of crumbling plastic and shrieking metal got lost when the airbag exploded in Worthington's face. Snapping back in his seat, he batted away the deflated bag and spit out the already dissipating acrid aroma which now clung to his uniform. As he unbuckled his harness, he let out a quick grunt and then ignored the stinging sensations tingling through his upper torso. The door to the patrol car opened with a scrunching noise and he stumbled toward the gate.

The force of the impact had pushed the sliding gate to the side; but not by much. Worthington twisted his body, barely squeezing through the narrow opening. After tumbling to the ground, he dug in and launched himself toward the front of the mosque. The failure of the flames glowing from inside the building to grow stronger puzzled him. He drew nearer, but except for trails of smoke seeping through small crevices around the entrance, the fire looked even less threatening. The cries emanating from inside the mosque had stopped, and that gave him a sinking feeling in his gut.

CHAPTER 7

Oroville, California
September 2
(earlier in the day)

Steve Casella pulled his old Itasca recreational vehicle into the Feather Falls RV Resort in Oroville, California. He whistled to himself as he finished leveling the rig, unhitching the Ford Explorer from the rear of the Itasca, and connecting the RV's utility lines.

His five-year-old daughter, Rosa, had been hands-on for most of the work until it came to attaching the sewer hose, when she decided to *'help Mom'* with her younger brother, T.C. In a bevy of rapid footsteps, she disappeared inside the RV with her thumb and index finger still clinging tight to her nose.

As Steve finished the remaining tasks alone, he glanced at Amber, who was resting under the redwood picnic table staring at the six-foot lead fastened to her collar with no one holding the other end. Steve liked to follow the park's rules, but only to a certain degree.

"I love it when my man's all sweaty and gets his hands dirty."

Still hunched on his knees, head partway under the side of the RV, Steve dropped back and turned to see Edie leaning up against the vehicle with her arms folded. He kept his features neutral, but felt his heart skip a few beats as he glanced at the woman who had changed his life. She was now a few years older and wore her straight black hair a few inches shorter—along with an added hint of curls. Her smile still radiated with the same power that made it difficult for him to catch his breath. Below her crossed arms and pale pink crop top he caught a glimpse of exposed belly. The crisp white shorts accented her smooth, light mocha complexion. After a long, hot summer, divided between Sonoma, in the sunny microclimate north of San Francisco, and Coeur d'Alene, in the Idaho panhandle, Steve's Sicilian skin-tone had darkened to the point where it rivaled that of his wife.

"You don't look like a middle-aged housewife who's churned out a bunch of kids."

Edie's eyes narrowed. "I'm thirty-three, and," she said, holding up two fingers, "only Rosa and T.C."

He got up and took a step toward Edie, about to cup his hands to her face. She pulled out a soft plastic pouch of antibacterial wipes and tossed it to him.

"Nice try."

"More notable," he whispered while pulling out a wipe and scrubbing his hands, "I'm not sure your outfit embodies the best image for the next president of the United States."

She smiled. "I'm too young to be president. And check your ballot, Steve. I'm running for the US senate."

"You're not campaigning at the moment," Steve said. "Want to work on baby number three?"

"Mommy," Rosa called, rapping her small fist on the RV's window. "T.C. needs help on the potty."

Steve handed the wipes back to Edie. He watched her disappear around the front of the RV as Amber nudged her graying snout against his leg. When he looked down, he saw she held the end of the leash between her teeth.

"Good idea, girl. Let's go for a walk." He led the dog around to the RV door and pulled it open. "Come on, Rosa. Wanna join us?"

Rosa leapt through the door and grabbed the leash from Steve. He grasped her other hand, and they walked off in the direction of the playground.

Edie stood in the doorway holding T.C. against her hip. Steve's parting image made her smile. She hadn't seen him this relaxed in ages. She couldn't remember the last time they'd gotten away for a real vacation. Steve's job as hazmat coordinator for his department in San Francisco and his expanded consulting role with DHS had kept him busy and on edge. His usual outlet for letting off steam—writing political action novels—had taken a back seat. And Edie winning a seat in the California state legislature hadn't made their home life any easier.

More recently, when Justin Mahorney, the senior US senator from California, unexpectedly announced that he would not finish his term due to health concerns, President Tyler Griffin, with Steve's reluctant consent, talked Edie into entering the race.

Until last year, the California governor filled any senate vacancies by direct appointment. Following rumors and innuendos surrounding the now deceased California Governor Nicholas Blackwell's abuse of power while in office, the state legislature passed a constitutional amendment requiring voters to select their new senator by a non-party primary and special election.

After a surprising performance, which gave her a narrow second-place victory in what's called the state's jungle primary, Edie Pauling had advanced to the special election. Due to the timing of the senator's departure, the special election would be held on the same day as this year's general election.

Edie still had reservations about her effectiveness as an elected official in congress. She'd spent most of her journalistic career fighting corrupt politicians and exposing government scandals. Several years ago, during President Tyler Griffin's first term, she'd worked in the White House as an advisor to the president. Although a key player in Griffin's inner circle, she always considered herself an outsider to the Washington establishment. Steve had asserted that she wore that as a badge of honor.

What would happen to my convictions when forced to play by the rules?

She'd seen the toll taken on Tyler Griffin and his family. She wondered if she had the stamina to fight for the kind of legislative changes advocated by the current president after he left office. He had only one year remaining in his second term. For the last seven years Griffin had garnered little congressional support, even from members of his own party.

The nation considered their government dysfunctional. Career politicians on both sides of the aisle gave no signs of acquiescing to the Restraint in Government Alliance—the grassroots voice of the people. Tyler Griffin had represented the core of this movement, but the Washington establishment only dug in deeper since his administration took over.

Without a surge in other RGA-supported candidates to oust the incumbent old timers at the ballot boxes, Edie feared she'd be drowning in a sea of self-absorbed, narcissistic, lifetime members of—

Calm yourself, Edie... calm yourself.

When she first announced her intentions to enter the national political scene, Steve had patted her on the backside and told her that after her victory in November, he'd pity the racist old white men in the senate when Senator Edie Pauling strutted her cute but fired-up black butt onto Capitol Hill.

These damn liberal firefighters could be downright sexist at times.

Edie still considered Steve a work in progress.

Well, I'm sure to lose the election anyway.

Edie's body shivered. She couldn't put her finger on it, but ever since getting into the public eye, she'd experienced feelings of unease. As if she or, far more worrisome, her family could be in danger.

She sighed and put all that aside. This could be the last getaway in the foreseeable future for the Casella family. She wanted to make sure Steve got the most out of their trip and could unwind before getting back to dealing with public safety and national security issues. This was the first stop on a short but leisurely drive through northern California. Tomorrow, they planned an early morning visit to a local German Shepherd breeder Steve was anxious to meet. After that quick detour, they'd be free to enjoy the remaining time before Edie's campaign appearance at a rally in Southern California, which coincided with the anniversary of 9/11.

* * * * * *

The remainder of the day and evening breezed by, and Steve felt the stress melt away from his tired body. After they'd wrestled the kids into the RV's bunkbeds and pulled the privacy curtain closed, he attempted to pick up from where he'd left off earlier in the day. Holding two glasses of wine, he stood next to the bed already occupied by two of his three favorite girls. The furry white one scooched to the bottom but refused to get off. Edie drained the offered wine in two smooth gulps, licked her lips in a provocative fashion, and placed the empty glass on the tiny shelf next to the bed.

Steve smiled. "Guess the foreplay's over." He did the same with his glass and climbed into bed. Edie sat up, stretching her arms to him as the sheets dropped to her waist. Steve looked on, appreciating a glimpse of his favorite politician. "That works for me. Makes me forget you're a gun-toting, narrow-minded—"

Much later in the night, Rosa called out, "Daddy! Your phone's ringing."

The Casella family never made it to their appointment with the German Shepherd breeder, Penelope Worthington, at Coyote Spirit Shepherds.

Nor did the rest of the trip go as planned.

CHAPTER 8

The next day's headlines might read:

'History Repeats Itself'

'Bigotry Rears its Ugly Face'

'President Griffin's Legacy: the Decline of a Divided Nation'

And at least a dozen more indictments aimed at the two-term presidency of a lone force in his waning fight against the established political system: reinforced by a media once again smelling blood in the water and all-too-ready to sink its teeth into President Tyler Griffin in the final days of his administration.

At the start of the last decade of the twentieth century, in the northern fringes of the Golden State's breadbasket, a local farmer and descendant of Muslim immigrants donated a portion of the family's peach orchard to the Islamic community for the purpose of building a mosque. Members of the fledgling Muslim population, who currently prayed in garages, banded together and collected the necessary funds to construct a twelve-thousand-square-foot mosque on the cleared five-acre plot.

Late one night, after evening prayers had finished and the worshippers had vacated the mosque, a fire broke out and destroyed the entire structure. The devastating loss to the Islamic community was thought to be perpetrated by individuals belonging to a local right-wing extremist group.

The message: *Muslims go home. You are not welcome in our neighborhood.*

To this date, although local law enforcement had identified key suspects, no arrests have ever been made. The original Islamic Center of Yuba City has the distinction of being the first mosque in the United States to be intentionally destroyed by an act of bigotry.

In sharp contrast to the fear and hate that denigrated the small number of Muslim families then residing in the area, other religious groups stepped up and spearheaded the rebuilding of the Islamic Center at the same location.

Until tonight's horrid event, the rebuilt mosque represented a rare voice of unity in an otherwise divided nation. In addition to the personal component bred from a demented mind, this act of terror foretold Jalal Ta'anari's goal for the next anniversary of 9/11.

The first salvo in a jihad poised to inflame the nation had been fired. The beauty of the spacious skies that nurtured oceans of amber grain was about to be challenged by a wave of violence not seen since the explosive origins of the majestic mountains as they spewed upwards from the ancient seas that coddled the North American continent.

CHAPTER 9

Yuba City, California
September 3
12:01 am

Sergeant Worthington approached the mosque, keeping his service weapon drawn and at his side. He saw no signs of the Ta'anari's Tahoe: the parking lot looked empty. The screams he heard had come from inside the mosque. But now the night had turned quiet. The earlier bright orange flames dancing in the arched windows were gone. He grabbed the heavy handle on the front door, but it wouldn't budge.

Jogging to a nearby window, he watched streams of water cascading down the inside of the glass panes. The mosque's interior continued to fill with smoke, and the sprinklers spit out torrents of water, dousing all vestiges of the flames.

The image of the dangling bodies of Faizan and Safura Ta'anari appeared hazy, but there was no mistaking the horrifying picture.

"Oh my God!" Worthington cried out and retraced his steps to the locked door. With his arm extended he fired several rounds from his service weapon into the door jamb, splintering the frame. He flinched as spiked slivers cut into his cheek. The heel of his boot kicked at the edge of the door and forced it free from the broken pieces of the lock. Holstering his weapon, Worthington charged inside. Sprays from the oversized sprinkler system pummeled his face as he sprinted toward the prayer room, his boots making loud squishing sounds on the soaked carpeting. The air reeked from a resilient coating, reminding him of old painting rags. He coughed out the remaining smoky particulates, now rendered sodden by deluges of water swirling down from above. He no longer saw any active flames.

When he reached the hanging bodies, he knew there was no need to hurry. The screams had stopped long before he'd gotten inside. He stared at the charred victims. At this point, he couldn't positively identify the bodies, but he had no doubt that he was staring at what remained of his neighbors.

He desperately wanted to cut them down but knew enough to leave the scene as intact as possible. Not that there'd be a whole lot of evidence with the sprinklers still running.

As if realizing he'd been wasting precious moments, he uttered a single word.

"Damn."

He ran outside and around the building, searching for the emergency cut-off water valve. By the time he found it, he heard sirens in the distance, responding to his call, and rapidly closing in on the location.

Whoever had done this had taken the time to deactivate the alarm system but hadn't accounted for the magnitude and efficacy of the sprinklers to spare the building from a similar fate to the one that had previously stood on these same grounds.

Chapter 10

As usual, Agent Mike Finley's phone call had been brief but left no room for questioning. Steve Casella hadn't bothered to check the time. He untangled himself from Edie's side, gave her a quick kiss, and stumbled from the bed. She murmured and fell back to sleep.

Steve ushered Amber into the rear seat of the Ford Explorer and pulled out of the dark and quiet campground. He yawned, fighting to stay awake as he drove south on California State Route 70. Silhouetted by the waning moonlight, the slopes of the Sierra Nevada cloaked the first light of the pending day.

The ride from the RV park in Oroville took him less than thirty minutes. Voice commands from the GPS system kept him company while Amber snoozed. The final announcement of his destination proved unnecessary as the typical light show associated with the emergency response vehicles served as a notifying beacon. As he neared the grounds of the Islamic Center of Yuba City and slowed down the Ford Explorer, he noted the presence of local media vans vying for space on the narrow shoulders of the road.

When he turned the SUV onto the short driveway leading to the entrance gate for the mosque, a uniformed deputy stepped in front of a wooden police barrier that blocked the path and raised a hand for him to stop. Steve noted the mangled condition of the heavy wrought-iron gate and the odd angle of its position behind the stone columns flanking the entrance. Parked between two palm trees on the interior side of the fence sat a Sutter County sheriff's patrol car with its shredded left front tire anchored against a low rock wall. It looked like someone had used the vehicle as a battering ram to force open the gate.

He lowered his window. "Good evening, deputy," he said, handing his credentials over to the man. "Agent Finley from DHS asked me to take a look at the scene until they can assemble a team to head the investigation."

The deputy sheriff grabbed Casella's fed creds and shined a small flashlight onto the ID. After an audible grunt, he swept the beam toward the SUV's rear side window. Amber responded by shifting her body away from the harsh intrusion. "Looks like Amber doesn't want to be disturbed tonight, Agent Casella." He handed the creds back to Steve.

Steve stared at the man and then glanced over his shoulder at the sleepy German Shepherd. Surprised by the use of Amber's name, he turned back and looked at the name tag on the deputy's uniform, but before he could get out any words, the man introduced himself. "The name's Worthington. Sergeant Cal Worthington. My wife's name is Penny. She runs Coyote Spirit Shepherds. I've seen more than a few pictures of your dogs. Especially the one you got in the back seat. I understand Amber's got one hell of a reputation."

Amber sat up on her haunches and chuffed.

Shaking his head, Steve extended his right hand through the window. "Nice to meet you, Sergeant Worthington." He nodded his head slowly, making the connection and solving the puzzle of where Finley got his information. "Agent Finley neglected to say how he knew I happened to be in the vicinity when he called."

Worthington shrugged and mumbled barely loud enough for Steve to hear. "Penny's wrong. I doubt you're just a part-time consultant like me." Raising his voice, he added, "You believe in coincidences, Casella?"

Steve thought a moment before responding. He narrowed his eyes and said, "Only for the bad stuff." He paused and then added, "So what have we got, sergeant? From the little I've been briefed on, this could easily qualify as bad."

Worthington pointed to the main parking lot where the emergency vehicles had gathered. "Go ahead and pull inside. I'll catch up with you in a sec." He pressed the button on his shoulder mike. "Copy this, Jackson. Haul it on up to the front gate and take over for me. But don't worry. I doubt this assignment is going to last much longer. Looks like Uncle Sam's about to give us the boot." He pulled the wooden barrier aside and waved Casella forward.

A few minutes later, Worthington and Casella stood in the circular turnabout facing the steps leading to the mosque's main entrance. Several county deputies were stationed at the door. At least for now, Steve decided to leave Amber in the Explorer.

"They ordered us to secure the scene," Worthington said, his voice sounded like he was reading a suspect his

Miranda Rights. "And to leave everything alone. Until the *appropriate* federal agency sent the *appropriate* agents with the *appropriate* authority. We did move my patrol car aside after prying open the gate the rest of the way so the first responders could get their rigs inside." He swallowed and his next words hitched in his throat. "The bodies are still... ahh... just like they were when I first approached the building."

Steve, who had been scrutinizing the immediate vicinity, turned to Worthington as he finished speaking. He remained quiet and then started up the steps to the entrance. When he reached the top, he turned again to Worthington, who hadn't moved.

"Sergeant?" Steve said. "You coming?"

Worthington's eyes shot up from where they'd been focused on the ground. He shrugged. "Didn't think I was invited."

Steve walked back to Worthington and placed a hand on his shoulder. "Can I call you Cal?"

Worthington glanced at Steve's arm and then looked at him. His eyes opened a little wider. He nodded, almost in slow motion.

"I'm a firefighter, Cal. We're both locals. First responders—trying to do a job." He pointed to a group of firefighters standing next to a hazmat rig positioned at the far end of the lot.

"Pretend I'm one of them, and we're working this scene together." Steve's arm dropped back to his side.

Worthington grunted and arched his head toward the rig and then back to Steve. A small smile spread across his otherwise ascetic features. "At the annual homeless benefit, our law enforcement football squad usually beats the crap out of those limp, pussyfoot, hose handlers."

Steve took a step toward the building and said over his shoulder, "Well then, Cal. I'm betting we'll get along just fine."

Once Steve passed through the main entrance to the mosque, his demeanor changed. His feet pressed into the soaked carpeting as he entered the main prayer hall. Aside from the damage caused by the sprinkler system, the interior looked mostly unscathed by the fire. He stopped short at the sight of the two charred bodies hanging from the steel cables attached to the ceiling fans. He'd had ample opportunities to discover burn victims, but never ones so ceremoniously sacrificed by such a gruesome act. The thought that this heinous deed had likely been perpetrated by the victims' own son chilled him to the bone. He hoped they at least had gone quickly and not endured much suffering but knew that was not the case. The anticipation alone would've driven them insane.

Steve's eyes fell on Worthington, who had been standing to the side staring at his boots. "I'm sorry, Cal. You knew these people, didn't you?"

"Yeah. They've been our neighbors for about two and a half years."

Steve could see him trying to damp down any personal feelings as he sucked in a huge breath. "Let me give you a quick rundown on the Ta'anaris' activities up until tonight."

Worthington gave a brief account. He cited no particular behaviors that warranted any second looks. Everything he and his wife observed had been chronicled in his weekly report summaries to DHS.

When finished, he stared at Steve. "You know. Sometimes working for the federal government sucks. I get that this is all for the good of our country and somebody needs to keep an eye on the bad guys, but these people were our neighbors. While they weren't the most hospitable family in the neighborhood—well, we still lied to them—pretending to treat them like everybody else...."

He let the words fade away.

Steve said, "No, Cal. I understand how you feel, but you're wrong. Neither you nor the government singled those people out because of their religious beliefs or because they were different. They were the best link to finding their son. And he's one bad character who needs to be stopped."

Worthington's eyes sharpened. "Speaking of which, according to the dossier on the Ta'anaris, Jalal fled the country almost three years ago. How the hell did he get back in?"

"That's an important question, Cal. One I'm sure the president is going to be looking at very carefully. But right now, a more critical one is what the hell is he up to?" He clapped his hands together and added, "Let's go over everything you did after speaking to Agent Finley."

Chapter 11

Agent Mike Finley stormed onto the grounds of the Islamic Center, accompanied by the usual cast of characters involved in any well-oiled government bureaucracy. They made quick work of establishing the new pecking order. One of the first items of business for Finley was to commandeer Sergeant Calvin Worthington. In the turnabout near the mosque's front entry, he found Worthington leaning against a palm tree and talking to Steve Casella. Amber was sitting at Steve's side.

Finley gave Steve a quick look and turned to face Worthington, moving his six-foot-two frame in between the two men. A nearby floodlight cast a dull reflection off Finley's shaved, fair-skinned head. When at home in the Florida Keys, he never left the house without a cap to protect him from the glaring sunlight.

Steve took a step to the side and caught a glimpse of Finley's chiseled features as the retired—but not retired—agent did his best to reprimand Worthington for not following orders to stand down until the feds could take over. Steve knew Finley's heart wasn't in it. He presumed Finley was grateful Worthington got on scene first, and his quick thinking to shut off the sprinklers helped preserve any possibility of recovering evidence.

"Mike," Steve interrupted while pointing to the media hysteria mounting outside the gate. "Looks like the natives are restless. I understand the local sheriff has been feeding out only minimal information. Now that you're in charge, are you planning on setting the record straight? The sergeant's boss says the satellite uplinks are all in place, and the media is poised to report this as another hate crime—an act of Islamophobia."

"And don't forget," Finley said with a tight smile frozen in place. "It's President Tyler Griffin's administration that encourages this bad behavior from the vicious right-wing lunatics."

"You mean his voter base?" Worthington said, but immediately waved his hands in surrender. "Just kidding guys. But that's exactly the sentiment you'll find from the opposition."

Steve snorted in agreement. "Yeah, Mike… welcome to California."

Finley shook his head. "Get your heads out of the sand, boys. In the last three years it seems like both sides of the aisle are screaming for the president's head. The left is still crying that Griffin stole the election from Blackwell." Finley pointed a finger at Casella. "And the corrupt republican establishment has all but deserted Griffin too."

Worthington's eyes narrowed as he turned his palms up. "But Blackwell's dead."

"That's gotta be his only redeeming quality," Finley retorted.

In the glare of the harsh lighting in the parking lot, a dark shadow spread across Finley's face. He lowered his voice and said to Steve, "That reminds me, when we finish up, I need a word with you in private."

Steve nodded. "You still didn't answer my first question. What about the media? It's well into the morning on the East Coast, and the sharks smell blood. Are you going to explain what really happened?"

Before answering, Finley swallowed. He looked directly at Worthington. "Were you upfront with me when you said you haven't told anyone about what your wife claims to have seen?"

Worthington stiffened. His hands clenched. "Look, Finley. Penny has worked just as hard as I have—in fact, she has a better handle on the Ta'anari household than me." He took a step closer to Finley. "So, if she says their fugitive son made a sudden appearance in his parent's house tonight and took them away at gunpoint and—by the way, *Mr. Federal Agent Man*—how is it this guy—Jalal Ta'anari—gets back into the country in the first place? That's the problem you should be working on. Not questioning whether Penny—"

Finley pressed his hand against Worthington's chest. "Why don't we all calm down and take a breath. No one is questioning your wife's story." Finley paused and exhaled. "Son, you did a good job tonight."

"Not good enough to save those two people."

Finley nodded. "We don't always win, sergeant. And nobody could've done it any better. In spite of what I said, we appreciate that you took the initiative. And tell your wife she did an excellent job too."

Worthington's features softened, but he said, "Time for us local boys to step aside so Uncle Sam can pretend to clean up this mess, and maybe tell a tale or two and generate a smoke screen from the public."

Finley smiled. "The media has been known to help us out from time to time, but usually they don't know it." He shook Worthington's hand. "Now if you'll excuse us for a moment, I've got something I need to talk to Steve about."

As Worthington watched Steve Casella and Mike Finley walk into the shadows, he picked up only a small part of the conversation, hearing the words 'Beale Air Force Base' and what he believed was the name of a small town in the Idaho panhandle called Coeur d'Alene.

He looked toward the front gate and the media mob growing along the road. He heard the first of the protesters starting to chant their Islamophobic rhetoric. Nearby, others shouted opposing views. The media floodlights began snapping on as two men who looked a lot like FBI suits stepped up to the makeshift podium where columns of microphones awaited their report.

Sergeant Worthington murmured to himself, "So… the spin starts here this morning."

Chapter 12

Coeur d'Alene, Idaho
September 3
9:40 am

Dozens of cars packed the small parking lot and overflowed along the lakefront drive near the historic dwelling. After parking the rented SUV on the closest side street, Steve Casella and Amber started walking toward the Jewett House. Completed in 1917, the three-story clapboard-sided mansion once owned by a local sawmill now hosted both private and public events. The covered porch with its ornate turned railings spanned the entire front façade and provided a welcoming venue for arriving guests.

Steve glanced at the stately homes lining the shores of Lake Coeur d'Alene. The scene brought back memories of his father who had worked as a property manager for several of these same estates. Steve swallowed a lump in his throat at those bittersweet memories and how he failed to come to grips with their strained relationship until long after his father died.

As they got closer to the Jewett House and its landscaped front yard that overlooked the lake, Amber spotted her first.

Steve's focus hadn't kept up with his body. In addition to the unbidden recollections of his father, he'd caught little sleep on the short flight from Beale AFB to nearby Spokane. The intensity of the crime scene at the Islamic Center of Yuba City and his upcoming task of informing Patas Ta'anari about the death of her parents had already started to eat away at his sanity. Deep in thought, he almost failed to tighten his grasp before the leash burned through his palm when Amber darted toward the beach. He settled down his canine companion and turned his attention to the lone person seated on a redwood bench. She was facing the angry, gray waters of the lake. When he saw the familiar outline of Amber's goal, he unclipped the lead and let out a lengthy breath.

The dog bounded through the public access gate to Sanders Beach. Without shifting her gaze away from the lake, Catori Torrence reached over and scruffed Amber's neck as the aging white German Shepherd scooted up on the bench and plopped next to her.

"How do you do that?" Steve said after catching up with the dog and cramming himself onto the small section of unoccupied bench next to Amber and Catori. "You never flinched when Amber invaded your space. It's as if you knew we were coming." He didn't anticipate an answer.

Catori turned her head. Steve watched a lone tear slip down her cheek as she wiped strands of windswept dark brown hair back from her face. Upturned lips confirmed the resilience he'd come to expect from her. Now in her early twenties, Steve first met Catori when she was fifteen.

He recalled how this brave little girl, showing no fear while leading him through a maze of underground dangers, helped find Edie and unraveled a deadly plot to destroy America's heartland. Her young body had now blossomed into a stunning beauty, but in Steve's view, her mind had always been light years ahead in maturity and perception.

He watched her lips twitch and mouth a few soothing words to Amber, as her eyes cast glances across the lake.

"Not far from this shore, the mythical creature led a small band of our tribesmen to their deaths." Centering her attention on Amber, her faint smile widened. "You remember Lomasi's legend of Coyott; the ghost of the ancient god of light?" As the words formed, a sudden blast of wind whipped her voice into a mournful tune, making her grandmother's tale sound even more mystical.

Amber chuffed and snuggled tighter. "Don't fret, girl," she said to her old friend. "We both know you're not that ageless trickster, but while Lomasi's life faded away—you stayed nestled at her side. And with her final breath—she still called you Coyott."

Steve felt the strength of Lomasi's presence, almost with the same force as when Catori brought him to that tiny cabin where the aging matriarch first set her eyes on Amber.

Catori let out a soft sigh, as if gently shepherding the memories of her grandmother aside. She rose from the bench, folded her arms, and stared at Steve. Standing motionless, with the graying swells mixing on the lake at her back, Steve imagined her small body shrinking inside herself. But that only made her bearing more prescient.

He listened to her next words. "This is going to turn ugly."

A more persistent gust, accompanied by the first large drops of rain, echoed off the weathered slats on the bench. Steve didn't respond. Instead, he stood up, and they strode toward the hundred-year-old mansion. He realized Catori's warning had nothing to do with the storm poised to sweep across Lake Coeur d'Alene.

"It already has," he mumbled under his breath, his mind flashing to the horrid images of Faizan and Safura Ta'anari at the mosque.

Amber turned more alert, picking up on his demeanor; her tired joints seemingly forgotten. Drawing closer to the Jewett House, his own awareness heightened. He raked his eyes over the perimeter. Although familiar with most neighborhoods in Coeur d'Alene, he'd never checked out this part of town. Perhaps avoiding it as a stark reminder of a lost segment of his father's life. The grand estate properties lining the northern fingers of the lake should have given him a sense of peace and safety. But today they did neither.

He gazed at the small crowds forming at the gate to the parking lot and near the mansion's front entrance. Local police worked to separate the protesters from the invited guests attempting to enter the building and listen to the compelling words of a provocative student activist.

The raucous mob didn't trouble Steve. With a final glance at the brewing storm, he predicted that one more wind gust would send these kids running for shelter. He noticed the crowd's energy wane as many already sought their safe space under the covered porch.

"Tell me how he did it," Catori said as they reached the bottom of the porch steps.

Steve paused and turned to her.

He thought, *Jalal Ta'anari.*

Of course she knew. That's what brought her to this location. While breaking news reports told a far different story, Catori's knowledge of past events and her own intuition would cause her to discount the hype and accusations formulated by a biased media.

He pulled Catori aside to allow people to pass and get inside for Patas Ta'anari's presentation. Although that was the young girl's name three years ago, the feds conveniently gave Patas a new identity. As part of the president's plan to clean up the mess surrounding a series of events that led to the deaths of Governor Nicholas Blackwell and his wife, they'd claimed to find Patas's body snagged at the bottom of the Sacramento River. The world had labeled her as another suicide bomber. The purported target—the governor of California. But this first attack had failed, and Patas Ta'anari, the suspected jihadist, had supposedly died. Catori was one of the few people who knew the real story. Her almost supernatural instincts played an important part in helping the investigators expose a cover-up and the depravity of the governor's actions.

Steve sidestepped Catori's question, and said, "How her brother killed their parents, or how he got back in the country?"

He could see her struggling with the need to either hear the facts or trust in her own visions. Distant thunder rumbled from the south, punctuating the grim task of telling Patas that her parents were dead before the authorities released the identities of the two victims. "Let's get inside."

Catori placed a hand on his arm. "Any back-up on the way?"

"Nope... it's just me." Amber barked and pulled forward. "Right now the murder scene at the mosque is garnering all the attention. That incident has raised a lot of red flags for the administration. The president believes it's the start of a surge in domestic attacks relating to the upcoming anniversary of 9/11." He paused before adding, "But not the same kinds being touted by the major news outlets. The media's not waiting. They're already spreading their own agenda of Islamophobia. Playing right into Jalal's design. It's no accident he chose that particular mosque. It has a history."

Catori bit her lip. "And the president isn't making any attempt to set the record straight?"

Steve looked into her eyes but remained silent.

"Why won't he do that?" she pressed.

To convince himself of the president's motives, he said, "Maybe he's tired. And at this point in his second term, the media would twist it around and still find a way to blame him."

Catori nodded and they headed up the steps. Once inside the central hallway, Steve sized up the packed seating areas, which included a spacious parlor and solarium. He signaled for Catori to follow, and they took up a position on the opposite side of the hall near the dining room. Lowering his voice, he leaned closer to Catori and said, "The president says heads are going to roll for letting Jalal Ta'anari slip through the cracks. He's been on the watch list since fleeing the country after the first incident with the California governor."

Behind him, the old windows creaked and rattled as the winds ratcheted up across the beach and spattered swirling grains of sand against the glass. In the soft glow of the interior lighting, Steve sensed a cold darkness unfurling over the bones of the old house.

He looked at Amber, listening to the quiet whimpering rolling from her closed jaws, knowing it grew from somewhere deep in her gut.

Catori interrupted his reverie. "If Jalal shows up today, how will you recognize him?"

CHAPTER 13

Movement near the front of the main reception hall prevented Steve from answering Catori's question. An attractive woman stood in the doorway. Steve knew Patas Ta'anari was a couple years younger than Catori. She wore a sheer headscarf, which did little to impose modesty, but succeeded in highlighting her honey-blond shoulder-length hair. The light fabric cascaded over her shoulders and muted the patterns of an embroidered blouse. Her faded jeans draped over scuffed, gray running shoes.

Many in the audience held fliers describing today's presentation. It listed the speaker as Patty Basara, a student activist who recently started touring colleges across the nation. The photo in the brochure depicted a headshot of the transformed image of Patas Ta'anari. The last time Steve had seen Patas, she had been a child of sixteen, with shining, long black hair. A grown woman now stood before him. Behind Patas's captivating features and wispy smile, he saw a little girl forced to grow up in a world she longed to change—one that would more likely make her a statistic—adding to the hate surrounding a faith she stood ready to die for. But unlike other jihadists, both past and present, Patas Ta'anari had a far different dream in mind.

Steve whispered, "Patas doesn't look like the same little suicide bomber who fled the failed attack on the California governor."

Catori shot him a look but let his lame attempt at humor ride. "But no doubt you think her brother knows where to find her." She rephrased her earlier question. "If Jalal shows up, how will you recognize him? I'm sure his looks have changed too. But I'd guess his alterations have a more deadly purpose."

Steve shrugged. "If he's close by, I'm counting on Patas to pick him out of the crowd."

He felt a sharp jerk from Amber's lead. He loosened his hold and studied the dog's actions. Her body swept from side to side and then halted with her snout raised.

Steve wasn't too concerned with Amber's behavior, which indicated the potential presence of any one of a long list of chemical substances. After all, the premises were chock full of college students to provide sufficient quantities of residual contraband odor to elicit this preliminary alert response. On the other hand, he had also trained Amber to detect far more virulent scents.

Patas stepped in front of the brick fireplace and faced the expectant crowd. When she smiled, her dark features shifted into a hopeful sign of the future. A concoction of jeers, threats, and applause greeted her.

Ignoring Amber's antics, Steve riveted his gaze on Patas's deep brown eyes.

Events played out in slow motion.

At first, Steve detected a hitch in Patas's breathing as she turned her head and scanned the room. She hadn't yet finished her opening remarks when her eyes widened, her face blanched, her body swayed.

Steve felt his own pulse quicken as he homed in on what had interrupted Patas's concentration. He saw a lone figure standing in the west corner of the solarium, and the perverse look in the man's eyes, which never once strayed from Patas. As she reacted to the instant acknowledgment, a tight smile creased the cheeks of Jalal Ta'anari, her fugitive brother.

Jalal's left arm stretched out to place a small object on a table next to the French doors leading to the side veranda. He took a moment to scrutinize the room before his gaze locked onto Steve. There was no mistaking the wrath that transformed Jalal's face. Turning, he pushed several people aside and grabbed for the lever on the patio door.

Steve ordered Amber to stay next to Catori.

The dog dropped to a crouching position and remained in place. Steve inched forward into the main reception hall, slipping behind the last row of chairs. He hugged the rear wall as he closed the gap, trying to reach Jalal before he could flee. His hand dug inside his jacket and withdrew the compact P229 Legion, keeping it lowered at his side.

His objective to maintain a low profile eroded when a number of nearby spectators spotted the drawn weapon. He knew that in a matter of seconds pandemonium would break out and increase the chances of people getting hurt, making Jalal's escape easier.

From off the lake, a distant, growling wind escalated and interrupted Steve's focus. Before he could react, the gust transformed into the roar of a runaway locomotive.

A splintering crunch followed the concussive blast of wind. The whole house shook, and the front porch structure disintegrated, spitting out shards of glass and debris. Pictures fell from the walls; bookcases spilled out volumes. Furniture—tables, sofas, chairs, antique cabinets—tossed about as if a massive earthquake had hit the lakefront structure.

Less than a second later, waves of wind, rain, and an unending sea of airborne particles assaulted the exposed interior of the stricken mansion.

This shocking act of nature that erupted off the northern shores of Lake Coeur d'Alene, left one dead, two critically wounded, and eight with minor injuries. But as fate would have it, the devastating storm played a role in saving the remaining lives of almost seventy-five people inside the Jewett House.

A falling bookcase slammed into Steve's shoulder, spinning him around like a ragdoll and knocking the handgun to the floor. His head smacked against the unforgiving plaster wall that separated the main reception area from the solarium.

He dropped like a rock.

His world turned black as the aftershocks from the impact of the falling tree punctuated the abrupt ending to Patas's speech.

Chapter 14

Seconds before the hybrid mountain ash—one of the largest and oldest trees in the city of Coeur d'Alene—devoured the Jewett House's front porch and ruined a good portion of the house, Patas Ta'anari had stared into the eyes of her brother, Jalal. The face of evil had somehow found its way back to America.

The president had told her she had nothing to worry about. He would never return, let alone seek her out. Although both siblings' appearances had changed in the almost three years since they'd parted, there was no question of recognition.

Patas froze, knowing her brother had returned to end her life for having failed to martyr herself for her perceived sins. Although she erased most of the bad memories of her father, and the far more deviant encounters with her brother, a sudden chill hit her when she thought of her mother and what Jalal's return heralded.

Deep in her heart, she reasoned it was already too late.

Patas shut her eyes and prayed to Allah.

Part of the past, she'd kept to herself. Buried it in some hidden corner of her mind. The shame, the self-loathing. She recalled the almost silent footsteps in the hall of their home in Sacramento. The slight scraping of the turning doorknob. The dreaded creaking of the old hinges as the door to her bedroom inched open. The silhouette of Jalal standing in the doorway. The depraved and sickening sneer on his face as he approached her bed.

When the governor of California got his chance—he thought he'd been the first. But Patas had already met the devil. He just came in different forms.

After being given a new life and a second chance, she'd left those dark days behind.

As a child, she had never shown any disrespect for her family's beliefs; especially the teachings of her faith. Patas cherished Islam and the beauty of a God that brought her love and comfort, but she isolated herself from the cultural aberrations orchestrated by misguided and malevolent individuals who wove their dogma into the souls of the masses.

She'd lost a vital part of herself, but prayed she had the power to make a difference and advocate against the intolerance, the hatred, and the bloodshed in a war with no end. She now tried to spread her vision across America, hoping to salvage the world from conflict and turmoil. But deep down Patas feared that no amount of forgiveness could defeat zealots, such as her brother and the countless numbers who spanned the centuries.

In a different part of her mind, she often conjured up images of a special boy she'd barely gotten to know—now a soldier—and what could've been if the world were different. The boy's father had pulled her from the depths of Hell when her discarded suicide vest exploded. This boy she often thought of from those brief and tumultuous times had been angered by his father's actions. He held a deep hatred toward Muslims. To him, Patas and her supposed behavior on that Halloween night in Sacramento represented those demons. And now almost three years after she last saw him, she feared his contempt may have grown deeper. But a small part of her heart still held on.

As the air around her imploded, she caught another look in her brother's eyes and understood his return signified a whole lot more than his hatred for her. The next phase of jihadism had arrived in her homeland.

While her whole world wavered, she never lost consciousness. But she did lose sight of Jalal when nearby furniture turned into weapons and tumbled across the room. Her body slammed to the floor. Stunned, Patas struggled against the bulky overturned sofa pinned against her. She saw a hand reaching from above, lifting the sofa and allowing her to twist free. When she turned to thank the person, she saw nothing but chaos. Whoever assisted her had moved on. For a moment she couldn't focus. The air remained thick with dust, clouding her vision.

Patas imagined herself either dead or hallucinating. And then her eyes settled on the large white dog and the beautiful Native American woman assisting a man near the doorway to the solarium.

All three looked familiar. A definite part of what she had left behind. But in that moment, she sensed they represented her future.

Frantic cries of frightened people and urgent voices of first responders brought Patas out of her trance. She scrambled to her feet and started helping as many as she could to exit the building.

CHAPTER 15

Slowly at first, then building in intensity, Steve fought off the murkiness. Aided by Amber's persistent pawing and licking, he returned from the abyss. Catori, nearby assisting others, jumped back and kneeled at his side. She spoke in such a rapid and discordant rhythm that many of her words didn't register. Piecing her story together, he got the part about the storm knocking over a tree which crashed down on the front porch. Steve racked his brain trying to recall the flickering images from right before the colossal tree fell. In a practiced move, he checked inside his jacket and discovered the empty holster.

Trying to focus on Catori's words, he grabbed her shoulders and looked into her eyes.

"He's gone, Steve," she repeated. "I saw the door open, and Jalal jumped through right before the tree hit. There's no sign of him."

Steve nodded and dropped his arms. Resting on his knees, his eyes searched through the rubble; he didn't see his gun. Under a scattered pile of books, he saw a bright object and picked it up, staring at the cracked screen of a cell phone with the digits of an alarm counting down. He rubbed a hand over his face and pressed his fingers against his forehead. The picture of Jalal Ta'anari placing the phone on a table and reaching for the door handle formed in his head.

The act made no sense to Steve.

Why the hell would he do that?

It's like a calling card.

Suddenly his eyes opened wide.

"That arrogant son of a bitch."

Fully awake and pumped, Steve sprang to his feet and again grasped Catori by the shoulders. His voice hardened and kicked into a professional mode. "We need to get everybody out of the house and cleared off the grounds—now. And that means you too." He looked around, relieved to see the inside of the house almost empty. The first responders had descended on the scene. He added almost to himself, "This storm damage is nothing compared to what Patas's brother has planned."

After looking from the cracked screen to the resolve on Steve's face, Catori said nothing and doubled her efforts to help escort any remaining people from the broken mansion.

Steve's eyes darted around the room and located his target. Pulling out his federal credentials, he painted the grim picture to the on-scene captain of the local fire department coordinating the evacuation and triaging the victims. The guy nodded and relayed new orders into his handheld without asking any questions. There'd be time for that later, but only if he did his job now.

"Ready, girl?" Steve said to Amber, once again taking off her lead. "Go find it."

Amber barked twice and jumped over chunks of plaster, padding down the central hallway. She bolted from room to room but gradually closed in on one particular area. Steve left her alone to work. He heard a change in her barking and rushed to catch up. When he rounded the corner behind the staircase, he found Amber with her snout pressed to the floor at the bottom of a closed door.

"Good work, Amber."

The dog barked again and backed up, sitting on her haunches. Steve pulled the door open. He flicked on a wall switch, surprised the electric still functioned in this part of the house. A bright light bathed the basement staircase. Amber charged down the steps and disappeared to the left. Steve followed Amber and flew by a labyrinth of passages connecting rooms hidden in deep shadows. All the while listening to paws padding over the concrete floor and accompanied by frequent vocalizations mapping her progress.

He switched on additional lights and snaked his way across the subterranean environment until he found Amber in a small utility room. The damp concrete walls and floor held on to ancient tangs of coal dust and fuel oil; vestiges of earlier heating systems now replaced by more modern units. The room was cluttered with metal ductwork, galvanized pipes, and a mammoth air handler and boiler. Steve crept into the room, his hand fumbling for the light switch. He ducked under the main trunk of the air return and squeezed around an auxiliary water heater to get a better look at Amber.

She stood motionless. Her nose glued to an army-green metal ammo container with numerous holes drilled through its sides. It was duct-taped to the natural gas main supplying the commercial-sized boiler. He praised her again and began working through the process of what to do next. He noticed that the earlier sounds coming from the upper floors had faded, giving him more confidence the house had been cleared. His mind focused on the obvious, immediate problem facing him.

And then once again Amber reacted before him and pivoted away from the explosive device now at the center of his world.

Steve picked up on her sudden movements and then heard the sound of rapid footfalls on the basement steps. He turned in time to see Catori and Patas running into the utility room.

His chest tightened and his eyes opened wide. "Are you two out of your—" Steve started to say.

"What's the plan, Steve?" Catori interrupted.

Chapter 16

After a final glare at Catori and Patas, Steve let out a long breath and pulled Jalal's cell phone from his pocket. He stared at the countdown timer, mentally checking off his short list of options. His eyes shifted to the presumed explosive device. "No time to wait for the bomb squad. I'm going to drop this contraption in the lake."

Before either woman could protest, he held up a hand. He took a small knife from a pouch on his belt and gingerly sliced away at the tape securing the device to the natural gas line. As he eased the metal container free, Patas snatched it away and pushed him aside.

She bolted out the door and up the stairs, shouting, "This is my fault. Besides, I'm the youngest and the fastest."

At first Amber set out after Patas as she bounded up the basement stairs. After taking a tentative step to follow her to the main floor, Amber's neck twisted, and her body arched around, almost colliding into Steve and Catori. Steve sidestepped Amber. When he got to the top step he turned back. Amber stood motionless in the basement; her eyes focused down a dark corridor. Steve called her. He repeated the command twice. Amber gave a final series of barks, hesitated, and then obeyed Steve, rushing to his side.

Close on Patas's heels, Steve and Catori crossed the Jewett House lawn and reached the beach at the moment Patas heaved the bomb as far as she could into the lake. She ran back and stood beside them, gasping for air.

Amber had taken two steps into the water when Steve called out, "Leave it, Amber."

Steve motioned them all back from the water's edge. He checked the grounds of the Jewett House, allowing himself to relax when he saw the area deserted and the first responders ushering people farther away from the house.

Amber padded to Steve's side, and they all turned back to the lake.

By now the storm had blown itself out. The skies showed signs of brightening, with blue gaps pushing away the last of the menacing clouds. The waters were still choppy from the lingering wind gusts. Steve checked the timer and watched the digits count down and stop at zero. They waited several more minutes; but nothing happened. Breathing a collective sigh of relief, they looked at the Jewett House.

Steve shrugged and started walking toward it. Amber placed her jaws around his wrist and tugged. He stopped and took one last glance at the phone's screen: his eye locking on the previously unnoticed small flashing icon in the upper left-hand corner. After freeing his arm from Amber's grip, he tapped the screen with his index finger. A new window popped open, and he watched a second timer counting down:

TWO... ONE... ZERO—

A deafening explosion slammed them to the ground. Debris rained down, obscuring the sun's attempt to ward off the daytime gloom.

When Steve wiped the sand from his eyes—the Jewett House was gone.

He helped Catori and Patas to their feet.

They stared at where the historic house once stood. A pile of burning debris in its place. For now, the residual winds blowing off the lake kept the smoke from the blazing inferno away from them.

In unison, Steve and Catori turned to Amber.

They gazed at the dancing flames unfurling in the rising smoke and mixing with the slate-hued skies reflected in the dog's eyes. Steve swore he heard a brief chuffing sound from Amber. Catori narrowed her eyes and whispered a prayer to Lomasi and her lost ancestors who had once followed Coyott to their death.

Steve remembered hearing Lomasi's tale of the ancient god of light when she had first set eyes on Amber.

Lomasi's words had stuck in his head.

"If Coyott chooses to lead you, you will have no choice but to follow. She can save the world from the fiery demons, but left to her own devices she can also be a trickster. To keep her truthful, she must be controlled by the stabilizing dark force."

At that point, Steve recalled, Lomasi had diverted her eyes to Edie. And bid her to provide the steadiness and make sure this creature would guide the world in the right direction to extinguish the deathly flames of the demons.

Amidst the rubble spread out before him, Steve chuckled to himself, caught between the harsh reality of a world he had sworn to make safer for his family, and the mystical incantations of a deceased matriarch.

But in the end, he had to acknowledge that back in the house—he was the one who ignored Amber's warnings.

Catori, Lomasi's successor to carry forward the tribal legends, placed a hand on his shoulder and nodded. No doubt she knew exactly what he'd been thinking. When their eyes met, he felt a knife stab deep in his heart, remembering why he'd come and what he needed to tell Patas about her parents. When he glanced over at the younger girl, he had the feeling she already knew.

CHAPTER 17

Sitting on the flagstone patio outside a popular coffee house on Sherman Avenue in downtown Coeur d'Alene, Steve and Catori kept a sharp eye on Patas, trying to decipher her reaction to Steve's words. Patas's emotions tumbled through a web of changes, but her face reflected only the dull edges that still clung to years of deceit and excuses.

Steve broke the news about the deaths of her mother and father, and the undeniable role her brother played. This was old news to Patas. She had seen it reflected in Jalal's eyes at the Jewett House the moment before Allah intervened and unleashed the storm's fury.

Her brother's return was inevitable.

Allah understood what devastation and terror Jalal had in store for this country. And after the brutal deaths served to their parents, she knew he still had one last personal matter to finish. To restore his twisted meaning of family honor, he needed to complete the job started three years ago.

Patas must die.

And above all, she was well aware of a more perverse need in her brother.

Three years ago, the current administration in the White House had fed the world a particular version of events relating to apparent assassination attempts on the presidential candidate, Governor Nicholas Blackwell, and the bloodshed that followed on election day. President Griffin had verified Patas's own account of what had led up to the bizarre scene outside the theater in Old Town Sacramento on that Halloween night prior to the election. To avoid dividing the country, he opted not to further tarnish California governor's record, who deserved no sympathy, but had come so close to the presidency.

A darker, personal story Patas chose to keep to herself. It wouldn't have changed the president's decision about announcing to the world that she had been killed by the blast of her suicide bomb, or for him to give her a new name and a new life. It would only serve to heighten the shame and fear she kept buried.

On that night almost three years ago, she dove into the Sacramento River, weighed down not only by the bulky, explosives-laden vest, but also the blackness engulfing her heart.

Patas should've died—wanted to die. But the unexpected appearance of a tormented Navy SEAL hell-bent on his own suicide mission had changed both their destinies.

And now Jalal was back to finish the job.

"It seems there's less time to spread my message than I anticipated," Patas said to Steve and Catori, tucking the memories from that night back into the recesses.

"But I believe if he wanted me to die today, he would have succeeded—regardless of the storm's intrusion. Leaving behind his cell phone was no accident. He could've easily slipped away and manually set off those bombs from a safe distance. He didn't need to show his face at all." A grim smile touched her face. "And planting the explosives in two separate locations with different detonation times? He was playing with us. Checking out his opposition. Don't blame Amber."

She glanced at the white dog sleeping under the table. Reaching down and stroking Amber's fur, she closed her eyes and continued, "I remember Amber from when we met in your training center, Steve. She has a history of making things happen—today is no exception."

Patas scrunched her face as she opened her eyes and looked at Steve. She asked the obvious question. "How did my brother avoid detection and get back in the United States? They told me he was on a watch list. That I had nothing to worry about." She shrugged and shook her head. "I never believed they could stop him. The borders are wide open. Must be a million ways he could sneak across. Is that how he did it?"

Steve's lips tightened. "It appears he used a fake identity and breezed through customs and passport control without a second glance. They determined his point of entry was Dallas/Fort Worth Airport. No wall would've stopped him."

"How's that possible? I thought the government used sophisticated technologies to prevent that from happening. Especially since he was more than likely traveling from one of several countries known to harbor terrorists."

"The president has signed numerous executive orders to implement better vetting processes and airport screening, but so far the courts have intervened and blocked those actions. By the time the Supreme Court weighs in, it will probably—no, not probably—as we saw today, we're already facing the consequences."

Catori chuffed. "Yeah. We should've learned an important lesson from my ancestors."

Steve tilted his head and raised his brows.

"If Native Americans had taken border security more seriously," she said smiling at Steve, "it would be your relatives living on reservations—not mine."

Steve's mouth opened and he took a deep breath. He appeared to consider several responses, but after a brief silence, he shifted gears.

"Patas." Steve's voice softened. "Agent Finley wanted me to reassure you we're taking additional measures for your protection. I know you have a full schedule of speeches and rallies, but we can do a better job if you stay out of the public eye until we find your brother."

A faint smile crossed Patas's face, while her eyes remained still. "Our country would be better served if you discovered Jalal's greater reason for returning to America." She shrugged. "But maybe I can help draw him out again. He's angry enough to perhaps get sloppy in his next attempt to confront me."

She felt Amber stir and stiffen under the table. The dog raised her head and stared at Patas. A cool breeze chilled the nape of Patas's neck: the last trace of the devastating storm or a stark reminder of what remained ahead.

As her thoughts seemed to do more often in recent days, they turned to Corey Galloway. She could still picture the expression on his face the last time she saw him. She had turned and walked away, leaving him and his father—the man who pulled her from the Sacramento

River—at the West Wing portico to the White House. That was almost three years ago. While the agents drove her away, she'd stared at Corey through the rear window until the SUV she rode in exited the West gate. At the time she had imagined him relieved by her abrupt departure—so much conflict prevented him from seeing inside her. The SUV's privacy glass had felt more like a high-powered microscopic lens compared to the layers of darkness that fought to keep Corey and her apart. To this day, she didn't understand the depth of her own feelings for a boy she'd just met—on the same night she had begged to die.

CHAPTER 18

Amber sat up with a start and bumped her head on the table, causing the coffee mugs to rattle. Ears perked and swiveled forward; her snout peered around Steve's legs. Before he could look over his shoulder, he heard the rising chants and the angry words of the advancing mob.

He stood and walked to the filigreed wrought-iron railing that separated the coffee house patrons from the sidewalk. The signs and the repetitious dialogue echoing from the crowd appeared almost identical to what he observed earlier at the Jewett House. But unlike those student protesters, the size and the volume of the current rhetoric quickly rose to much more dangerous levels. He knew exactly what that meant—the media had arrived to fuel the flames.

Steve supposed the usual outside advocacy groups had organized a large part of the protesters, but taking a closer look, he recognized a number of professors from the local college.

A few years back, Steve had spent several semesters at the Panhandle Institute of Technology and Sciences, enrolled in classes to supplement his field work for a special hazmat program under development by the San

Francisco fire department. This acclaimed technical institute was located on the northwestern shores of Lake Coeur d'Alene. The PITS, as the students affectionately referred to the school, was associated with the North Idaho College, or NIC, campus.

Steve had attended a number of lectures given by NIC professors. He remembered that compared to the San Francisco Bay Area's liberal faculties, NIC had appeared somewhat conservative in its views. But with the growing wave of intolerance to dissimilar viewpoints sweeping the nation's campuses, those relative differences had slipped precariously close to silencing the principles of free speech.

Steve's phone buzzed. After plucking it from his pocket, he punched the screen and listened for several seconds. "Got it." He turned to Patas who had stepped up next to him. "Come on, we're going through the restaurant and out the kitchen door."

Catori grabbed Steve's arm, her eyes begging the question.

"A little late, but back-up has arrived."

They scooted toward the door to the coffee house. Steve chanced a quick glance behind him, sensing the mob breathing down his neck. For the moment, the horde appeared lost in a cloud of indecision. He arched an arm around Patas's shoulder, prodding her forward, and said, "From the venom pouring out of the opposing demonstrators, they may kill each other before they can get to you. I'm having trouble telling the players without a scorecard."

A few stragglers from the angered crowd surrounded Steve's rented SUV, smashing rocks against the windows.

Appearing out of thin air, someone lobbed a Molotov cocktail inside the vehicle, the blast overshadowing the crackling glass fragments and issuing forth fountains of flames and acrid smoke.

Amber barked as they charged through the kitchen, heading for the rear parking lot. Patas looked up at Steve. "How'd they know it was your SUV?"

Without a moment's hesitation, Steve said, "The mob itself appears disorganized—on purpose—but obviously somebody's directing the show. And once they spot our tattered clothes, they'll have no trouble linking us to the incidents at the Jewett House."

Catori added, "I'm not sure anyone can control these thugs. It looks like a lot of innocent people are going to get hurt." As she said this, the crowd splintered into at least three opposing factions and temporarily directed their fury at one another rather than seeking out the young female activist.

Steve caught the painful expression on Patas's face. He scanned the parking lot and cursed—no sign of any cavalry. Then he heard tires squealing around the corner. Three black Suburbans bounced across the lot's entry apron, skidding to a halt about ten feet from the back door. Two men jumped out of the middle vehicle, waving and shouting. Steve, Patas, and Catori made a dash toward the open doors to the SUV while Amber pounced over the rear seat and landed in the rear cargo area, looking years younger than her aching joints usually tolerated. Before the doors slammed shut, all three vehicles started moving. Protesters, finally getting their priorities straight, had begun spewing from the rear door of the coffee house, but the more immediate concern came from the stampeding mob bursting around the corner of the building and blocking the exit to the street.

The lead Suburban's tires skidded, spraying gravel and traces of burning rubber as the agent behind the wheel abruptly changed course. He plowed through the hedgerow separating the coffee house's parking lot from an adjacent business. The remaining two vehicles followed, and the small caravan shot through the adjoining lot and sped off down a narrow connecting alley onto a side street. With the crowd still converging on the coffee house, the Suburbans maneuvered through the residential neighborhood, trying to stay clear of any locations clogged with cars and more protesters. Tensions eased when the SUVs hit the west-bound onramp to the interstate.

Steve's phone buzzed again. He listened, his face blank. "Yes sir, Mr. President. I understand. Your guys have been a little busy. No, I was not informed you wanted us to—" Steve glanced up at the guy holding the shotgun in the front passenger seat. The agent returned a thin smile before refocusing his attention out the black-tinted windows.

"What's that, Mr. President? Oh, yes, that should cover it. That's a much more generous tip than I usually leave. I'm sure the owner will be pleased. That is if the mob doesn't torch the coffee house. Can you get the local health department to overlook the owner's fines for allowing a dog in the food preparation area?" Steve held the phone away from his ear. "No sir, that was a joke." He listened for several more seconds. "Right. Edie appreciates my sense of humor about as much as you do, sir."

When the call ended, Steve turned to Patas. Before he could speak, she said, "Do I get my old name back?"

Steve almost answered with, *"How many more enemies do you need?"* While he was one of the few who knew the real story regarding the assassination attempts on the governor of California—most of the nation did not. Right now the media was focused on castigating the young female activist, Patty Basara. If they knew Patty Basara didn't exist and Patas Ta'anari had arisen from her presumed watery death in the Sacramento River, they'd have one more nail to hammer in President Griffin's coffin. The media was always on the lookout for another high-level cover-up.

Instead, he said, "We're heading toward Spokane— actually to Fairchild Air Force Base."

"But I need to get to Berkeley," Patas said. "I'm speaking at a—"

Steve placed a hand on her shoulder. "The president anticipated you wouldn't listen to my advice and made arrangements for your transportation to the Bay Area. Someone will meet you at the air force base and accompany you."

"Oh? You're not going with me?" Patas's face muddied before their eyes met. She looked at Catori and then back to Steve.

Steve's features relaxed. "You remember Agent Davenport? She's heading a team in charge of your safety and making sure Jalal doesn't get anywhere near you." He took a deep breath and added, "The president wants me and my wife in D.C. as soon as possible, although Edie doesn't know it yet. Right now she's driving our RV back to Sonoma with the kids."

Catori tapped his shoulder. "Sounds like you guys could use a babysitter for Rosa and T.C."

Smiling, Steve shrugged. "You're a sweetheart, Catori. I think that might work out for the best. I'll arrange transportation for you and Amber. Do you remember the last time Rosa visited the first family? She and Sean—the president's youngest—tried to help the contractor hired by the first lady to install new hardwood floors at their New Jersey retreat. The kids got tired of playing with the Lincoln logs, and the wide-plank oak flooring boards made excellent building blocks. Sean's been posting excerpts of their little project on his Facebook page. He's been giving Rosa hints on the best use of social media."

Catori raised her brows.

Steve winked. "The president thinks it's kind of cute."

"I thought the White House advisors frowned on anyone close to the president engaging in any of the social media platforms."

"He's just a kid. What harm could there be in that?"

CHAPTER 19

San Francisco, California
September 4
6:05 am

Slivers of light darted through the crevices of the closed drapes. The motel room reeked of stale cigarette smoke, plus an underlying stench of corporeal secretions that took on a life of their own in the soiled and sagging mattress. Rising above the petri dish concoction that defined the dank space, Jalal Ta'anari breathed in a more carnal odor that competed with the adjuvant brew.

He pulled off the tattered sheets and swung his legs over the side of the bed. His bare feet pressed onto the grimy carpet and then stepped into the oily remains of an open pizza box with a lone slice glued to the cardboard. He lunged toward the bathroom. Gobs of congealed cheese and dried tomato sauce stuck between his toes. Jalal's hands grasped the corners of the toilet tank, almost wrenching it from the bowl as he puked up last night's indiscretions.

Pushing away from the iron-stained porcelain, he flipped on the light switch. The harsh glare sent a lightning bolt of pain through his head. He grabbed the edge of the sink counter and twisted his mouth under the faucet. He gulped down mouthfuls of the sour water and tried to spit out the regurgitated food particles stuck between his teeth. After splashing several handfuls of tepid water over his face, he reached for a towel—finding it buried in a pile of discarded clothing on the cracked tiled floor.

Jalal tossed the threadbare towel into the tub and chanced a look at his frightful reflection staring back from the broken mirror above the sink. Behind him, from under the clumped bed sheets, he heard a shallow cough and a cloying sigh. He inhaled; then swallowed a tang of their earlier animalistic coupling. The scent hung in the air and gripped his sweat-soaked body, making a viler and more forbidden craving jump to the surface.

An image of his younger sister usurped his own face in the mirror. As always, his mind perceived her flesh—raw and hot—tempting him again and again. He imagined Patas's voice pleading him to ravish her one more time.

Jalal smashed his fist into the mirror, causing the existing fissures to rupture, sending shards of glass into the sink and scattering across the counter. He looked at the blood dripping from his hand and slowly licked the wounds before turning toward the sleeping female on the bed.

Patas's face faded from his thoughts.

For now, he'd use this whore to quench his lust. But he knew the time would soon come when he'd again face the real target of his depravity. And he'd make the most of their last moments together.

Jalal hissed out the words, "Yes, Patas, I will come for you, but the next time we meet I will pierce your demon soul with a far more fatal weapon."

Taking a deep breath and releasing a primitive growl, he pounced on the girl, ripping off the sheets and thrusting himself over and over at the helpless creature in an act far more abhorrent and demeaning than his forthcoming deed of simply killing her.

His sister would be next.

When he had finished with the girl and dumped the mutilated body in a dumpster located miles from the seedy motel room, he drove onto the freeway. It was time to get to work. For now, his urges were temporarily sated, but he still savored the thought of dealing a similar fate to his sister.

Chapter 20

Washington, D.C.
September 4
4:20 pm

After completing the typical security formalities, the duty officer escorted Steve Casella and Edie Pauling through the Watch Center and down a corridor to an unmarked door in the underground state-of-the-art communications facility. This opened into a recently constructed, but little-known suite. The operational security for these particular private meeting rooms in the White House Situation Room complex precluded any monitoring or recording of what took place inside, following a philosophy similar to the popular Las Vegas motto.

The duty officer punched in the first segment of an access code on the panel adjacent to the door labeled *Jersey Shore*. Steve looked at Edie and raised his brows. She smiled with a feline expression but otherwise remained quiet.

When the light blinked yellow, the duty officer nodded to Steve and Edie while he retreated to the suite's outer entry door. After exiting, with the door closing in front of him, he waved to Steve and Edie from the other side of the glass and punched in the final coded digits on the exterior keypad. They watched as the symbols appeared on the *Jersey Shore* access panel display. When the flashing yellow light turned a steady green, a disembodied computer-generated voice dictated, *"Please enter. You have ten seconds before access is denied."*

Steve reached for the doorknob and whispered to Edie, "You guys don't get it. It's *coast*. Jersey *coast*—not *shore*."

Edie tried to pinch his ear, but Steve already had his hand pushing her butt through the open door and saying a little louder, "I hear the Taylor Ham and egg sandwiches in the White House are the best."

Having caught Steve's last words, President Tyler Griffin looked up from his conversation with Mike Finley, the only other occupant in the small conference room, and said, "Too bad we can't serve them down here—triggers the radiation sensors."

The president rose, kissed Edie on the cheek, and shook hands with Steve. He motioned for them to sit across from him at the rectangular conference table. Steve pulled out a chair on Finley's left side and Edie did the same on Finley's right.

Finley glanced back and forth between them. "If you two plan on continuing your bickering—I don't want to be in the kill zone."

"Don't worry, Mike," Edie purred. "I'm a politician now—thanks to the president—and Steve is a constituent."

Steve peered around Finley. "You should be playing to your conservative base, dear. Not the opposition."

The president coughed and shook his head. "Now I'm beginning to understand the depth of the political divisiveness in the country. Looks like we need a marriage counselor sitting in the Oval Office instead of an aging New Jersey businessman."

Spreading out his arms, the president sat. "Congratulations, Edie. Glad to see you're one step closer to the White House."

She shrugged. "Don't go there, sir. And right now the senate race is a longshot at best. At least the Prop 14 legislation got me on the ballot. But now the full forces of the establishment machines are set to bury me."

Griffin tilted his head and narrowed his eyes. "So, it's *sir* now, Edie?" He smiled. "If I didn't know better, I'd say you're trying to distance yourself from the current president."

Before Edie could object, he added, "Good move, young lady. If you recall, I gave the same advice to your new campaign manager last week. Right now, I'm more radioactive than Steve's Taylor Ham and egg sandwich."

The president gestured to Finley. "Mike's kept me up to date on the search for Jalal Ta'anari, and the steps taken to protect Patas."

Steve broke in. "Mr. President. If I may. We're taking a real gamble with Patas's safety. It's like feeding red meat to a hungry wolf. There's no telling what her brother's next move will be or how far he'll go to stop her." He paused before adding, "And you saw what happened in Coeur d'Alene. Not only did she narrowly escape being blown up by her brother, but this new wave of violent dissenters tracked her down and tried to finish the job."

Finley said, "We've gone over this, Steve. We both know that since Patas has refused to cancel her speaking engagements, there're no options left but to—"

"—treat her as bait," Edie sighed.

Steve nodded.

Finley retorted, "Olivia Davenport is not going to leave her side until Jalal Ta'anari is found. As far as the growing violence by the protesting factions, we think that may all be tied together with whatever Jalal Ta'anari has planned. We need more intel—and we need it now." He locked eyes with the president and hesitated before adding, "For the record, sir, I'm not completely on board with Olivia's assignment—at least not without having the chance to—"

"Yes, Mike. That's why Agent Davenport texted you *after* she boarded the flight to Fairchild Air Force Base to meet up with Patas and escort her to the next appearance." The president tempered his voice. "I understand your concern, Mike. And to be clear, Olivia's got a lot of back-up and support—you included—so she's not out there alone."

Steve thought Finley was about to object further but instead let out a resigned sigh and opened up a folder he pulled from his briefcase. "Sir. There's one more item to fill you in on before we discuss the larger issues surrounding the intel reports from Yemen."

The president glanced at the secure phone in front of him and checked his watch before nodding to Finley. Steve thought he looked distracted and anxious.

"Angela grabbed me on the way down," Finley said, referring to the president's press secretary. He tapped the top sheet in his open folder. "She wanted to make sure you got a heads-up on a story that's breaking tonight on one of your favorite cable news channels."

Griffin's lips thinned and he leaned back in his chair, spreading out his arms toward Finley. Steve watched Edie make a reflex move that looked like she was reaching for a pen and a notebook from her purse. He smiled to himself, thinking, *she'll never lose her instinct of smelling a possible story in the works.*

Neither the president nor Finley noticed her reaction, and Finley continued to speak. "The lead story in the nine o'clock time slot is *'the smoking gun'* on the administration's ties to a foreign entity. This time it's Russia, not ISIS or Al Qaeda or any one of the usual suspects. And once again they cite a single source close to the president." Finley paused and glanced at Griffin, who seemed to breathe a sigh of relief.

"I have got to give them credit for tenacity," Griffin said. "These stories have plagued my entire second term. Starting with the claims of the last election being illegitimate. We made the decision last year to refrain from responding to such nonsense. This will fade away like all the other dead ends they've tried." He shook his head. "Why is Angela bothering you with any of this?"

"Well, sir, like always—even with no official press release statement from your office—we do our own investigation to keep tabs on potential leaks. Just in case someone on the staff thinks it's okay to distribute sensitive or classified information to the media."

Steve caught a definite change in Finley's demeanor. He saw that both the president and Edie picked up on this too. The president's chair creaked as he leaned forward and rested his elbows on the table, tenting clasped fingers under his chin.

Finley lifted the top sheet from the folder and picked up an envelope. He pulled out a stack of photos and, one by one, placed them on the table in front of the president while describing their details.

The president stared at the assortment of photos, which highlighted a number of industrial structures in a suburb of Minsk—a major city in Belarus—an eastern European country to the north of Ukraine. Finley pointed a finger at one building labeled as the old KGB headquarters: a stone's throw from the industrial site at the center of the cable channel's lead news story. Steve noticed Finley held several more photos in his hand, but instead of putting them down, he sorted through the remaining documents in the folder. He dug out a paper with the Customs and Border Patrol insignia imprinted on top, explaining that customs officials had recently placed a temporary hold on a shipment at the Canadian border. The shipping papers listed the origination point as Minsk. Finley read off the name of the company and pointed to one of the photos showing the industrial complex.

He concluded by saying, "The destination address was a contracting firm in Morristown, New Jersey. The contractor eventually received the goods last May."

The president looked like he was poised to tell Finley to get to the point when Steve felt his body sway as a wave of nausea crept up his chest. Under his breath, Steve muttered a few curse words and cleared his throat. He started to speak but swallowed his words in a pool of bile and remained silent.

Finley placed the last of the photos on the table and said, "And this is the White House source, sir."

Griffin looked from the photos to Finley. "Is this a joke, Mike?"

The red light on the secure phone in front of the president started blinking, and a sharp bleeping sound screamed. The president picked up the handset, listened for a few seconds, and then slammed it down.

"Let's go." He looked at Steve and Edie. "There's no time to go over the details as I had planned. You'll get the official briefing along with my cabinet. Things are moving faster than expected."

Griffin paused for a second, jabbing a finger at the last photo Finley had placed on the table.

He glared at the selfie of his youngest son, Sean—with the shadow of a much younger girl off to the side—taken in the renovated family room at the president's Stillwater retreat in northwestern New Jersey. "And my advisors told me *my* use of social media was a problem."

The president took a deep breath and turned toward Steve. His virtually black eyes grew larger, and his expression transformed several times. With a slight shake of his head and a raised finger pointing like the barrel of a gun, he said, "Later, Casella."

As they exited the small conference room, Finley smiled at Steve, and Edie gave her husband a questioning look.

CHAPTER 21

The atmosphere in the main conference center of the White House Situation Room complex buzzed with excitement as it filled with the president's cabinet members and the required intel committee chairs from Capitol Hill.

Steve and Edie squeezed into two open seats along the side wall to the right of where the president took his place at the head of the oversized conference table. They waited for the meeting to get underway.

In a hushed voice, Steve took the opportunity to finish telling Edie the story of how the president's building contractor from Morristown, New Jersey—working at the first family's retreat in Stillwater—came to install the wide-planked oak hardwood flooring purchased from a company headquartered in Minsk. The one with purported close ties to the former Soviet Union.

"Canada?" Edie whispered. "You told the president that the company was Canadian based? Why would you do that?"

"Well… that's where Liliya was from."

"Who the hell is Liliya?"

"Liliya Ivanshinski. The sales rep from the company. I dealt with her when I purchased the materials for our own remodel. Her office is in Ontario—near Toronto." Steve paused and shrugged. "Found out later that the company is headquartered in Belarus, once part of the Eastern Soviet Bloc. At the time, when the first lady asked about the flooring, I didn't think to mention it."

"I hope the trees didn't come from Chernobyl," Edie said. She added, patting his knee, "Maybe I should be distancing myself from you instead of the president."

Steve's mouth opened, but before he could answer the president slammed down the secure phone. After exchanging a few words with Vice President Evander Patterson, the president called the meeting to order.

"As outlined in the documents you received, we're acting on a solid tip regarding a newly discovered Al Qaeda training camp in the Taizz Governorate in southwestern Yemen. Over the last several weeks, our intelligence agencies have intercepted data suggesting attacks on our homeland for the upcoming 9/11 anniversary are being planned by this particular Al Qaeda in the Arabian Peninsula group." Nodding at the phone sitting in front of him, the president added, "I've given the final approval for this mission, which will commence immediately." He motioned for General Davidson to update them on the scope of the SEAL operation about to start in Yemen.

When the general finished his summation, the junior senator from California, Butch Carlisle, got the president's attention and threw out a statement. "When I read the intelligence briefing regarding this operation, it was unclear as to whether or not the Yemeni government had been properly notified about any military maneuvers taking place on their soil. In General Davidson's description, I didn't hear any specific remarks concerning the Yemeni military, and if they'd been briefed or were taking part in this mission."

Senator Carlisle had replaced Senator Justin Mahorney, also from California, as the chairman of the Senate Intelligence Committee soon after Mahorney announced his plans to retire for health reasons. The president's interactions with Mahorney during his brief tenure as committee chairman had been cordial, unlike his dealings with the man's predecessor, the half-wit pain in the ass from Georgia, Senator Henry Whitcome. For a moment he contemplated the dynamics between Butch Carlisle and Edie Pauling if she pulled out a victory in the upcoming special election in California to replace Mahorney.

President Griffin gave Carlisle a tight smile. "As we speak, a special courier is delivering my message to the prime minister at his headquarters in Aden."

While the occupants in the Situation Room stared at the monitors, General Davidson provided a simplified description of the ongoing operation. The general was also receiving live updates via a secure satellite uplink from the command center at MacDill.

From time to time, Senator Carlisle checked his watch. At one point he shook his head and turned to his aide. The aide jumped to his feet and listened to the hushed words from the senator before nodding and heading toward the door.

The senator turned back to the president, but never got the chance to speak. The monitors on the rear wall had gone dark, and General Davidson slammed down his secure communications device. He cleared his throat and informed the president, "Sir, we have a problem."

Steve had caught the exchange between Senator Carlisle and his aide. He now focused his eyes on the senator and watched the man's deep California tan turn a deathly shade of white. He noticed the vice president had looked hard at Carlisle before tapping the president's arm and whispering in his ear.

As the general scrambled to circumvent the sudden communications blackout, a harried duty officer charged into the conference room and handed the president a document. In contrast to the waxy image frozen on Carlisle's face, the veins on Griffin's forehead bulged, and a purplish hue highlighted the level of his anger.

CHAPTER 22

Taizz Governorate, Yemen
September 5
5:54 am

The clear night with comfortable temperatures and low humidity had transformed into a firestorm that shook the heavens. Even now, hours after the bombing had stopped and the conflicting forces had either fled the scene or been left for dead, a thick, pungent cloud hung over the rough terrain in a remote region of Yemen's Taizz Governorate.

The training camp, belonging to Al Qaeda in the Arabian Peninsula, the target of a clandestine Navy SEAL operation, had been leveled. Until recently, US intelligence had not been aware that AQAP operated in this part of Yemen. Smoldering remnants of once camouflaged structures and disseminating wafts of incinerated human flesh marked the perimeters of the devastating zone of destruction.

After completing the first phase of the mission, the SEAL team was regrouping on the periphery, when the gates of Hell opened and the skies lit up in an apocalyptic display of firepower. Unfortunately, the elite team had not been far enough away from ground zero to avoid being part of the carnage reaped upon the hidden terrorist stronghold.

The sudden appearance of the airborne barrage had been unexpected and not part of any support for the SEALs. Although the lines of communication to command headquarters at MacDill Air Force Base remained sporadic, from all accounts, an entire Navy SEAL platoon had been snuffed out by the unknown forces that had hit the training compound.

Local inhabitants in the mountainous districts to the south of the city of Taizz lived a quiet existence that dated back through centuries of conflict in one of the world's most war-torn regions. The sudden arrival of Al Qaeda represented another chapter in the unending fight for a beleaguered populace with nothing left to lose. The Yemeni tribes in the Taizz Governorate had a long-standing distrust of not only outsiders to the region, but perhaps an even greater animosity toward the centralized government in the state of Yemen.

Any outsider to this struggling agricultural expanse, whether it be one of many Islamic extremist groups or larger states such as Saudi Arabia, Russia, or the United States, represented a potential force to be avoided or neutralized, but the more real and continuous threats from the self-proclaimed official governing bodies on Yemeni soil warranted a much more direct peril to their continuing existence.

Two older men with scraggly beards and weather-carved leathery skin stood beside a much younger man: clean-shaven and looking out of his element. They hovered on a precipice overlooking what was once the Al Qaeda training camp they had learned to tolerate in a mutually agreed existence. In the complicated interaction of non-tribal relationships, tribal leaders sometimes sided with a particular group one day, and then aligned with the opposing forces the next. These tribesmen cared little about the ideological composition of their competitors, but instead focused on how best to gain access to needed resources for their communities.

When one studied the countenances of the two Yemeni farmers who gazed down upon the death and devastation before them, it was difficult to gage their allegiances or level of interest in the current state of conflict.

The younger man, Nadheer, standing at their side, could have been considered an outsider, although one of the men next to him was his father. He had recently returned following years of education in Saudi Arabia—an almost unheard-of circumstance for one of the local tribesmen. While the three conversed using a Ta'izzi dialect of the Arabic language, as their tribal ancestors had done for centuries, Nadheer also possessed a respectable command of English.

The sun nudged above an eastern ridge, imparting a gingery contradiction to the gory spectacle at their feet. As the sky brightened, Nadheer's father shielded his eyes and pointed to something beyond the outer rim of the camp, about a hundred yards from where they stood: A strange reflection rippling in an otherwise stationary landscape.

The three climbed down the rocky incline and trekked across the battle-strewn plateau. They passed numerous bodies which needed little inspection for them to conclude that death had been swift and violent. As they approached the object noted from their earlier observation point, they detected a definite movement from a section of crumpled steel roofing panel.

Nadheer forged ahead. When he got close, he abruptly turned and told the older men to hurry—he thought he heard a muffled groan coming from underneath the mangled panel. The three worked feverishly to extricate the wounded body. As they scouted the area looking for anything usable to fashion a makeshift stretcher, they also checked for signs of any additional survivors of the bloody battle. They found no other bodies, living or dead, in the immediate vicinity of the wounded soldier. Most of the dead had been cut down closer to the camp itself, along the path they'd just followed. The magnitude of disfigurement in the fallen warriors horrified the farmers. While the injuries of the wounded soldier looked severe, it appeared he may have been saved from a sure death by the heavy roofing panel shrouding his body.

After securing the soldier on the hastily built stretcher and gathering up what remained intact of his gear, they began the arduous journey back to the fertile valley of their home.

It was then that Nadheer realized the soldier was not from the Yemeni military. It was also clear he was not an Al Qaeda fighter. No, this man was an elite special ops combatant. Nadheer revealed to his father that the sole survivor of the massacre that took place at this remote Al Qaeda training camp was a US Navy SEAL.

Chapter 23

Washington, D.C.
September 5
10:38 am

President Tyler Griffin isolated himself in the Oval Office. As he paced his inner sanctum, it felt more like a tomb than the official hub of the most powerful man in the world. Having sent sixteen brave young men to their deaths, he felt more like an executioner than the leader of the free world.

The routine business of the nation ground to a halt while the president struggled to deal with one of the most disturbing decisions in his life. It had seemed like only minutes had gone by from delivering the go-ahead for the mission when the world's most sophisticated communications system crashed. And then, in agonizingly slow bits and pieces, the news dripped in with the shocking outcome of what was supposed to be a relatively low-risk reconnaissance and intelligence-gathering operation. Someone had staged an attack on the Al Qaeda camp at the exact moment the Navy SEALs were on scene. All of our special ops team had perished. The president didn't believe in coincidences. He slumped into the leather seat behind his desk.

When a sharp knock on the private entrance to the Oval Office interrupted his thoughts, he knew it was time to put any personal feelings aside and get back to work. He called out for the person to enter. Another knock sounded on the northeast door. Both doors opened at the same time. Mike Finley walked through the private door, and the president's secretary scurried in from her office. She placed a sealed communique on his desk and disappeared before Finley had a chance to close the other door.

Finley crossed the spacious office and glanced at the envelope delivered by the secretary as the president picked up the antique letter opener.

With his eyes locked on the letter opener gripped in the president's white-knuckled fingers, Finley said, "Mr. President, I think I can tell you what's inside."

The president looked at the United Nations insignia embossed on the upper left-hand corner of the envelope. "What the hell do you know about this UN document?" He placed the letter opener on the desk but started tapping it lightly with the tips of his fingers.

"Rumor has it that Yemen's prime minister has filed an official complaint with the UN security council demanding immediate sanctions against the United States for conducting a military operation on their soil without prior notification to his government."

"That's impossible. These things take time to work through channels, and this—"

Finley watched the president's face turn a purplish hue as he came to the grim conclusion.

President Griffin smacked closed fists against the top of his desk, causing the letter opener to catapult in the air and land point down, impaled in the plush carpet. The president didn't seem to notice it. Finley took a step back.

He looked on as Griffin pieced together his own thoughts about what had happened. After the pulsing veins protruding on the president's temples and the fiery redness on his cheeks subsided, Finley took a chance and spoke.

"Sir. We have a leak."

The president turned so abruptly with his eyes stabbing at him that Finley contemplated using his right foot to kick the letter opener farther away from the desk and out of the president's reach.

Griffin didn't utter a single word at first. He continued shooting darts at Finley while tilting his head as his lips formed a thin tight line. After taking a deep breath, the president spoke. His voice sounded eerily calm. "Mike. Sixteen of our boys are presumed dead. I sent them to that God-forsaken land. What they were looking for could possibly have saved thousands of American lives. But right now, all we have are sixteen dead soldiers. And you're telling me somebody from our government may have leaked the details of this mission to the prime minister in Yemen?"

The president took a breath and glanced at the unopened official U.N. document sitting on his desk. He stood, and briefly looked out at the South Lawn. The tension in the room was palpable, and Finley sensed the president had already dismissed any sanctimonious noises coming from the U.N. None of it was binding, since the security council vote needed to be unanimous, and unless the current United States ambassador had a death wish—

like the previous man in his position—this letter was just posturing on the part of the secretary-general.

"Mike, I—"

Finley spoke over the president, "Sir, no stone will be left unturned. We've got every resource looking into—"

The president held up his hand. "I'd expect no less, Mike, but let's be clear about priorities. We needed the intel from that mission. I've got no doubts those bastards have something big planned for the 9/11 anniversary. And that's less than a week away. If we don't get a better handle on the targets, I got a bad feeling that we are going to wind up with a bloodbath."

Finley gave the president a quick nod.

"Right now we don't have a lot to work with. Only vague threats and the usual pre-9/11 chattering," Griffin said. "I want you prepared for every contingency. At the first sign of trouble, you need to get your ass on scene and squeeze whatever you can from witnesses and any suspected terrorists. I'll press the intel analysts to double check what little data we've got." He walked closer to Finley and placed a hand on his shoulder. "When we get through this—we'll tear this town apart until we find the sonsofbitches behind all these leaks. As you know, this isn't the first. We've been plagued for almost the entire seven years in the White House. I didn't expect to spend the last days of this administration investigating my own people, but—"

The president sighed, shaking his head. Finley sensed a sudden chill running through Griffin, who never found the words to finish.

CHAPTER 24

Berkeley, California
September 7
11:06 am

Olivia Davenport glanced out the window at the San Francisco Bay and the never-ending traffic tie-ups on the Bay Bridge. In a few minutes they'd be leaving the Marriot and heading to the University of California's Berkeley campus, a short fifteen-minute ride from the hotel.

She turned back to the room and observed Patty Basara, whom she knew by her real name, Patas Ta'anari. Patas sat on the bed, legs crossed underneath her, pencil tucked in one ear, leafing through a tattered notebook. She looked like she was studying for a high school geography test.

Do they even teach geography in school anymore?

The girl appeared so young and fragile, but she seemed relaxed. Patas's appearance had changed dramatically since Olivia first met her as part of an investigation into the attempted assassination of the governor of California.

Part of the investigation?

Patas Ta'anari had been seen running from the scene of the purported attack. She had been wearing a suicide vest. It had exploded in the Sacramento River. To the rest of the world—Patas Ta'anari had died that night during a failed attempt on Governor Blackwell's life.

Patas was sixteen at the time.

Olivia Davenport and Mike Finley had played pivotal roles in the investigation. With the help of an ex-Navy SEAL with an axe to grind against the governor, they'd uncovered the sordid events that had led up to that night. Patas Ta'anari, along with a number of other people, had been the real victims of the governor and his wife. The president exonerated Patas and gave her this new identity. She was now pushing close to twenty.

I could have a daughter that age.

Olivia's face blanched and she thought of Mike Finley.

Let's not go there.

Patas turned from her notes and smiled at Olivia. "With any luck, Jalal will try to kill me today and then you can go home."

Olivia's mouth opened wide.

Patas waved her hands. "I'm joking, Agent Davenport. I really do appreciate you looking out for my welfare. You and all the others searching for my brother."

"Olivia. We agreed for you to call me Olivia."

Certainly not Mom.

Olivia's cell phone rang. Several moments later she ended the call. "The rally's still on. The university decided not to cancel—despite all the threats. Time to get ready to go." She hesitated; then trying to lighten the moment, she added, "What're you going to wear when you speak?"

Patas cocked her head and smiled. "What you see is what you get. I'm a college student." She got up from the bed and spread out her arms. She had on a similar outfit to what she'd worn for her presentation at the Jewett House in Coeur d'Alene—faded jeans and running shoes. Although they were new since her previous wardrobe had suffered serious damage at her last appearance. In place of the embroidered blouse, she wore a gray and black T-shirt.

Turning serious, Patas opened up the top dresser drawer and chose a delicate headscarf. She stood in front of the mirror and started wrapping the garment in place. "As you can see, Olivia, I'm not trying to dismiss my faith. But I want to show Muslim females it's possible for our culture to coexist with others." She shook her head. "Not only possible, but imperative."

Trying to hide her skepticism, Olivia looked at Patas's reflection in the mirror.

"For too long, Muslim females have remained silent. My mother…."

Her voiced faded and Olivia could see the loss and helplessness Patas felt at her mother's recent death. She also sensed a deep anger at her brother for what he had done.

"Right now I'm not trusted by anyone. Muslim men—and the majority of Muslim females—want me silenced for betraying Islam. And in this country, non-

Muslims—usually divided when it comes to Islamic traditions and jihadism—appear united against me. Although for different reasons. Seems I'm accomplished at offending pretty much everyone. Many fear my goal is to replace the laws of this nation with Sharia. That I'm using false rhetoric to disguise my ultimate plan. Others look at me as an Islamophobe—that I'm not a real Muslim."

Patas finished with her headscarf and turned toward Olivia. She took in a deep breath, heaving her shoulders as she exhaled. "I *am* a Muslim, Olivia. But first I'm an American. Every bit as much as you. So let's go exercise my right to free speech. And while we're at it—let's keep an eye out for my sonofabitch brother."

So much for studying high school geography, Olivia thought.

CHAPTER 25

San Francisco, California
September 7
1:05 pm

Following the fiery reunion with his parents after returning to the United States, Jalal Ta'anari shed his former identity as an Egyptian businessman and, for the moment, assumed the guise of an American tourist. Since he'd grown up in the Sacramento area, this role fit him much better than he would've liked. His hatred for America and everything it represented had been compounded by the years spent in the Al Qaeda training camp in Yemen following the failed assassination attempt on the California governor.

Jalal, dressed in a Navy-blue blazer, a white shirt with the top two buttons open, and a pair of tan chinos, placed his hands on the weathered railing and stared out across the tarnished emerald waters of the bay. His head pivoted from side to side, but never strayed far from the image of Alcatraz Island. His vantage point on the upper level of Pier 39, not only afforded him an excellent view of the many popular tourist attractions in San Francisco, but the crowded venue gave him an air of anonymity. While fixated on the distant waves crashing against the jutting rocks of the former federal penitentiary, his peripheral vision took in the outlying silhouette of the Golden Gate Bridge and the arrival of the solitary figure standing at his side.

Without turning his head, Jalal said, "You would blend in better if you lost the striped business suit and silk tie." He cupped a hand across his brow to shield his eyes, still gazing to the north and west. "And at least pretending to enjoy the scenery—instead of darting your head about as if waiting for the authorities to drag you away."

A sheen of sweat broke out on the man's forehead, but he remained mute. Jalal had dealt with this pathetic specimen back in Yemen and knew the fool feared him more than any federal agents hauling him off to an American prison. Word had just gotten to Jalal that their camp in Yemen had been wiped out. There were rumors of a US Navy SEAL platoon on a secret mission when the Yemeni Air Force intervened. When the sun rose the next day, no survivors had been found. Jalal put those pictures out of his head. He had an important job to do while in America and couldn't be distracted by a few more deaths in a war that had been fought for centuries. With no SEALs left standing, it seemed unlikely his mission had been compromised.

"Unless you're waiting around for someone to incarcerate you—get going. We have much work left to complete, and the time grows short."

The man was smart enough not to acknowledge Jalal's words or to make any overt gestures. He turned, and although he attempted an air of casualness, Jalal detected an anxious rhythm in the man's footsteps as they gained purchase on the slippery deck. He all but ran back toward the street.

It wasn't until the man had disappeared down the stairs that Jalal chanced a furtive glance at the spot where his inept accomplice had been standing. The large forest green vinyl shopping tote was exactly where it was supposed to be. In one smooth motion, Jalal turned away from the bay and swept up the bag. He headed inside one of the nearby touristy restaurants. After placing the bag at his feet, he took a seat at the bar in a position that gave him an excellent view of the pier's upper-level concourse. He ordered a club soda and scanned the area but saw no signs of any activities to suggest either he or his courier had been followed or had raised any suspicions.

The wall-mounted TV, tuned to a local news channel, caught his eye. He swiveled to look at the screen. The lead story was the breaking news on the disturbance and violent rampage at the Berkeley campus of the University of California on the eastern side of the bay. He frowned as a photo of his sister popped onto the screen. Of course the name underneath was not Patas Ta'anari. Neither the media nor the public had discovered her true identity. Earlier, he had debated whether or not to make an appearance at that rally to complete his personal jihad. But after discovering another, more meaningful upcoming engagement which spotlighted his sister, he chose to wait a little longer. The thought made his eyes focus on the shopping bag at his feet. He knew that among other relevant data inside it, there would be more precise details pertaining to his sister's schedule which coincided with an important event. He drained his glass and slapped a few bills on the counter. Grabbing the forest green tote, he left the restaurant without looking back at the angry rhetoric spewing from the TV.

Jalal had also kept up with two other stories involving his family: The gruesome findings of the burned bodies of two local Muslims at the mosque in Yuba City, and the bombing and subsequent rioting at a local college event in the Idaho panhandle.

As expected, the media jumped in with little hesitation or fact-checking and salivated over the latest outburst of Islamophobia and the growing bigotry that divided the nation. One thing perplexed Jalal. He found it odd that the White House had been silent on these latest attacks of supposed acts of hate aimed at a frightened population of Muslim Americans. While there were many holes in the intelligence community, he expected his presence and the role he'd played in those two events would've been discovered by now. He wasn't sure what to make of this silence from the president and how it impacted the rest of his plans.

CHAPTER 26

Sonoma, California
September 7
1:50 pm

At the president's last-minute request, Steve Casella had remained in D.C. with Mike Finley to prepare for the threatened attacks on the 9/11 anniversary. So far they only had vague intelligence reports and desperately needed the data from the Al Qaeda camp in Yemen. Instead, recovering the bodies of the sixteen SEALs was all that remained of the failed mission.

After flying home from D.C., Edie primed herself for a heated campaign battle. Catori volunteered to help with the kids until after the election.

With Steve's busy schedule and Edie's career in politics on the upswing, Catori had taken over most of the management duties at the Mayacamas Shepherds dog training facility. Several years ago, Steve had expanded the operations to include specialized K9 instruction techniques in addition to breeding and boarding. The training building was located across the road from Steve and Edie's house which overlooked the beautiful Sonoma Valley.

Ever since leaving the Kootenecti Reservation in the Idaho panhandle to attend college, Catori had played a role in Steve's canine enterprises. Last May, Catori had completed her biology degree at Sonoma State University. She was preparing to enter the UC Davis veterinary program in January but intended to continue working at Mayacamas Shepherds as much as her schedule allowed.

The afternoon sunbathed the Sonoma Valley and radiated its warmth through the expansive windows of the Casella home perched in the eastern hills. With T.C. sound asleep in his bedroom, and Rosa studying Disney cartoons in the den, Edie and Catori worked on Edie's campaign strategy in the family room. Edie hoped Rosa's current obsession with Disney characters would keep her busy until bedtime. She'd been fantasizing non-stop about their upcoming trip to Disneyland.

Edie sat on the sofa and reached for a drink of water after practicing her campaign speech in front of Catori. She planned on delivering this message to supporters at the Disneyland Hotel on September 11th to officially launch her senate race.

Seated across from Edie, Catori smiled and nodded. After a brief hesitation, she said, "That was great, Edie, but—"

Edie tilted her head and placed the water glass on the coffee table.

"Didn't Ms. Gregory advise you to distance yourself from the president?"

Earlier in the day Edie had a video conference with her campaign manager, Evelyn Gregory. She had given

Edie a series of talking points for her appearance at the Disneyland Hotel. Edie had asked Catori to sit in on the conversation.

"Well, I could hardly ignore mentioning the most prominent leader in the RGA movement."

Catori checked her notes. "I counted eighteen times."

Edie shrugged. "That's all? Evelyn will never catch it."

"Ms. Gregory must be a saint," Catori mumbled while glancing over the rest of her notes.

Before Edie could respond, Catori leaned forward, dropping the notepad on the table. When she settled her gaze on Edie—Edie's cheeks turned to ice and her throat felt like sandpaper. She glanced at the water glass and the drops of condensation running down the sides, but knew the cold, inviting liquid would have zero effect on her ability to swallow.

She'd experienced this look on her friend's face before.

"This is none of my business, Edie," Catori started.

Not capable of speaking, Edie gestured for Catori to continue.

"When you first ran for a spot in the state legislature, I figured that was a good thing. No more fighting behind the scenes to expose corruption and make enemies." She shut her eyes. "But now… I don't know… look at what the president has faced. Over this last year, everything seems to be spiraling out of control. The nation is at a crossroad. I'm reminded of Lomasi's tale of Coyott. You recall the day you met Lomasi?"

Edie nodded, still failing to swallow. Every time she looked at Catori, it reminded her of Lomasi. Catori carried the spirit of her grandmother with her. She had been destined from birth to continue the task of passing on tribal lore.

"On that day outside her cabin, when Lomasi looked at Amber," Catori said, her voice barely above a whisper, "she didn't see a white German Shepherd. She believed she had witnessed the return of the creature from the times of our ancestors: The ghost of the ancient god of light. According to Lomasi, when this creature, Coyott, chooses to lead you, you will have no choice but to follow. This ancient trickster can save the world or lead you astray."

Edie at last found her own voice. She stared at Catori. "Lomasi pointed at me and insisted I was destined to provide stability and make sure this creature would guide the world in the right direction to extinguish the deathly flames of the demons."

Catori opened her eyes and looked at Edie. "This is the second time in less than a week this familiar vision has visited me."

Edie waited for Catori's next words.

"I'm not sure when or how, but I fear that soon, many people could die."

CHAPTER 27

San Francisco, California
September 7
2:01 pm

Jalal Ta'anari exited the restaurant on Pier 39 carrying the forest green shopping tote and headed toward the closest BART station. In a matter of minutes, the Transbay Tube channeled his commuter train under San Francisco Bay. Switching rail lines in Oakland, he found a seat and placed the tote on his lap. Jalal sat back and listened to the garbled announcement declaring that the two Berkeley BART stations remained closed until further notice due to undisclosed security issues at the Berkeley campus.

He smiled and closed his eyes, thinking about his next encounter with Patas. He praised Allah for keeping his sister safe on this one occasion at the liberal college campus. It seemed fitting that he himself should impart justice on her. Her lustful actions had played a deciding role in taking down the governor of California, but Jalal had a far greater score to settle with Patas. Allah, of course, understood Jalal was not responsible for succumbing to the wickedness of his evil sister's flesh.

He disembarked the BART train at the northern-most station in El Cerrito, stepped onto the elevated platform, and rode the escalator down to street level. Unfolding the bus route map pulled from inside his jacket, he checked his bearings and walked the short distance to the transit stop near a time-worn strip mall on Cutting Blvd. In less than five minutes he climbed aboard a city bus for the thirty-minute ride to his destination in the city of Richmond.

Today was his first visit to this critical location. This segment of the mission—in essence, the defining moment of the jihad—was his prime responsibility, and he needed to assure himself that the laboratory operations had produced sufficient quantities of the toxic agent.

When he stepped off the bus, he paused at the intersection and stared at the morbid skyline of towering catalytic stacks and distillation columns. He noted dozens of storage tanks threaded together with a labyrinth of pipes snaking an unending web across the behemoth Chevron oil refinery like some prehistoric creature's vascular system. Inside the metallic vessels flowed the precious fluid whose sordid journey to the home of the Great Satan heralded the spilling of blood for the sole purpose of squandering vast quantities of this liquid gold.

A gaseous cloud of hydrogen sulfide, imparting its familiar reek of rotten eggs, perpetually infused the entire Richmond neighborhood. A shroud more impenetrable than any physical barrier in keeping the inhabitants imprisoned by a resource from which they'd never reap any benefits.

Jalal strode off with an added purpose, inhaling the foul gases as one would crave the burst of sweet-smelling oxygen after being pulled from a burning building. He smiled. So Allah had a purpose to bring him here. A glowing flame ignited in his head, fed by the hydrocarbon-sated atmosphere. An extra venture shouldn't compromise his original goal. And with a little bit of luck, it would feed the authorities another dose of misdirection. He nodded. Plus a parting gesture to the community, which much like the denizens in Yemen—the poor souls in this hellhole had nothing left to lose. He'd gladly give them their freedom.

Jalal approached the site of the operations laboratory, making a mental checklist of the defense measures in play and how vigilant the workers monitored the perimeter of the sprawling single-story brick structure. His entry proved difficult, satisfying his concern for security.

Most of the personnel working at the site were scientists and engineers, not soldiers. He couldn't be sure if years of higher education had dampened their thirst for Islam and the glory of the jihad. He knew, more than most, of the temptations this decadent nation espoused, and the enticements to stray from their holy cause.

Not a scientist, Jalal had little patience for overseeing the complex chemical reactions and laboratory procedures. He had called ahead and asked for proof that the arduous steps produced the necessary results to obtain maximum carnage.

Dressed in a crisp, clean white lab coat, the head chemist, stereotypically gaunt and bespectacled, rubbed his sweaty palms together and swallowed. "Jalal." He hesitated and diverted his eyes from the bright lights of the two tiny cubicles seen through the two-way observation mirrors. "I can assure you, the potency of the VX gas is—"

At Jalal's glare, the rest of the man's words stuck in his throat.

"Of course, Jalal." He pressed a button on the control module in his hand. Jalal noticed his index finger shaking at the act and inwardly smiled at the tremors in the man's voice as he described the demonstration. "In the room to the left you can see the half-dozen twenty-pound sacks lined up on the steel shelving." As he spoke, a young man wearing a lab coat walked into the chamber through a door in the center of the rear wall.

Jalal scowled. "Were you not explicitly told to use females for these tests?"

Before the chemist could answer, the man who'd entered the room unbuttoned his lab coat. He removed it, revealing that underneath he wore only a pair of white boxer shorts and a thin, sleeveless T-shirt.

"I did not wish to insult you by allowing such a display of female flesh."

Jalal stared at the chemist and then turned his attention back to the left cubicle. He watched the man place the lab coat over the back of a chair. The chemist explained the actions as the man wheeled a utility cart over to the shelving unit. He grasped each of the six sacks and placed them on the cart. As the man carried the last sack, Jalal observed beads of sweat pooling on his exposed forearms. The heavy bag dropped to the floor when his arms twitched. The man's eyes flitted around the room, and he attempted to cross over to the door. Before he could reach for the door handle, his back arched in a violent spasm, sending him crashing to the concrete floor. His limbs jerked at odd angles before turning rigid—his spine appeared pinned to the floor. The man's head—unmoving. His eyes bulging as streams of vomit spilled over gaping jaws.

Jalal checked his watch and nodded his approval. The chemist pressed another button on the control module. In the cubicle to their right, a female carrying a small brown paper bag entered the room and placed it on a round steel table. She pulled out the lone chair and sat down. She wore a white lab coat. Below the hem of the coat, Jalal could see loose-fitting blue jeans and a pair of heavy work boots. Her headscarf left only the fine features of her face exposed. Her eyes reflected a dull veneer of resolve as if she had knowingly sensed her fate. Steady hands unfolded the edges of the bag, and she removed an apple and a small container of yogurt. She fished inside the bag again and pulled out a clear plastic spoon.

Jalal leaned forward and pressed his hands against the mirrored glass panel. For a moment he imagined the young female's eyes returning his stare. The chemist standing next to him droned on and pointed to the ventilation grill in the ceiling, directly over the table.

Moments later, Jalal watched the female's pupils constrict. And then streams of tears intermingled with watery secretions flowing from her flaring nostrils. She dropped the spoon and clutched her chest. Her mouth opened and closed like a dying fish stuck in the sand. At first, her upper body fell forward against the tabletop. Next her legs kicked out and the force of her convulsing frame sent the chair skittering sideways and toppling over. She slipped to the floor, and all her movements ceased.

Jalal shrugged and again checked his watch. He looked at the chemist. "Not as dramatic as I expected, but it appears either direct exposure to the skin or inhaling the vapors is equally effective."

The chemist busied himself leafing through a notebook before responding. "We have processed the precursors separately and the packaged products remain in their binary forms. This gives us maximum flexibility for transportation and ultimate detonation. I assure you, Jalal, many will die. Many will die."

About to leave, Jalal spun around and slapped a hand on the chemist's shoulder. "I will let you in on a secret." His eyes pointed to the dead scientists in the cubicles. "I anticipated watching the skin melt and drip from their faces and limbs." He smiled and shook his head. "Goes to show you how Hollywood gets it all wrong. Those arrogant filmmakers continue to sell their garbage to the American fools." He patted the chemist's cheek. "And you look nothing like that sad-faced actor. Besides, I believe Dr. Goodspeed was a biochemist in the Nicolas Cage movie. Soon we will demonstrate to these infidels what a real terrorist attack can accomplish."

Jalal laughed so hard the glass panels on the cubicles shuddered almost as much as the chemist's shoulders. "Come, what else do you have to show me tonight?"

After completing the remainder of the inspection tour and pleased to see that by tomorrow morning the containers would be packed, sealed, and ready for transport, Jalal took a moment to sort through the papers from the tote delivered to him in San Francisco. He picked a quiet location in one of the smaller offices along the partitioned area on the south side of the building; far from the bustling activities surrounding the laboratory equipment. Deep in thought, he didn't hear the soft tap on the doorframe. But he did detect the smell of fear radiating from the man standing on the threshold. Sweat dripped from the man's forehead and disappeared into the bushy nest of an unruly beard.

"What is it, Assad? I need to finish up. I must be on the road before daylight." When he had entered the laboratory building, Jalal had spotted the vehicle procured to take him south, parked near the entrance. The previous BART trip and foray with the local bus system would not be repeated. His next ride, a gleaming Sterling Blue Metallic Corvette, although conspicuous, tended to lose itself on the LA freeways. It mildly disturbed Jalal that he preferred such a garish means of transportation. It should have troubled him that he was more of a Californian than he cared to acknowledge.

Assad looked like he would soil his pants as he summoned up the courage to address the leader of this jihad. Jalal leaned back in his seat and folded his arms across his chest. One hand resting underneath his open jacket. A gesture that might have been taken as a harbinger of reaching for his weapon. Exactly the scene Jalal wished to stage.

Still standing in the open doorway, Assad found his voice—a trembling, hesitant tone akin to a child approaching a parent with news of a dreadful act committed. "Yes, Jalal, I am sorry to interrupt. I... my family... I must ask you—"

"Assad. Either make your point or get back to work."

Lowering his head, Assad continued in a more constricted air. "I believe I understand the need for the deaths of so many fellow Muslims living in America. But—"

Jalal stood so abruptly his chair kicked back against a metal file cabinet, making Assad almost lose his balance as the sharp clanging reverberated across the tiny space.

"Do you?"

The words spit from Jalal's mouth, slapping at Assad, who staggered back into the corridor. Jalal closed the gap. In a lightning move he grabbed Assad by the collar and flung him back into the office.

"Do you?"

Jalal thought of his own perceived sacrifices and the ease—no, the perverse pleasure—with which he dispatched his mother and father.

"You are a weak and pitiful fool, Assad. You think mere acts of death and destruction thrown at the infidels are enough? No. We must set the stage so they can tear themselves apart from within. The time is right for this to happen. Those pretending that Islam, a peace-loving religion revered throughout the world, can coexist with the decadent, self-righteous infidels, are poised to condemn the opposing views of those labeled as hateful, bigoted, and privileged Americans. The ones convinced we are out to overtake and destroy the west. To desecrate their beloved US Constitution and replace it with the Sharia doctrine."

Jalal continued, ignoring the fact he was also an American. "And more to the point, the Muslims in this country have become soft. The call to jihad has been replaced by the evils of this infidel society. They worship their gadgets more than the Prophet."

Assad flattened himself against the wall. Somehow, he summoned the nerve to answer Jalal's wrath. "I swear, Jalal. My faith is as strong as ever. And I have kept my promise not to tell a soul. But is it necessary for my family to die? I can forbid them to go—they do not need to hear the real reason. I know thousands of Muslims will die. Jalal, I beg you to spare my family."

At the mention of *family*, Jalal's rage erupted. His hand reached inside his jacket and pressed against the cold steel of his handgun. He shook his head as he leapt at the wretched image of this failed jihadist in his midst. His fingers pulled away from the gun as if stung by a deadly serpent. He thrust the hand into his pocket and latched onto his switchblade. His other hand gripped Assad's hair, twisting the trembling body until it rested against his shoulder.

He hissed into Assad's ear, "You have proven my point. Consider it a favor that you will not live to see your family perish." The blade swished open, and Jalal slid it across Assad's throat. A second jab went deep into the flesh, stuttering as it scraped bone. Assad's final words gurgled, lost in the spurts of blood spattering the wall and dripping down the sleeve of Jalal's jacket.

CHAPTER 28

Taizz Governorate, Yemen
September 8
4:15 am

Soft music hummed in the background. He reached into the sterling silver ice bucket and lifted the dripping brut Champagne bottle from the icy slush. Not able to keep his eyes from the form gliding across the room, he failed to notice the bubbly liquid overflow and cascade down the sides as he filled the two glasses. When he picked them up, they almost slipped from his grasp. He didn't really care and decided to skip the drinks, placing the glasses back on the coffee table.

As she neared the sofa, he jumped to his feet and took her into his arms. For several moments they clung tight in a warm embrace. He listened to the rhythmic beating of her heart. She gently pulled back and lifted her arm. Grabbing the end of the hijab, she unwrapped it. Her deep brown eyes reflected a willful desire. He could feel the heat radiate from the delicate blush on her cheeks as her long lashes fluttered under prominent arched brows. Jet black hair caressed her shoulders and framed a chiseled jawline. She used the untethered headscarf as a lasso around his neck to draw him in for a quick, but passionate kiss before she turned, grabbed hold of his hand, and led him to the bedroom.

Transfixed at the image of this stunning creature, he watched the silky garment slip from her shoulders and drop to the floor. With one graceful swirl of her foot, she cast it aside. He smelled the moist fragrance emanating from smooth olive flesh as pure as her heart.

He opened his mouth to speak.

A scream spilled from his lips as an agonizing pain slammed his body and wrenched him from the dream and into the nightmare. Voices bounced around him and hands grabbed his body—pulling, tugging at his arms and legs. The words had no meaning—they sounded urgent—but not threatening. The world remained black. He inhaled a strong, reeking vapor and felt as if he were glued to the festering underbelly of a primeval swamp. Now and then he caught a whiff of an unfamiliar cooking odor, making his gut revolt.

He again opened his mouth but failed to work up another scream. He allowed the fatigue to take over, vaguely thinking it masked the pain—praying to once again lose himself in his unfinished fantasy.

When he awoke, the pain felt veiled, taking a back seat to an underlying curiosity. The dream had eluded him and the real world stayed black. He no longer heard any voices. A shifting sea of aromas shaped a tangible hint of hunger. About to call out, a voice close to his ear spoke in crisp, clear English, "I am going to remove the compresses from your forehead. Do not be startled."

He felt the damp towels being pulled from his head and blinked open his eyes. A pair of penetrating black eyes stared back at him, studying and calculating, as if forming a decision.

"My name is Nadheer." The man's voice sounded concerned, but pleasant.

Not sure of the circumstances, he allowed several seconds to pass while trying to get a better glimpse at his surroundings. His head was propped slightly, but he couldn't see much; except the olive face of a young man, who looked about his own age.

Taking a short breath and exhaling, he closed his eyes. Aware of the absurdity of his next words—given whom his imprisoners logically must be—he recited, "My name is Corey Galloway. United States Navy Seaman. Rate, E—"

His narration got cut off by a sudden outburst of laughter.

Nadheer patted him on the arm. "No, no, no, Seaman. No, you are not a prisoner. You are in the home of my father. He is a farmer, a local tribesman. We found you at the site of the decimated Al Qaeda camp and brought you here. You suffered many injuries."

He lost the fight and slipped back into temporary darkness. Over time, the episodes of consciousness grew longer. Bit by bit he retained parts of the stilted conversations, and the painful conclusion that the mission had failed and every one of his SEAL teammates had perished.

* * * * * *

Corey Galloway, sitting up in his bed, allowed Nadheer to lift the empty tray of food off his lap. He watched the young man carry it from the room. Through most of the morning, he'd listened to Nadheer describe the massacre. Still confused about the sequence of events that had led to the demise of the ill-fated mission, Corey grappled with something that gnawed at the discordant images swimming in his head.

Physically, he felt strong enough to attempt getting out of bed, but his head remained clouded and dark, consumed by the loss of his fellow SEALs. The overwhelming guilt kept him paralyzed. He needed something to jumpstart his way out from this spiraling hole of remorse and self-pity.

From the corner of his eye, he noticed his torn and blood-stained fatigues heaped in the far corner of the room. His weapons and other equipment were stacked next to his clothes. This triggered a memory. He stripped back the blankets and stumbled to his feet. After losing his balance and landing on the floor, he crawled over to his gear. Tossing aside his boots, tactical vest, and the assortment of weapons, he clutched at what remained of a torn and battered backpack. When he peeled back the flap on the mobile forensic pack, he sighed and leaned his aching body against the wall. He quickly shrugged off his frustration and extracted the items from the damaged container.

He worked with such intensity that he never noticed Nadheer slipping back into the room until he spoke. "I am impressed with the technological gadgets you guys have at your disposal, but I do not believe you will find anything functional." Corey looked up at Nadheer and watched him shrug before continuing, "Sorry... I took the liberty of examining much of your equipment. Are you looking for something in particular?"

Before answering, Corey did a quick rundown of his predicament, as well as his options. As the fog shrouding his consciousness waned, he concluded that this young man had saved his life and could be trusted.

And now Corey needed something else.

He nodded to Nadheer. "We entered the camp, extracted data from their computing devices, and then retreated to evaluate the intel before initiating phase two. My orders were to withdraw to the western flank and do a quick rundown on the data—uploading anything critical to the com center—and report back to the mission commander before completing the operation." He paused and looked to the ceiling. "That's when all hell broke loose. The sky lit up, and I never saw my team again."

He looked back to the mangled piece of gear sitting on the floor in front of him. "Nadheer. There's crucial information locked inside this unit. I downloaded the encrypted data from the camp's mainframe equipment, plus cell phones and other mobile devices left carelessly around." He pointed to the universal forensic extractor device. "Right now this baby appears dead, but according to the manufacturer, if the damaged unit looks at least halfway recognizable, none of the data has been lost."

The room again began to close in around him. He needed to get this data transferred and deciphered. "Do you have a way to communicate with the Yemeni central government?" He was desperate. Maybe they could contact the US military.

Nadheer slowly shook his head. "When my father was in Taizz, he heard many stories about what happened at the Al Qaeda camp. It appears with almost one hundred percent certainty that the Yemeni Air Force sent in fighter jets to bomb the camp. Our prime minister is claiming the US military raided the camp without our government's knowledge or approval. He has stated that your military commanders made a last-minute request for support when your troops started taking heavy fire from the Al Qaeda fighters. But by the time the Yemeni ground forces assembled near the site, an entire squadron of Navy SEALs had been wiped out. The Yemeni Air Force then conducted an air attack which annihilated the camp. With no reported survivors. I understand our government has demanded that the United Nations place sanctions on your country for conducting an unauthorized military action on Yemeni soil."

While Corey deduced that part of those statements contained slivers of truth, no one called the Yemeni military for help. Nor did they show up with ground troops. The air attack came without warning amidst the clandestine Navy SEAL operation. And the odds were pretty good that the appearance of the Yemeni Air Force at that particular moment was not a coincidence.

Corey glanced at the scattered equipment from his mobile forensic pack and began returning the damaged but critical items to the bag. He got to his feet. Trying to hide any unsteadiness from Nadheer, he said, "Thank you, my friend. I'm indebted to you for saving my life." The words made his voice hitch. He swallowed and continued, "I appreciate your hospitality in nursing me back to health. But now I think it's time for me to go home." After completing his statement, he looked around the room. His body swayed and he staggered back to the bed. "Give me a couple minutes, and then I'll collect my gear and go."

Nadheer raised his brows and nodded. "Perhaps I can be of further assistance in seeing you to the door. Or better still, back to American soil." He looked at Corey's pile of equipment before continuing, "You should not trust anyone in the Yemeni government if you need to export those items."

Corey stared back. "Not a lot of options to consider at the moment. My communications equipment has been damaged beyond repair. And my gut tells me this data is extremely time sensitive. Our intel guys need to work on it now. A lot of good men died to get this. I still got a job to finish."

"You get a few hours rest while it is still daylight. Gather all the strength you can. I have a few resources of my own which might help. I learned more than English while attending the university in Saudi Arabia."

CHAPTER 29

Waiting for Nadheer's return, Corey Galloway relinquished all futile attempts to sleep. He paced the room he'd spent the last few days in recovering from his wounds. Once or twice, he checked other parts of the house, but it remained empty. Not unusual. According to Nadheer, his father awoke before dawn and never returned from the fields until after sunset. Nadheer had told him that his mother died while he attended the university in Saudi Arabia. His uncle lived in a similar dwelling about two kilometers to the east.

Impatient, Corey got dressed. Next, he cleaned and inventoried his weapons and supplies. In a last-ditch effort he checked his communications equipment again, but confirmed nothing was salvageable and tossed it aside. He packed, then repacked his equipment bag several times, choosing which items could be left behind. His primary concern was ensuring that the data from the Al Qaeda camp would not be confiscated or destroyed. Realizing the current date and the symbolic meaning of the looming 9/11 anniversary, he concluded that if he didn't get the info back to central command at once, the gathered intelligence would be useless, and his platoon had made the ultimate sacrifice for nothing.

Gazing out a west-facing window, Corey watched the sun easing behind the distant hills and transforming the evening sky into a cotton candy-like illusion. He knew the old farmer would soon be trudging up the winding trail, expecting Nadheer to have prepared the evening supper.

Still no sign of Nadheer.

Corey rummaged about the simple food preparation area but had no clue as to where to start. His mind remained hazy, not even sure what he'd been given to eat and drink by his kind hosts.

For the first time in his life, Corey began to build a kinship regarding his father's battle with reality after returning home from his last tour of duty in the Middle East. Although physically stronger, he experienced a seesawing sensation of a disturbing rollercoaster ride which threatened his sanity. This emotional weakness caused him no small degree of shame. He was alive, and his fellow teammates were all dead.

The front door burst open and Nadheer stood silhouetted in the waning sunlight. Before Corey spoke, Nadheer hurried inside and disappeared into a storage area at the rear of the house. He returned carrying a bundle of clothing and tossed it to Corey.

"You need to get out of those desert fatigues."

Corey stared at Nadheer.

"Hurry. Do as I say. If you are caught wearing anything resembling a United States military uniform, you will be shot on sight—no questions asked. At the moment, the Yemeni government is not your friend."

"Where are we—"

"Corey. We must leave before my father returns. He knows nothing of—"

"So you were able to contact—"

Nadheer raised both hands and slapped them against his temples.

Corey nodded, shed his fatigues, and scrambled into the clothes Nadheer provided. When finished, he joined Nadheer who'd gone into the bedroom. Nadheer had pulled a ratty-looking leather satchel from underneath the bed. He looked up at Corey. "Get those fancy devices from your bag. Everything should fit—with plenty of room to conceal it using my dirty laundry. All your other gear—you must leave behind."

Corey extracted the instruments from his bag and handed them to Nadheer. "What about my firearms and—"

"Your weapons *especially* must not be found on you."

"But—"

"What? You think you are going to shoot your way back to the United States?"

Nadheer finished stuffing the satchel with the dirtiest articles of clothing he could find. He then scraped up a few ripe leftover food bits from the breakfast trash and scattered them on top.

"Why don't you toss in a rotten fish too?"

Nadheer shook his head. "That would raise suspicion. We will be heading toward the Red Sea, not coming away from it." He slammed down the lid, pressing the loose, rusting snaps closed. He shook his head and reached for a length of rope hanging on a hook. Wrapping it around the satchel several times, he secured it with a complicated variation of a bowline, which served as a crude reinforcement for the damaged leather handle. This impressed Corey, but before he could comment, Nadheer had already started for the door, signaling him to get moving.

Looking like a pair of nomadic laborers off to scrounge up work to get a scarce meal in their bellies and a decent night's sleep, Nadheer and Corey disappeared over a slight prominence to the west, before Nadheer's father stepped into the house.

They flagged down a local khat grower heading to the city of Taizz and settled into the back of the slow-moving oxen-driven cart. If Corey thought Nadheer's father appeared old and wizened beyond his years, the driver of the cart looked like he had died sometime in the twentieth century, but nobody had thought to take him from his cart and place him to rest in the ground.

A cloud-covered half-moon provided little light for the journey, and Corey wondered how the driver navigated the narrow winding trail as the cart worked its way down the mountain toward the distant lights of the city. He gazed at the stacks of green vegetation that filled the cart. He inhaled the aromatic leaves and sensed a familiarity with the wafty bouquets. Raising his brows to Nadheer, he said, "This guy isn't delivering coffee beans to market, is he?"

"Ahh... my friend. The sacred leaf of this evergreen helped you through the worst of your wounds. And perhaps contributed to a pleasant dream or two."

Corey stared at Nadheer but remained quiet.

Shrugging, Nadheer added, "But now it is time to kick the habit, unless you intend to retire from the Navy and live on a farm in Yemen. For centuries, khat has been both a blessing and a curse to our humble tribal communities."

After stopping at the outskirts of Taizz, near the Al-Ashrafiyyah Mosque, Nadheer thanked the driver and hustled Corey down a dark alley, leaving him with the satchel and telling him to wait. Before Corey could question him, Nadheer's footsteps faded down the narrow street as he dashed left at the first intersection. Fatigue hit Corey like slamming into a wall. He leaned back against a cracked and faded brown brick building which contrasted with the gleaming towers of the renovated mosque he saw rising above the aged structures that spread out from the holy shrine.

It couldn't have been more than a few minutes when Corey, who had fallen into a deep, dreamless sleep, snapped open his eyes at the noise of a sputtering engine. Screeching brakes echoed in the quiet alley, and Corey watched a battered old car bounce over a curb, sideswiping a line of trashcans. The closeness of the buildings magnified the clattering sounds. He blinked as the car jerked to a stop and Nadheer shouted from behind the wheel. A cloud of bluish-tinged exhaust smoke swirling in the dim light of a streetlamp made his eyes tear.

"Get in. Hurry. We have at least a two-hour drive to Mocha, and it would be to our advantage to travel in darkness. Plus, we must keep on schedule."

"According to the Navy's mission briefing, it's ill-advised to drive the Yemeni highways at night. The chances of an attack by the local bandits—"

Nadheer smiled. "You need not worry, Corey. Not in this piece of crap. And look how we are dressed. Even for Yemen, any respectable thief would avoid wasting his time. As far as the Yemeni military or the PSO—same thing goes."

"PSO?"

"Political Security Organization."

Corey nodded. He fought with the rusty hinges and yanked on the passenger door, sending mechanical screams of protest up and down the alley. Climbing in, he lifted the satchel over the seat and placed it on the rear floorboards. An even more chilling repeat of metallic cries sounded when he closed the door.

Nadheer yanked on the gearshift and the car lurched forward while Corey's neck snapped against the headrest. At the end of the alley, Corey's arms extended as he barely avoided being cast into the dashboard by Nadheer's erratic braking.

The car accelerated down a larger but, at this hour of the night, deserted thoroughfare.

Corey chanced a quick glance at Nadheer. "I didn't know you owned a car. This is a real classic."

Nadheer shook his head. "I do not. But someday I hope to afford a decent car—not something like this." He patted the steering wheel. "Thanks to Allah, some fool left a set of keys tucked on top of the sun visor." He hit the brakes again, whipped the wheel around, chomped on the gas pedal, and bounced the rear tires over the curb as he followed the signs leading to the highway to Mocha.

Corey had enough. "Pull this heap of junk over." He had to repeat his request two more times before Nadheer complied. Tires scraped and sparks flew from the rims, but Nadheer managed to stop the vehicle without any major catastrophes.

"What is it?"

"This is just a wild guess, Nadheer, but I get the impression you've never driven a car before."

Nadheer shrugged. "I am a quick learner, and you are still not well."

Corey stared back at him.

Rather than fight with the stubborn doors again, both men shimmied around the inside of the car and switched positions. Most of the trip to Mocha, an important port city on the shores of the Red Sea, proceeded with little conversation. After a few short words directing Corey to the correct route, Nadheer had fallen asleep.

Chapter 30

Washington, D.C.
September 8
7:57 pm

Steve Casella slipped away from the suffocating confines of another urgent meeting in the Situation Room and wandered outside on the White House grounds. He leaned against one of the West Colonnade's white pilasters. Although the sun had set, with fall a few short weeks away, the hot, humid air in the nation's capital showed no signs of letting go.

Focused on the nearby sounds coming from the Rose Garden, he didn't notice the shadowy image until it spoke.

"If something doesn't break soon, the president is going to fire his cabinet, the entire intelligence community, his advisors, and—with a little bit of luck—me."

Steve glanced over his shoulder at the sudden appearance of Agent Mike Finley, but one ear still engaged the frolicking noises coming from the far side of the hedges. He nodded, knowing the recent mission that took the lives of an entire Navy SEAL platoon had hit President Griffin hard.

* * * * * *

Four days ago, Steve had sat in the Situation Room while the drama unfolded in real time. He'd seen the haunted look on the president's face after realizing that the mission to gather needed intelligence on suspected threats from a recently discovered Al Qaeda group in Yemen had failed. The intelligence agencies now worked to determine the source of the leak that compromised this critical operation. But that didn't stop Tyler Griffin from carrying the burden of sending his elite warriors to their deaths. Although the president accepted full responsibility, Steve understood that once the traitors who leaked the information to the Yemeni government were discovered, Griffin would crush the culprits with every weapon at his disposal.

Finding the specific data on what Al Qaeda had in store for the upcoming 9/11 anniversary, however, took precedence over punishing those responsible for sabotaging the mission.

After leaving the White House only hours after the disastrous SEAL operation, Steve and Edie had been standing in line to board a Boeing 787 Dreamliner at Dulles International Airport for their flight back to the San Francisco Bay Area. An agent from the president's security team muscled his way through the queued passengers and pulled them from the crowded jetway. Following an urgent discussion, Edie proceeded to board the flight without Steve.

Due to the secret service's intervention, the flight departed fifteen minutes late. The president had decided that Steve Casella and Mike Finley would work together on investigating the potential terrorist threats.

When Edie got home, she made immediate arrangements to fly Amber back east to assist Steve with his assignment. Catori Torrence had already persuaded Edie to let her help with the children while she worked on preparing a campaign strategy. Edie's first scheduled appearance was a rally at the Disneyland Hotel on September 11th.

Rosa, excited about meeting Goofy and the rest of the Disney cast of characters, only pouted for several minutes after learning of Amber's abrupt departure. It wasn't difficult for Edie to sell the Disneyland trip as a much better substitute for their abandoned RV tour of the northern foothills of California.

* * * * * *

Steve remained quiet after listening to Finley's words. At the moment, he felt like he'd been stuck in D.C. for a month, instead of the few hectic days since the tragic events in Yemen. He took a step closer to the Rose Garden, intending to ignore Finley's complaints. They both looked up toward the south-facing Truman balcony off the first family's private residence when First Lady Alison Griffin called down to her youngest son.

"Sean, it's time to come in now. You need to get washed up and ready for bed before your father gets home. He hasn't finished talking to you about your social media activities." She turned her head and waved down to Steve and Finley before disappearing inside.

The two men watched Sean hand over Amber's lead to one of the secret service agents while three others from the detail escorted the president's son from the Rose Garden.

Finley punched Steve's arm lightly. "So far the president has come down harder on Sean than you."

After a brief smile, Steve shrugged his shoulders. "You gotta admit it, Mike, the Russians make an excellent hardwood flooring product."

Steve signaled for the agent holding Amber to release her. Amber barked twice and squeezed through a slight separation in the dense privets. That made Steve a little sad as he recalled earlier visits when Amber had gracefully leaped over them. As she approached, her speed ratcheted up. She barked again, shifted her head, and darted right past him.

Steve spun around and watched Amber's pace accelerate, reminding him of her younger days when she hadn't been all that obedient. She closed the gap between the South Lawn and the southeast visitors entrance near Pennsylvania Avenue at a rate that dropped his jaw. As she got closer to the gate, the White House grounds erupted in a display of glaring floodlights, blaring alarms, and hordes of uniformed guards materializing out of thin air.

A scuffle had started just outside the wrought-iron barricade which served as the symbolic line of defense to protect the most powerful man in the world and his family.

CHAPTER 31

Steve and Finley charged toward the epicenter of the unexpected disturbance. It appeared no one had as yet breached the perimeter of the White House grounds. Outside the fence, security personnel hardened up the west sector of lawn adjacent to the General William Tecumseh Sherman monument. Steve entertained a fleeting thought that a new generation of protesters had determined that not only should the Confederacy be written out of American history, but it was time for the Union to disappear as well. They might as well go straight for George Washington instead.

Then he realized that a lone man had been wrestled to the ground by at least four agents, but no other intruders could be seen in the immediate area. Steve remained so absorbed with the scene on General Sherman's turf that he had neglected to consider Amber's actions. When he checked out her behavior, he noticed she wasn't concentrating on the man half-hidden by his captors and surrounded by teams of armed agents ready for a fight. In fact, she was ignoring the whole spectacle.

Amber stood at the now taller, stronger, anti-climb-equipped, wrought-iron fence, staring at a black German Shepherd on the opposite side of the barrier. The dog was sitting on its haunches, one paw raised against the fence while he licked Amber's snout as she stretched it through the iron pickets.

"Holy—" Steve started to say as Finley grabbed his shoulder. When Steve turned toward Finley, the face on his long-time colleague looked like he'd seen a ghost—or the devil.

Steve raised his brows. "Ahh… I seem to recall… you've met up with Kobe before. Wanna go say hello?"

Finley, who'd drawn his weapon seconds before, took a breath and slipped the gun back in his shoulder holster. He wiped both hands across his face in a failed effort to cleanse away the gritty sweat.

Steve ambled toward the fence and the touching reunion between Amber and one of her grown-up pups from an earlier litter. Finley followed but kept a half-step behind. As Steve approached the canine family, he glanced at the bizarre sight transpiring about a dozen yards from the two dogs. His attention focused on the confrontation between the White House security officers and the man pinned to the lush lawn surrounding the monument. The perimeter search outside the White House widened as they hunted for additional intruders. The entire area adjacent to 1600 Pennsylvania Avenue quickly locked down.

"What in the hell is *he* doing here at the White House?" Finley uttered in a resigned voice.

As Steve clipped on Amber's leash and edged her back, he called over to the black German Shepherd on the opposite side of the fence, "Don't worry, Kobe, I don't think Mike means you."

With Finley in the lead, Steve guided Amber toward the gate. A sudden thought flashed through his head regarding the identity of the man subdued on the other side. The appearance of Kobe left no doubt that the guy being pulled to his feet, arms yanked behind him, and cuffs squeezed onto his wrists was retired Navy SEAL, Master Chief Ethan Galloway. Steve had given Kobe to Ethan Galloway and his son, Corey, about three years ago.

That immediately sobered Steve up. "Jesus, Mike. Corey Galloway—Ethan's son—was one of the SEALs killed in the Yemeni operation. This doesn't look like a guy coming to thank the president for—"

Although Ethan Galloway was in cuffs and surrounded by at least a dozen agents; weapons drawn and trained on him, he didn't seem intimidated, frightened, or angry. He looked like he was waiting for someone to invite him inside. His face remained calm while his eyes scanned the area.

After gathering up Kobe, Steve and Finley rushed toward the scene, holding credentials high and picking their way through the crowd. When Galloway spotted them, his shoulders relaxed and he exhaled. His eyes locked onto Finley, giving him a quick nod and a tight smile.

Steve hung back, keeping short leads on Amber and Kobe. He watched Finley stride deliberately over to the agent-in-charge and pull him aside for a heated conference. The two men got in each other's faces and argued. The agent-in-charge continued shaking his head until Finley raised his hands and pulled out his cell phone. He hit one of the speed-dial buttons and spoke rapidly into the phone. He signaled for the agent-in-charge and handed him the phone.

Narrowing his eyes, the agent shrugged and yanked the device from Finley's hand. "I don't give a rat's ass who the hell you are—I'll tell you how this is gonna—"

The agent's spine arched back like he was hit with a round from his own service pistol. In the glow of the spotlights aimed every which way, illuminating the spectacle, Steve, standing at least ten feet from the two men, could see the color drain from the agent's face. For a split second, Steve entertained the idea that the man had indeed been shot. Then he listened to his words and thanked God he wasn't the one holding the phone.

"Yessir! Yes—sir, Mr. President. I understand. We'll clear up this matter right away, sir. I'm—" He stopped speaking and listened to the president. Steve could see his body relax and the frozen contours on his face loosen up. "Thank you, sir. Yes, Mr. President, you have yourself a good night as well." After a brief closure of his eyes and a fleeting smile, he handed the phone back to Finley. He glanced around. Looking satisfied that his team hadn't noticed his transitory change in disposition, he lifted his body back to its full six-foot-two stature and pointed a finger at Finley.

"You guys, including your handcuffed buddy, are cleared to enter the White House." He paused and continued in a louder tone, "But—this guy's not going one step closer until we do a complete body search. You understand that Finley?"

Finley nodded. As the agent-in-charge walked over to relay the situation to his men, Finley, called out, "Nice work tonight, Agent Cocheran."

Cocheran swung around and stared at Finley.

"I mean it, son. Everybody did their job. This is the way it's supposed to work. I'll make sure the president is made aware of the caliber of your unit's performance."

Cocheran's face showed nothing, but Steve detected a definite swagger when the agent turned away and strode over to the center of the action and shouted out orders to his men.

Finley walked back to where Steve and the two dogs stood. Steve noted that Finley kept his distance from Kobe.

"Who's going to pat down Kobe?" Steve asked.

Finley snorted. "If it turns out Galloway's got his custom sniper rifle stashed anywhere in the vicinity, I might volunteer to frisk the dog myself. His bite is nothing compared to the president's."

CHAPTER 32

Thirty minutes later, four secret service agents escorted Ethan Galloway, Steve Casella, and Mike Finley into the Oval Office. The president's chair swung around and he stood. Tyler Griffin wore a pair of faded jeans, a red plaid flannel shirt, and scuffed black cowboy boots. Steve knew for a fact that the president would have rather been splitting firewood at his Stillwater retreat than stuck at the White House. Griffin had long since given up on fighting with the secret service to allow him to let out his frustrations with a splitting maul on the South Lawn.

After a slight hesitation, the president walked over to Ethan Galloway, his hand extended. "Ethan, I'm…." Instead of grasping Galloway's hand, he attempted an awkward embrace and said, "I just learned Corey was on that mission. I'm so sorry, Ethan." He pulled back but held on to Galloway's shoulders.

With a short nod, Galloway looked into the president's eyes. "Mr. President. I have a solid reason to believe Corey did not die at that Al Qaeda training camp." He blinked and his eyes dulled. "But it does appear the rest of the platoon perished." Before continuing, he took a deep breath. "Based on what I've learned, there's a good possibility you can still salvage this mission, Mr. President, so those boys didn't die for nothing."

Steve looked at Finley, his own eyes widening. To his surprise, the president's next words did not challenge Galloway's conclusion or his source of information.

Griffin stared hard at Galloway before saying, "Ethan, if anybody survived that devastation, it would be nothing short of a miracle. I hope to God you're right." He swallowed and cleared his throat. "What you discovered about the mission… is it time-sensitive?"

Galloway gave a quick nod. "Yes sir. Plus the latest info I received—moments before your security detail greeted me—suggests we've got little time left to stop the triggering of an international incident. Not to mention the loss of my son and valuable intel data."

The president spun around and grabbed the phone on his desk, punching down on one of the buttons and rattling off orders.

"I don't care if he hasn't slept or seen his family in a week. Get him back downstairs. A fifteen-minute break is long enough. This is a non-union outfit." He spoke a few more words and slammed down the handset. Pointing a finger at Finley, he said, "Escort Ethan to the Situation Room. General Davidson will be waiting to hear his story. I've got a few details to take care of."

Steve glanced nervously between the president and Finley, finally settling his eyes on the two German Shepherds at the end of the leads he held. Both dogs avoided eye contact with Steve. As he handed over Kobe's lead to Ethan, the president placed a hand on Steve's shoulder.

"Go ahead with them, Steve. Don't worry. What I need to do, doesn't involve you."

With a crooked smile, Steve nodded. He exhaled and turned to catch up with Finley and Galloway. As he reached the door, the president added, "I do look forward to speaking with you soon though. Once I get finished with Sean."

* * * * * *

Ethan Galloway sat alone with Kobe in one of the smaller conference rooms of the Situation Room complex, staring at the clock and wringing his hands together. He knew time had all but run out. The general had listened to his story. He made Ethan go over it two more times. When Steve and Finley tried to come to Ethan's aid, General Davidson held his hand out, his eyes commanding them to remain quiet. That failed to work, so he directed them out of the room. Amber resisted, but Steve convinced her to follow the general's orders.

When the interrogation ended, Ethan closed his eyes, stroked Kobe's neck, and asked Kinsley for forgiveness if he couldn't convince the military of the situation. Maybe she expected him to fail—just like the mess he'd made of their marriage. Kinsley had been dead now for more than four years. He'd gotten that part of his life completely wrong.

Ten minutes had passed since the general had risen, thanked Ethan for the information, and left without informing him of his decision. Before the general turned away, Ethan noted the skepticism on the man's face. He also recognized the tiredness in the man's stride as the door slammed shut and the general's footsteps faded.

Ethan whispered a silent prayer for Corey and the slaughtered men of his platoon. If he had failed to persuade the general, not only would Corey be dead, but what he told the president about an international incident would likely not be avoided.

CHAPTER 33

Mocha, Yemen
September 9
3:28 am

Corey Galloway's body ached, screamed, cried for rest, but his mind raced forward. The adrenaline coursed through his system, fighting to keep him going. He had to deliver the gathered intel data before the looming deadline hit. Maybe the ill-fated mission could still accomplish its goal and his buddies hadn't given their lives in vain. In the rearview mirror, only darkness followed his thoughts as he drove toward the Yemeni coast.

Several more hours of night remained. Nadheer said they needed to reach the rendezvous point before dawn. So far he hadn't given Corey any details of the plan to get him and the electronic files out of Yemen. Corey had no idea whom they'd be meeting in Mocha.

When the first twinkling lights of the port city of Mocha took shape through the smeared windshield, Corey decided to wake Nadheer and get some real answers. After repeated prods, Nadheer raised his head, rubbing his eyes and stretching out his arms to the dashboard. He took several deep breaths and glanced at the signs at the side of the highway. Looking startled, he blurted out, "Take this next road coming up on the right." He drummed his fist on the dash for emphasis.

"But the arrow points straight ahead for access to the port. I thought that was the destination. You implied we were meeting someone on a ship."

"Yes, but not anywhere near the main docks and shipyards. Make a right turn—now."

Corey hit the brakes, decelerating enough to navigate the turn without fishtailing. All four wheels barely hugged the pavement.

Nadheer patted Corey's arm and smiled. "You are a very good driver." Five minutes of silence followed. "Now I must look for... ahhh... I think... yes. Please make a left just beyond those two white concrete structures. Yes. This is the correct road."

Corey slowed and eased the car off the pavement, hanging on tighter to the wheel as the useless suspension did little to dampen the consequences of the rutted, narrow dirt path he found himself negotiating. He glanced over at Nadheer who was nodding his head.

"We should reach our intended destination in about ten minutes."

"Good. That should give you time to explain what we'll find when we get there, and where we'll be heading."

Nadheer hesitated before answering. "Part of your question may have to wait a bit longer. The prince sounded a little vague on his intentions. I suggested that the US Air Force base in Riyadh would be an excellent destination, but the prince—"

"Riyadh? That's almost all the way to the Persian Gulf. Across most of Saudi Arabia. You said we'd be traveling by boat, didn't you?"

Before Nadheer could answer, Corey slammed on the brakes and turned to Nadheer. "Prince? Did you say prince? What prince are you talking about?"

"Yes, yes." Nadheer beamed. "My very good friend. The prince of Saudi Arabia. Prince Al-Waleed bin Majiid Al Saud. It is him I called. He was my very best friend at the university. Where I spent many years away from my home in Yemen. At Jazan University in Saudi Arabia."

Nadheer drummed his fist again on the dashboard. "We must hurry. He said it is important we board the vessel and reach the open seas before daylight."

Corey shrugged and shifted back into drive, spinning the tires and sending plumes of dust into the dark night air. "The prince of Saudi Arabia? Prince Al-Waleed bin…."

"Yes. Prince Al-Waleed bin Majiid Al Saud. My very good friend. The prince of Saudi Arabia."

Corey narrowed his eyes, glancing at Nadheer. "You do know there are—I'd estimate—thousands of princes in the House of Saud?"

Nadheer waved a hand in a dismissive motion. "Of course, Corey. I am not some ignorant farmer. I have a degree in biology from the university. If this school is good enough for the prince, I am pleased with the education I received."

"I'm sorry, Nadheer. I never meant to question your education or your intelligence. Go on. Do you have any idea about the prince's plan?"

"Of course. We are to board his yacht. And you will be smuggled out of Yemen so you can deliver this vital information to your command center. When we spoke on the phone, he said he would explain the details when we meet. He had several minor issues to work on first. So beyond getting on his yacht, I know little else."

Nadheer reached into a pocket and pulled out a cell phone, holding it up to show Corey. "He said not to call him again on this device unless a serious emergency arose, or if we could not rendezvous as planned. He is sometimes a very paranoid person and thinks there is always somebody intercepting, listening; tracking him every time he uses his cell phone."

Corey wasn't going to argue with the prince's security concerns. He recalled his own father had always preached this same advice to him. And on more than one occasion had been proven correct. Instead, he said, "I didn't know you owned a cell phone—but I don't mean anything negative by that."

"I purchased this phone when I attended the university. But it is, of course, no use on my father's farm or in most of the mountainous regions throughout our governorate. To use it I must go near the city of Taizz. That is why I left the house earlier—to speak to the prince. When I called, he sounded skeptical. Asked many questions. Then he ended our first call—"

"First call? You spoke more than once?" That sounded alarm bells in his head, but at this point he had few options.

"Yes. The prince told me to stay close to Taizz, so as not to miss his call, and about an hour later we spoke again." Nadheer hesitated and added, "To be precise, the prince called me two additional times and I called him back to relay a piece of information I had forgotten to tell him. Plus, he texted me the coordinates of where we are to meet."

Corey struggled to keep the car on the obscure path which now snaked through an increasingly rugged terrain filled with scraggly trees and dry foliage, but Nadheer's words concerned him. They should've had this conversation hours ago. He tried to keep his voice casual. "What information are we talking about, Nadheer?"

Nadheer leaned forward, straining at the darkness ahead. "The names. He wanted to check out the names."

"Names? What do you mean? Whose names?" The car swerved as Corey swung the wheel at the last second to avoid a twisted branch encroaching on the treacherous route.

"Your name specifically, but he also inquired about the identities of the commanders and your platoon designation too." Nadheer grabbed onto the center console and the door's armrest as Corey narrowly missed another tree limb. "Be careful, Corey. None of this will matter if you get us killed. We are almost to the end. Of course, I had no idea of the names of your commanders, so I just summarized what I knew about the fighting at the Al Qaeda camp. Plus the details you provided. We can talk more about this later."

The road continued to narrow and became almost impossible to follow. Although close to dawn, the night appeared as black as anything Corey had ever encountered. It gave him an ominous feeling about what would come next. Nadheer's words had him worried. His mind drifted to his father's admonitions about the increasing lack of privacy and the ever-intruding reaches of the government intelligence agencies into the lives of American citizens.

To be honest, that didn't sound so bad at the moment.

Under his breath, he whispered, "Can you hear me now, Dad?"

Louder, he said to Nadheer, "Yes, later, we can talk."

The copse of trees thinned. After the car crested a small hillock, a faint glimmer spread out ahead as far as his eye could see.

"This is it. Stop the car."

Corey let the car roll to a stop, killed the headlights, and shut off the engine.

"Now, you must switch the lights on and off. Two times. Then wait. Good. Now three more times. Then wait. Good. Now one final time."

Corey did as directed, and they both got out of the car. Corey reached into the back seat and grabbed the tattered satchel before slamming the door. The protesting hinges assaulted the stillness surrounding them.

Nadheer pointed at an old wooden pier jutting out to the isolated cove and led the way. They stepped across the weathered boards to the end, about fifty feet from shore. They listened to the gentle lapping of the waves against the aged pilings while sea breezes swept briny trails across their faces. The night remained quiet for several minutes and then they heard a rumbling engine noise echoing somewhere out near the inlet.

Squinting, Corey gazed into the black waters. "It could be tricky steering a large yacht into this tiny cove. Especially in the dark. I can barely see the dock, and we're standing on it."

"Do not worry. These luxury vessels are equipped with smaller launches for getting close to shore. This should be no problem for the prince. I am sure his crew is experienced in maneuvering through much tighter places."

The sounds reaching them grew louder, but still they could see no craft approaching. And then about hundred feet from where they stood, a motorboat appeared to form out of the blackness. Its engines throttled back to a steady chorus as the boat neared the pier. The size of the vessel surprised Corey. It was no small dinghy or inflatable launch, but rather a good-sized cabin cruiser—at least thirty-five to forty feet in length.

He turned to Nadheer. "This prince must own one mega-yacht to keep a boat like this for shuttling people back and forth to shore."

Nadheer's head bobbed. "Yes, Prince Al-Waleed is a very important man in the royal family. I have seen yachts large enough to moor crafts—such as the one now approaching—within the interior of the yacht. They steer the launch right through a garage-like door and can control the water level inside the yacht's chamber once the vessel is secured."

As Nadheer finished speaking, Corey heard the reverse thrusters kick in, slowing the sleek craft. The timing of the thrusters came too late, and Corey and Nadheer had to jump back to avoid being hit as the side of the boat crushed the last few feet of the pier decking before shuddering to a complete stop.

From on board the vessel, a voice pierced the night air. "Nadheer?"

"Yes. It is me." He turned to Corey and whispered, "That sounds like the prince himself. He has personally joined his crew to greet us. This is an honor."

Corey remained quiet. He stared at the boat now slapping against the pier and making it difficult to stand on the shaking boards. The pier shifted as the weakened pilings began to give way to the weight of the assaulting hull. He could see a lone person silhouetted in the glow from the bridge's instrument display. No other crew members were in sight.

"Nadheer," the voice said. "You must hurry. You and your friend should climb on board immediately."

Both men boarded the boat seconds before the damaged pier succumbed to the massive weight crushing against it and splintered. Before they could approach the bridge, the engines revved up. The craft made a sharp turn to port and headed out to sea.

The ship's pilot concentrated on navigating the craft across the shallow waters in the cove. At the speed they were traveling, if they hit any rocks protruding near the water's surface, the gleaming white fiberglass hull would be torn to shreds. The large man at the helm shouted over his shoulder, "Please, gentlemen, you should go below. It is much more comfortable in the cabin." One hand left the wheel and pointed to the narrow stairway. "We are not home-free yet. Once we reach the open waters, we can talk."

CHAPTER 34

(several days ago)

Retired Navy SEAL, Master Chief Ethan Galloway, still resided at his modest home in a small farming community close to Davis, California. At the moment he and his black German Shepherd, Kobe, lived alone. When Corey, his only child, announced he'd enlisted in the Navy, Ethan had been both proud and anxious at the same time. His own military experiences, coupled with the consequences of a failed government project, had cost him his marriage. Those memories still haunted him.

His wife, Kinsley, had been dead for years now so he could never fix the pain he'd put her through. Even after the discovery of the mind-altering drugs and hypnotic episodes fed to him by a joint military-intelligence operation, he never forgave himself for doubting Kinsley's love. All he had left now was Corey.

With Corey, now a Navy SEAL and stationed overseas, Ethan had more than enough time on his hands to rehash old issues and dig up new reasons to question the elected leaders in the nation's capital. His once manipulated mind had been purged of those past conspiracies which drove him to the brink of a suicidal tragedy, but when the clarity resurfaced, it left him with an even greater mistrust in the government.

Surprisingly, he hadn't been fired from his security position at UC Davis. President Tyler Griffin certainly had a hand in that. Three years ago, after calling in sick for his night shift, he disappeared for over a month. The extent of his involvement with the events surrounding the deaths of Governor Nicholas Blackwell and the governor's wife had never been made public. Few individuals knew the real story behind the bloody scene at the Blackwell estate in Jackson Hole, Wyoming, that transpired while the voters cast their ballots during the last presidential election. And on many a long, lonely night, Ethan's mind questioned the details of how the incident slipped out of control, and how he had reacted in the heat of the moment.

To this day, Ethan tended to peer over his shoulder, thinking the government might want to make sure the truth behind the election night carnage could never reach the light of day. He epitomized the proverbial loose end that could be made to disappear in the blink of an eye.

The TV in Ethan's living room droned on in the background. While he remained a news junkie, always watchful about potential new scandals, this evening he couldn't concentrate on the rehashing of the week's recycled headlines or the predictable opinions of the talking heads. He sat on the sofa stroking Kobe's neck. Kobe, Ethan's black German Shepherd, found his new rawhide chew toy far more captivating than tonight's talking points, exclusive interviews, or closing remarks.

While the flickering images on the screen dominated the fading light, and the sun settled behind the western hills, Ethan felt the room close in around him with a sudden vengeance. Thoughts that had remained submerged in the subconscious recesses of his muddled brain fluttered to the surface and gnawed at his senses.

In general terms, he was aware that Corey's SEAL platoon would be part of a clandestine operation but knew better than to grill his son on any of the classified details. Something bothered him about the impending mission, but Ethan couldn't put a finger on the bad feeling in his gut.

That gave birth to a new strategy.

He hadn't seen Archie Schlessinger since barging unannounced into Schless's house in Seattle three years ago. With no questions asked, his old SEAL buddy had assisted Ethan in his quest to locate where Governor Blackwell and his wife had sequestered themselves before making his election night appearance.

Tonight, as he flipped through the cable news channels, Ethan made a spur of the moment decision and placed a phone call to his old friend. He then booked the next available flight from Sacramento to Baltimore.

* * * * * *

Following the non-stop United flight and retrieving a disgruntled Kobe from his crate in the luggage compartment, Ethan rented a car at a Hertz airport counter at BWI and headed south on Interstate 97 toward Annapolis.

Schlessinger had given Ethan an open invitation to visit him at his summer home in Epping Forest, an exclusive community on the Severn River north of the Naval Academy, but until today Ethan had not made the journey. Several years ago Schlessinger had inherited the property from a rich aunt: a prominent resident and board member of the Epping Forest homeowners association.

Behind the wheel of the rented Cajun Red Malibu, Ethan turned to Kobe. "This a little better ride than the cross-country flight in the luggage compartment?"

Kobe chuffed and refused to look at him.

"I told you not to get used to jetting around in one of those government-owned luxury planes. That only happens when you got something they want."

Unlike his unannounced appearance in Seattle, Ethan had called ahead, and Archie Schlessinger expected him. When he arrived at the entrance gate to the Epping Forest community, a uniformed guard slipped back the window of the brick-walled security building and smiled. "Welcome to Epping Forest, sir. How may I help you?"

Before Ethan could respond, Kobe stretched to the limits of his seat restraint, placing his front paws on Ethan's lap, and growled at the guard. "Knock it off, Kobe." He grabbed Kobe's collar and eased him back onto the seat. "Sorry. He's a little cranky from the long flight."

The guard tipped his hat. "No problem, sir. When I was growing up, we used to have a German Shepherd. Great dogs."

That line had become familiar to Ethan since acquiring Kobe. The key phrase he had come to realize was *used to have a German Shepherd*.

Ethan smiled in return. "We're here to see Archie Schlessinger."

The guard nodded and turned back toward a computer monitor. He punched a few keys and Ethan saw a photo of himself and Kobe appear on the screen. After glancing back and forth between Ethan and the monitor, the guard said, "May I see some ID, sir?"

Ethan fished for his wallet and pulled out his California driver's license. "Is this acceptable?" Ethan meant his tone to sound facetious.

"It is for now, sir. Next month, at the request of one of the residents, the board will be voting on the validity of driver's licenses from certain states due to the criteria many are adopting regarding the issuance—"

Kobe leaned toward the open window and barked at the man, causing him to stop in mid-sentence. This time Ethan shrugged and smiled.

After scanning it into the system, the guard handed Ethan back his license. "One moment, while we wait for Mr. Schlessinger's response."

Making small talk, Ethan inquired, "Doesn't this procedure back up traffic if you get a lot of visitors arriving at the same time?"

The guard laughed. "Oh no, sir. I'm just a little slow. It's the first time I've used this computer. This is Mr. Schlessinger's prototype personal security system. He asked me to beta test the software program created by his company before it's cleared for sale." He stopped and grabbed a shabby memo pad on a rusty clipboard, holding it up for Ethan to see. "For everyone else, I just jot down the name and—if I'm quick enough—I try to record the license plate number too. Mr. Schlessinger's security suggestions at the board meeting have started to shake things up a bit though."

He paused as a long beep, followed by two short beeps, came from the tiny speakers on the monitor. He punched a key and reached over to the printer as a single sheet of paper slid out. "Here you go, sir." He handed Ethan a directional map to the Schlessinger residence.

"I've already got the address." Ethan waved his own piece of paper at the guard.

"I'm sure you do, sir. Please be sure to stay on the roads indicated on Mr. Schlessinger's map. And you have a good day, sir."

"Do I need to burn this map once I've located the house?"

The guard's face turned serious. "That won't be necessary, sir. I have a military-grade shredder hidden under my desk. We'll take care of it during your debriefing session on the way out."

Ethan narrowed his eyes, and he started opening his mouth.

The guard broke out laughing and slapped his hands together. "Gottcha! Mr. Schlessinger said you were a real hoot."

Ethan gave a weak smile and proceeded through the open gate. He drove slowly, following the specified route, gawking at the subdued elegance of the stately homes he passed. Many stood partially veiled behind dense groves of towering white oaks and lush landscaping. The last turn brought him closer to the river. Through the trees he noted a number of boat docks jutting out below along the rocky banks.

He slowed the car and checked the house number engraved on a small placard attached to a weathered post. With no room to park on the narrow lane, he turned onto the crushed stone driveway. He didn't see any signs of a house until the second sharp curve where the sloped drive led him even closer to the Severn River. He stopped the car in front of a small bungalow. The modest weathered wood-shingled structure looked old but well-kept. He removed Kobe's restraint and they both got out of the car. The place seemed almost preternaturally quiet with the nearby echoes of seagulls flying somewhere over the river.

No sign of Schlessinger.

Although tempted to scour the taller trees for evidence of a sniper hiding in the boughs, he reckoned if Schlessinger was in position, the best clue would be when the killing round penetrated his skull. He'd be dead before the reverberating blast from the high-powered rifle reached him.

His cell phone shrilled, and he dropped to the ground, hand digging toward his holstered Glock—the one he'd left back in his bedside nightstand in California instead of hassling with airport security—before the intruding sound registered in his mind as a ringtone. His nerves were wound tighter than he thought. He let out a long sigh. Still on his knees, he leaned back against a nearby black locust tree. Kobe sat on his haunches and stared at him. The caller ID screen flashed the expected *'number restricted'* notification.

He swiped the screen and listened. "Hey, chief. You're damn nimble on your feet for a feeble old man. But I gotta tell you—you drive that conspicuous rental heap like a freakin' old lady."

Ethan's eyes raked the area but found no traces of Schlessinger.

"Grab your gear from the car and walk back up the driveway till you get to the last turn. Head north, straight toward the big old oak with the tarred portside broken branch. Sidestep twenty paces to the left and then continue north. At ten paces you'll see a small gap in the hedgerow. You won't see the gate. It's lowered and the juice is off. Once you're through, it's programmed to re-engage and power-up. So don't dawdle or you could get castrated. Then again, I've been catching snippets of your pathetic life—and that might be the most fun since they threw your sorry ass out of the Navy. And don't let the dog get his tail stuck. Kobe looks like he might hold a grudge, and I'd like him and me to stay on neutral terms for now."

Ethan followed Schlessinger's directions and found himself staring at a multi-level stone mansion. On one of the wraparound cantilevered decks showcasing the glistening waters of the Severn River flowing toward the Chesapeake, stood Archie Schlessinger. He waved and disappeared inside through a set of French doors. Moments later, the door to the side porch opened and he motioned for Ethan to join him.

Once inside, Schlessinger didn't waste time with a lot of small talk. To Ethan, he seemed a bit wired, like a rodeo bull waiting to rocket out of the gate. "I've been working on this since you called last night. A couple links are still giving me trouble, but I'm almost there."

"What can you tell me?"

Schlessinger fidgeted some more. "Not a whole lot, so let me get back to work."

Ethan nodded. A useless question, but he asked anyway. "Okay. What can I do to help?"

"Haven't had time to eat today, and I'm guessing you're a little hungry yourself."

Kobe barked and pawed the floor as Schlessinger rattled off instructions.

Ethan filled two large cast-iron kettles with water and placed them on the oversized burners on the patio cooktop. He and Kobe descended to one of Schlessinger's docks and hauled up a heavy crab pot from the river. Making sure Kobe's nose stayed clear, he wrestled with the paddled tongs to grab onto the main course. They rounded off the meal with two loaves of crusty sourdough bread and a half-dozen grilled corn cobs Schlessinger had earlier picked up from a local market. Kobe rounded off his meal of pan-fried hamburger patties from Schlessinger's freezer with a scoop of grain-free kibble from Ethan's suitcase.

Schlessinger had eaten in silence. Although anxious, Ethan bided his time cleaning up the dishes. He was drying his hands on the dish towel when his old SEAL buddy called to him from his office. The room appeared to be about the same size as Schlessinger's high-tech computer lab back in Seattle, but to Ethan's untrained eye the stacks of equipment spread across the curved desktop looked less intimidating than what he remembered from Schlessinger's setup in Seattle.

He couldn't mask his reaction.

"Don't worry, Ethan. I'm linked to my mainframe system in Seattle." He pointed Ethan to the second office chair. "By the way, these new algorithms I've been tweaking are finally paying off. Most of the stuff hackers intercept are mountains of either routine bullshit or unending streams of gibberish. The trick is to isolate and cut the diamonds from the shitload of… well… shit." He smiled and continued, "And thanks to your taxpayer dollars, the NSA, to name one of a few key players, has the ability to harvest enormous amounts of public and private information. Not only from domestic carriers, but also from key foreign carriers too. Along with every electronic transaction you ever made. They accumulate so much data, they don't even know what they've got. Somewhere in this vast ocean are all your personal, medical, and financial documents; phone conversations, internet logs, and what you've purchased, including where and how much you paid. But unlike Google or Amazon, they can't use the data—at least not legally. To tell the truth, these mega-internet conglomerates scare me more than the government. They are the real gatekeepers of who sees what. If they decide your opinion is not to their liking—they simply change an algorithm or two and it all goes away."

Schlessinger glanced up at the digital wall clock. He then tabbed through several pages and brought up a map on the center monitor. Each of the two side monitors were filled with small print too tiny for Ethan to read. Schlessinger tapped a key, and Ethan watched the map zoom in on a region in the Middle East. "This has got to be what you're talking about, Ethan. All the data points to this sector in Yemen. There's a site in the mountains near Taizz. From all indications, Corey's platoon is poised to raid what has been identified as an Al Qaeda training camp. And the communication links are configured for the highest levels. If I got any better at this, I could show you a live picture from the White House of all the president's men sitting in the Situation Room. And you know what this all means, don't you?"

Ethan bit his lip and swallowed. "Everyone's waiting for the president's go ahead. This is going down a lot quicker than I imagined." He shook his head. "Guess that's not unexpected. Could be related to the 9/11 anniversary. But that's not what's bothering me. My gut's been screaming ever since I talked to Corey before the mission blackout."

Schlessinger stared at Ethan. "Give me a second. This could have something to do with your worries." He started scrolling the data lines on the two side monitors. Every several seconds different colored highlighting began appearing, then disappearing on the screen as streams of words flashed by. Ethan leaned closer, but the screens changed too rapidly to comprehend. He thought he detected several languages.

"Don't even try, Ethan. Although this is one of the last stages of filtered data that gets fed into my new software, it still contains enormous amounts of garbage. I started to see a definite trend in particular threads of data from sources which are about a week old." He punched a few more keys. "Let's shift to the analyzed portions. This is still updating. The last hour or so has shown a lot more specifics."

Confused, Ethan asked, "What are we looking at?"

"For now, the origin points are still unclear, but I'm seeing a communication link with a government source in Yemen describing a SEAL operation about to start."

"So the administration is informing the Yemeni government about a military operation set to take place on their soil. That's the expected protocol, correct? I remember last-minute authorizations communicated for many of our missions—that's SOP for avoiding any potential international incidents. This way all the necessary parties are informed—but the timing doesn't allow for any loose lips to compromise the operation."

Schlessinger shook his head. "In this case, I don't think so, Ethan. Did you hear what I said before? The first messages I intercepted were sent about a week ago."

"A week ago?" Ethan said, pushing up from his seat and staring closer at the monitors. "That's suicidal. I can't believe Griffin would inform the Yemeni government about a clandestine mission until the last minute. He's not stupid enough to compromise—"

"You're absolutely right, Ethan. I think that—"

Ethan turned toward Schlessinger, his eyes bulging. "Some son of a bitch is leaking classified military intelligence to a foreign government? Jesus Christ, Schless—Corey—"

Schlessinger spun back to the computer screen at the sound of three loud beeps. "Hold on, Ethan. I'm getting a relayed intercept from MacDill." He watched the screen for several seconds. With tightened lips he faced Ethan. "The president has given the green light and the mission is under way."

Ethan dropped back into his seat and wiped his hands over his face. "May God help those boys."

Chapter 35

The Red Sea
September 9
7:20 am

From below deck, the rumbling engine noises were muted. Corey and Nadheer sat across from each other at a galley table. Nadheer's lips were plastered into a frozen smile, but his eyes flitted about the well-appointed cabin, never resting on Corey.

Corey tried to get through to Nadheer. "Isn't it a bit odd the prince piloted this craft by himself? Where are the other crew members?"

Nadheer's head slumped, his eyes staring at his hands. But then he nodded as if an answer had just occurred to him. "I think the prince is a cautious man. A very wise and cautious man."

Corey raised his brows.

"It is much safer if fewer people know of his intended mission."

Corey cocked his head. "How often do you think the prince picks up an American combatant in the middle of the night at an abandoned pier?"

Nadheer shrugged. "I am sure the prince has an excellent strategy."

Corey, poised to challenge Nadheer's retort, stopped when he felt a definite shift in the engine's high-pitched whines. Then the swift-moving vessel slowed. Several seconds later the engines stopped. The accompanying silence broken by the gentle waves slapping against the hull.

"Is this not exciting? We must be close to the prince's yacht. I have only seen such luxury vessels from great distances. Come, Corey. Let us go up on deck and have a look at the prince's magnificent ship."

Both men stood and climbed the short stairway to the main deck. Morning had arrived. The sun cast a fierce glow across a crystal-clear blue sky. Corey watched Prince Al-Waleed bin Majiid Al Saud fumbling with the Saudi flag, attaching it to a sizeable staff mounted on the stern. The prince waved and then continued completing the task. To Corey, the whole exercise seemed odd.

With only a subtle westerly breeze, the water appeared calm. At this early hour the air remained crisp and refreshing. Corey shielded his eyes, looking over the bow—absorbing the undulating façade of the Red Sea.

He scanned the placid waters but saw no sign of the prince's yacht nearby.

Due west, close to the horizon, he did spot a vessel, but from this distance he could not identify its type. It appeared larger than any yacht he'd ever come across, but perhaps Nadheer had not overestimated the prince's wealth.

The prince approached, taking each stride as if apprehensive of stepping on a land mine. Nadheer greeted his friend, who responded by embracing him in a huge bear hug. This seemed to help the prince stabilize his bulky frame, although if he lost his balance Corey feared Nadheer's slim body would be crushed.

Nadheer introduced Corey to the prince. Corey hesitated, not sure how to respond, but the prince thrust out his right arm and grasped hold of his hand, welcoming him aboard with a hearty chortle.

Nadheer chimed in, "Prince. Is that your yacht so far away?" He pointed to the same vessel Corey had observed.

The prince looked confused, but he recovered quickly and slapped Nadheer on the back. He laughed more vigorously than before. "My good friend. Those monstrosities of the sea are a thing of the past. I represent the modern House of Saud. We have no need to flaunt our wealth to the world. This fine craft on which we sail is the future of the royal family."

"Of course, Prince Al-Waleed," Nadheer said, dipping his head. "That makes perfect sense." But his crinkled face suggested he had no clue as to what the prince meant.

Corey nodded, glancing again at the distant vessel.

"Yes. And one day I shall own a craft as sleek and as swift as this splendid cruiser."

That drew Corey's attention back on the prince.

Nadheer worked up a smile. "Oh?" he muttered to the prince while shooting a look at Corey.

The prince lowered his voice as he turned his head, eyes cast over his shoulders. "On such a secret—perhaps *illegal* mission," the prince said, forming the words with deliberation, "I deemed it wise to borrow one of the fastest boats at my disposal."

Corey and Nadheer spoke together, "Borrowed?"

"Yes, yes." The prince's whole body shook as his head bobbed, causing the flabby layers on his chin to roll. "It is my uncle's dinghy. It is utilized to transport him and his guests to shore and then back to his yacht." He paused and shook his head, frowning. "This craft has a berth within the hull of his oversized pleasure yacht."

Nadheer looked at Corey and shrugged.

"My uncle is from the old school, Nadheer. But it was fortuitous that he dropped it off at our family's boatyard for servicing last week." He pointed to his generous chest. "It is my responsibility to oversee the technical staff while they perform the necessary repairs."

Corey tried to move things along. "That's all fascinating, Prince Al-Waleed. Your skills are indispensable to the House of Saud." He paused, struggling to keep his huge smile in place. "But I am eager to hear your plan for getting me and my equipment back to the US military commanders."

"Of course." The prince started moving toward the helm. "We must get underway." He pointed to the only vessel, still near the horizon, that could be seen. "That is one of yours. It is the USS Oscar Austin. Part of a large fleet of Arleigh-Burke class destroyers out of Norfolk, Virginia. Quite an imposing warship—and our destination."

Corey perked up and Nadheer smiled, patting Corey's shoulder.

"I'm impressed with your knowledge, Prince Al-Waleed." Corey said. "And I'm amazed at your influence in arranging for my transfer to this naval vessel. These are considered hostile waters and rapid decisions are usually hampered by miles of red tape and bureaucratic nonsense from Washington."

He noticed a slight change in the prince's demeanor as he positioned himself at the helm. "No arrangements are necessary. Much too dangerous to communicate our intentions using such a direct manner. The sources I rely on are much more discreet. The enemy is always ready to intercept my messages."

"This is true," Nadheer added in a weak attempt to assuage Corey's concerns.

"I needed to use more subtle methods and trusted allies to work out this plan." The prince started the engines, the hull vibrating to the throaty rumbles of the idling high-powered diesels. "We are now flying the colors of the House of Saud. We shall be welcomed with open arms by the gallant commander of the USS Oscar Austin. But we must hurry, my uncle is expecting to pick up his boat early tomorrow morning."

Corey lost his balance and grabbed at a side rail as the prince pushed on the throttles and the craft sprang forward, gaining momentum as the engines reached maximum RPMs. He shouted to the prince over the escalating noise, "It might be best if we hail the Oscar Austin before getting too close. I can relay the mission evacuation codes to the ship's captain. Then they can verify the authenticity of our request."

Part of the prince's response got lost in the cacophony, but Corey got the gist of his story. The craft's communications system was being upgraded. The radio had been removed yesterday and the new equipment was waiting at the boatyard. The work needed to be completed by this evening for his uncle to pick up the boat on schedule.

Their speed continued to increase as the prince maneuvered the craft into the correct planing attitude. Corey locked his gaze at the once distant destroyer that now loomed straight ahead. While it had first appeared set on a southerly course, it now came about and faced them. Corey was familiar with the powerful capabilities of the Arleigh-Burke class warships. They carried a deadly arsenal of Tomahawk missiles. But at the moment he was more concerned about the ship's CIWS, or Phalanx Close In Weapon System.

As part of his training, Corey had studied the sequence of events, the standard procedures, and the rules of engagement in effect on October 12, 2000. The USS Cole was on a routine refueling operation in the port of Aden when a small, motorized rubber dinghy laden with explosives approached the Cole without being challenged. The terrorist attack killed seventeen sailors and injured thirty-nine other crew members. The powerful bomb punched a forty-foot hole in the Cole's hull, resulting in massive flooding, and causing the destroyer to list before the crew stopped the deluge.

This event proved to be a harbinger of Osama bin Laden's attacks in New York, Washington, D.C., and the Pennsylvania countryside less than a year later on September 11, 2001.

Corey, confident the captain of the USS Oscar Austin was well aware of the revised protocols now in force, doubted he would make the same mistake. As if to reinforce Corey's deduction, when he grabbed the binoculars offered to him by the prince and lifted them to his face, he witnessed the crew repositioning one of its CIWS platforms and preparing to fire. Before Corey could get the prince's attention, a series of warning shots whistled overhead.

The prince started waving his arms and pointing to the Saudi flag rippling above the stern. He shouted to Nadheer and Corey to stand on the bow and gesture to the destroyer. Corey remembered that Nadheer had convinced him to shed his military attire in favor of peasant clothes to better blend in during their journey through Yemen. When Corey turned to Nadheer, he saw him disappearing down the stairs to the below quarters.

The prince maintained speed and direction.

They were now within five hundred yards of the USS Oscar Austin. The next volley from the warship landed in front of the bow of the cruiser. Each shot closer to its designated target. Corey rushed forward and grabbed the prince's arm. The prince told him to take the helm and maintain course as he clamored to get to the bow, still waving his arms.

Instead, Corey throttled back the engines, trying to avoid dropping the bow too quickly and losing control. But by now they were less than one hundred yards from the Oscar Austin. Two more rounds hit close to the bow. Corey knew their vessel had penetrated the warship's safety zone and presumed the next round would blow them the hell out of the water.

He'd waited too long.

The boat's forward motion stopped, and it began bobbing. With nothing to lose, Corey jumped below and retrieved the satchel with his equipment. He climbed back up the stairs. Standing on the bow, he held it up and waved. They were now close enough to see crew members lined up along the destroyer's railings. In that instant, Corey came to the realization that he probably looked like a suicide bomber gone mad.

Focused on the CIWS weapons aimed at their boat, he hadn't seen or heard the approaching SH-60 Sea Hawks until almost overhead. The satchel slipped from his hand, and he lunged for it before it could tumble overboard. He slid precariously close to the side, but the prince who had been squatting on the bow reached out and pulled him back. Corey clutched the satchel in his arms.

From above—a powerful bull horn sounded. "Nice save, Seaman Galloway. Let's all take a deep breath and relax. You've gotten this far. We need to get you and your equipment safely on board." The air filled with several bursts of static and then the voice continued, "Oh! I almost forgot, Galloway. Your dad says '*Hello*'. Too bad we didn't get the president's message sooner and avoided some of the theatrics."

Clutching the tattered satchel, Corey rolled to his back and stared skyward.

Prince Al-Waleed patted him on the cheek. "My friend. Did I not tell you this would work? To be honest, I thought we might have a more difficult time, but as you can see, the House of Saud is welcome everywhere in the world."

Between deep breaths, Corey said, "And your uncle gets his fine craft back in one piece."

CHAPTER 36

Santa Cruz, California
September 9
10:30 pm

Jalal Ta'anari had one final stop to make before heading to his final destination in southern California. He didn't relish the idea of meeting with this man, but his handlers had given him little choice. He remained thankful for one thing. This man did not know Jalal's real identity. That could have been a game changer. On the other hand, he always looked forward to a challenge.

With traffic unpredictable even at this late hour, Jalal put his Corvette to the test and carved a fast and furious route. He needed to get through the meeting as quickly as possible and continue south to oversee the final details for the attack. The man he was to meet had provided major funding for the upcoming mission. And last week he had made an extraordinary request to Jalal's leaders. Jalal's goal: to assure this man that he'd organized the steps to carry out his newest wishes so the first half of the additional fifty-million-dollar fee would be transferred.

After negotiating the complex highway system around the southern tip of the San Francisco Bay, he continued at a slower speed over the narrow and winding California SR 17 for the twenty-six-mile path over the coastal mountains to Santa Cruz on the northern-most stretch of Monterrey Bay.

Turning south on Route 1, he followed the directions to the Chaminade Resort & Spa, where he pulled into the rear parking lot. He had instructions to not wait in his vehicle but to start walking toward the ATM kiosk outside the main conference center. He had orders to feign a transaction and then proceed to the rear service area of the building.

Jalal completed these directives. Growing impatient, he stared up at the giant redwoods, whose tops disappeared above the glaring floodlights lining the resort's perimeter. A voice from behind told him not to look back but to begin walking and take the first path on his left. Without acknowledging the man's presence, Jalal followed the commands. After less than ten yards, darkness engulfed him. The voice directed him to stop. He felt a hand press down on his shoulder and a hood slipped over his head.

Under different circumstances, the individual performing this act would have already been dead, but Jalal's leaders told him to comply with every request, no matter how puerile the demand. He handed over his weapons as instructed. The man grabbed hold of his left arm and elbow as a second person joined in and repeated the act on his right side. With no further conversation, they led him along a steep, rocky trail with many turns.

Jalal relaxed and let his mind form an image of where these fools were leading him. Before arriving at the resort, he had studied digital maps of the terrain adjacent to where he parked his Corvette. He went along with this inane game, not in the least concerned about where this meeting took place. When they guided him down a long set of what he envisioned as wide railroad ties and gravel steps, he smiled to himself under the hood. In his mind's eye he could picture the neighborhood they approached. He'd saved the Google street map images on his phone.

After led a short distance on what felt like a concrete sidewalk, the men whisked him around and hustled up a sloped paved surface. They ushered him through a doorway. He heard the door click closed, and someone pulled off his hood.

"Good evening, Mr. Mohammad. I apologize for these antics, but we must be careful as I'm sure you can appreciate."

Jalal blinked his eyes, letting them adjust to the bright overhead light in the two-car garage where he stood. The voice had come from a large man wearing a suit that strained to keep its seams from bursting.

"Mr. Jones is waiting for you," the man said through thin lips and pale features. He gestured for Jalal to follow. He wrenched open the heavy steel door that led them inside the house.

As Jalal entered the modest family room in what appeared to be a typical, upscale California chalet, he entertained the notion that for someone poised to transfer the initial twenty-five-million-dollar down payment, this could not be the man's actual residence. These Americans must play their games. He almost laughed out loud when he remembered that he too was an American. But his benefactor did not need to know his secret.

Jalal's own sources had uncovered Mr. Jones's real name: Daniel H. Chauncey. He surmised that if Chauncey knew this, his own existence would be short. Not much of a setback, since he had little hope of surviving the next anniversary of 9/11. He focused on completing his final mission and leaving the rest to Allah.

The meeting went off without a hitch, and the two men escorted Jalal back to his car using the same routine by which he'd been brought to see Mr. Jones.

* * * * * *

As soon as his men had escorted Mr. Mohammad from the family room, Daniel H. Chauncey pulled a cell phone from his pocket and punched in a number.

"Send in the senator."

He ended the call, walked to the L-shaped bar, and poured a generous portion of vodka over the ice cubes he'd plunked into the glass tumbler. After taking a healthy swig he smacked his lips and settled into an armchair facing the fireplace.

By the time the door eased open and Senator Butch Carlisle took a step into the family room, he'd finished the drink. Chauncey looked away from the fireplace and smiled at Senator Carlisle. He rattled the ice cubes in his empty glass and extended it toward the senator. "Get me a refill. Will you, Butch? Vodka on the rocks. And go ahead—pour one for yourself."

Chauncey had been working on a plan with key players in Washington ever since his daughter and Governor Nicholas Blackwell, his son-in-law, were found dead at the Jackson Hole estate. He never believed the story concocted by President Tyler Griffin and his flunkies. But even if he did, none of it mattered. Nicholas

Blackwell had lost the presidential election in a dramatic, bloody conclusion, so Daniel H. Chauncey needed to chart a new course.

He considered himself a patient man, but he wasn't getting any younger. What he had in mind would speed things along, but that wasn't the only benefit. This was something personal, and he would enjoy this perk almost as much as completing his lifelong ambition of owning the Oval Office. He realized long ago that he could never be elected to the highest office in the land, but he'd spent many years working on the next best thing.

Owning the man who sat in the Oval Office.

Of course, President Tyler Griffin could not be manipulated by Chauncey or anyone else. While Chauncey had bought and paid for Senator Butch Carlisle, he recognized the senator had limited usefulness in the greater scheme. His new position on the intelligence committee had proved valuable on more than one occasion, but Chauncey noticed that the senator's grandstanding actions garnered far too much attention, and his excessive drinking habits offered too many opportunities to talk to the wrong people. Plus the man's ego and ambitions far outweighed his capabilities.

The time was drawing near Chauncey acknowledged, for Senator Butch Carlisle to meet an unfortunate accident, become the victim of a senseless criminal act, or succumb to a sudden medical emergency. Selecting the exact nature of the man's fate represented an appealing part of Chauncey's game.

"Here you go, Daniel." The senator handed Chauncey one of the glasses he held. Chauncey had watched Carlisle top off the vodka in his own glass two times before pouring the drink for his host.

Carlisle sat across from Chauncey and nodded. "The last information you gave me proved dead-on accurate, like all the previous leaks." He raised his eyebrows. "Care to tell me your primary source, Daniel? I could deal with him directly and save you the effort. He must be someone close to the president."

Chauncey smiled and gave the appearance of considering this idiot's proposal. He had no intention of divulging the name to anyone, especially Carlisle. His thoughts shifted to the meeting with Jalal Ta'anari. He'd given this terrorist the final piece of key information from the same person Carlisle had called his *'primary source'* and offered immense sums of money for Ta'anari to arrange the strike.

Jalal Ta'anari had been introduced to him as *Mr. Mohammad.* Chauncey stifled a grunt. Almost as believable as referring to himself as *Mr. Jones.*

The irony was that Ta'anari undoubtedly believed that if Chauncey knew his real identity it would make a difference. Chauncey was well aware of Jalal Ta'anari's role in the attempted assassination of Nicholas Blackwell. Although Jalal's sister had worn the suicide vest, and the authorities had claimed to find her body after the bomb exploded in the river; the investigation into the incident quickly led authorities to her brother, Jalal, as the mastermind of the plot. He'd fled the country before they could apprehend him. Based on the purported evidence suggesting a hidden sniper near the theater, they had originally sought another potential accomplice, but that road had seemingly led nowhere. At least according to the White House's interpretation of the events.

Another loose end? Possibly something to consider for the future.

But right now all that was ancient history. As it turned out, Chauncey's daughter, Anita—the governor's wife— was the most likely culprit in Nicholas Blackwell's ultimate demise a week later; followed by her own apparent suicide. Knowing his daughter's devolving mental state, Chauncey deemed this a reasonable explanation. But even today he still harbored doubts about the events at the Jackson Hole estate on election night when the gruesome scene revealed the bodies of Nicholas Blackwell, his wife, and his chief of staff.

One should never trust the government's version of the truth.

Too much at stake to rely on honesty.

Chauncey took a sip of his drink and glanced at Carlisle, who had an expectant look on his face. "Daniel? Did you hear what I said?"

Chauncey ignored Carlisle's question and steered the conversation to a different topic.

Yes, he thought, after next week, the senator's usefulness will have evaporated.

When Senator Butch Carlisle departed, Chauncey stood up and walked over to his desk. He settled into the high-back leather chair and considered how close he was to fulfilling his dream. An interesting piece of information Carlisle had reported stuck in his head. One of Griffin's closest friends had once again stepped into the spotlight. Chauncey's local informants had kept him up to date on California state politics, and he'd been mildly concerned about this particular candidate's past victory in the state legislature.

Edie Pauling's recent surprising performance in the jungle primary—to replace the ailing Senator Justin

Mahorney—had raised his trepidation. And now Carlisle informed him that the president had requested Pauling's attendance in the Situation Room when the special ops mission in Yemen had been approved and implemented. At the moment this new development appeared trivial, but in the future, he didn't want any obstacles to stand in the way of the next president—the one he'd already chosen.

He thought, *if the opportunity arises—*

Chauncey jotted down a few notes. Including a big incentive in the form of another huge monetary bonus. Reaching into his pocket once again, he plucked out his cell phone. "Harrison? I need you to deliver an urgent message to *Mr. Mohammad*—as soon as possible."

CHAPTER 37

Virginia countryside
September 11
4:05 am

President Alice Andersen had always been a morning person. While the years of dealing with her Parkinson's disease gradually took their toll, the former president's habit of waking before the first light of dawn had stuck with her through it all.

She stood in her den and pulled back the drapes, watching the taillights of the black Suburban disappear down the country lane on its journey to Arlington County, Virginia. The two remaining agents on duty secured the wrought-iron gates and walked back to the guard house. The small brick structure abutted a larger dwelling which served as the headquarters for the former president's security detail at her farm in rural Virginia.

Andersen had insisted that all members of the detail take the day off to attend the 9/11 ceremonies at the Pentagon, but the agent-in-charge tried to overrule her instructions. They compromised, and he ordered the two rookies to remain on duty at the farm until the others returned.

Andersen let the drapes drop back in place and smiled. She had already turned on her desk lamp and coaxed her failing body to navigate the short distance to the leather desk chair. She stared at the computer keyboard, uttering a hollow chuckle. "Well, it's time to get reacquainted with the sequel to my memoires. I'm sure the world is dying to read one more tired journal from another forgotten politician."

She pressed the power button on the PC console, but instead of sitting at her desk she ambled over to her favorite rocking chair and eased herself onto the well-worn seat cushion. The old chair creaked from age, dried-out wood, and constant use. This made Andersen smile again. "As long as we're both groaning and complaining—it means there's at least an ounce of life still in us." She'd always been self-conscious about talking to herself, but now she had the whole day to spend alone. Just her and Curly, her aging calico—actually Curly number four—in a long line of feline companions.

Rosa Pauling, Edie Pauling's grandmother and a dear friend of the former president, had always chided Andersen on never becoming a dog person and following tradition while residing in the White House. She did, however, have a special place in her heart for Steve Casella's white German Shepherd. Amber had saved her life, but better yet, whenever Steve and Edie visited the farm with Amber, the dog seemed to get along with Curly.

Andersen allowed several tears to snake down her wrinkled cheeks. "Oh, Rosa. I do still miss you. You could always put a smile on my face." Those thoughts produced a steadier flow of tears. She let them run their course and then blinked her eyes closed.

In her mind's eye she watched Rosa Pauling sitting on that gentle mare, on its slowest gait across the open meadow. The picture changed in a flash when the horse reared up after encountering a snake. Rosa was flung from the saddle. As Alice rushed to Rosa's side, she noticed her friend's head canted in an unnatural position. A nearby rock stained with fresh blood. Rosa never regained consciousness.

Rosa Pauling had repeatedly nagged Andersen for the chance to ride one of her horses. She told Andersen the story of the only other occasion she'd been in the saddle. On her fifth birthday. Her parents took her to this place in Saddle Brook, New Jersey. The ponies would go around and around in wide circles inside a small corral. But Rosa swore she was a cowgirl in the foothills of western Montana.

Since the day Rosa died, Andersen had never ridden again. She tried to tell herself that her Parkinson's made it much too difficult.

Her eyes fluttered open, and she grabbed onto the padded wood arms of the rocker, pulling herself up. That routine act became more difficult with each day. Andersen knew it did no good to dwell on her illness and thanked God for the life he had given her. Against all odds she had fought her way to the top of the legal system. From a local county prosecutor in Bergen County, New Jersey, to the attorney general of the United States. And then the vice presidency. She ended her career as the first African American—and also the first female—to sit in the Oval Office.

The way that happened—ascending to the presidency when her impeached boss had been removed from office and eventually thrown in prison—hadn't made her proud of the democrat administration that she was a part of, but she liked to think that in the little time she'd spent in the Oval Office, she did her best to make a difference. After being sworn into office, appointing the newly elected republican senator from New Jersey as her vice president was the first step in draining the swamp of the D.C. establishment. If anyone could pull the plug, the new vice president, Tyler Griffin, was the man. He now sat in the Oval Office.

A sudden chill swept across her wrinkled brow. "Tyler, I'm thinking you got more than we both bargained for. After almost two full terms, are things any better now?" She shook her head. "And look at all the enemies you've made."

Andersen regained as much stability as her illness allowed and turned toward the door. She worked her way to the front porch and paused to garner the strength to walk down the steps and make the trek to the stables.

"I'm too old to ride, but that doesn't mean I can't visit those majestic creatures. When I get done in the barn, I'll make a cup of tea and turn on the TV to watch the president's speech in New York. I always get anxious on the anniversary of 9/11."

The brightening sky provided sufficient light as Andersen turned down the path and headed toward the barn. She felt a cold wind ripple through her thinning gray hair and wished she'd remembered to grab her shawl before leaving the house. "I hope those preliminary threat assessment reports of potential terrorist attacks prove wrong, Tyler. Let's get through this day one more time."

Her stride remained slow, and from time to time she paused to recalibrate her stability. Inhaling the sweetness of the damp air filled her with more than life-giving oxygen. This farm was her special part of the universe. She kept her gaze straight ahead, and the sight of the russet-colored Dutch barn clad with dark green metal roofing panels softened her heart and pushed the dire thoughts of the world's problems to the side. In such a tranquil setting, one could easily forget the vicious nature of ideological zealots and the wrath they forced on the rest of humanity.

Entering through the door off the barn's south-facing side porch, Andersen's senses relaxed further when she caught the familiar wafts from the aged, sweat-imbued leathers in the tack room and the perfumed sweetness of the alfalfa. Her cherished horses instilled their own accustomed fragrances, unique to each mount.

She busied herself with chores that had at one time been simple—and performing them taken for granted. The damp soles of her boots produced a soft squishing sound on the basket-weave patterns of the brick pavers lining the center aisle. The hired stable hands would arrive in the late morning to perform the bulk of the tasks, and she planned on being gone, so as to not get in their way. While she went about her work, delighting in the labors, she realized how fleeting life was and what a gift it was to wake up each morning to enjoy this beauty.

Absorbed with the chores and her thoughts, she didn't hear the same side door to the barn that she just entered, once again open. The footsteps approaching the stall where she now stood also escaped her awareness.

A mare in the stall across the way whinnied and stomped its hoof against the black rubber matting covering the coarse granular flooring material. The gestures imparted a chorus of muted thuds. Andersen glanced over her shoulder and noticed two men standing on either side of the closed doorway to her stall. The man on the left grasped a bar on the door grill and started sliding back the gate.

For no good reason Andersen fixated on the fact that the door glided silently in the well-oiled track. Slowly her eyes swept across the faces of the two men now blocking her exit from the stall. When her gaze focused on the larger man with a gleaming knife blade held at his side, the stark realization of what would come next gave her a sense of resolve. It wasn't the concern for the man's weapon, but the look of pure evil in his eyes. She gave a brief thought to the two young agents stationed at the security gate. Not that she wished for them to storm into the barn and fight with these terrorists. In her heart Andersen knew they were already dead, and she said a silent prayer for them.

At that moment, President Alice Andersen acknowledged her fate, but that didn't mean she'd surrender without a fight. For an old woman with a chronic disease and failing health, she moved with remarkable dexterity. Her right arm shot toward the corner of the stall, and a shaking hand grasped the wood handle on the pitchfork leaning against the wall. This move had been so unexpected by the two men that she succeeded in jamming one of the tines into the foot of the man holding the knife. He screamed out in pain and the knife dropped to the floor. Her victory was short-lived as the second man drew a knife from his belt and completed the task they'd come to perform.

Andersen's last act was to press the emergency response button on her wristwatch. This sent a distress signal to the guard house on her farm which would go unheard as the two lone agents were nowhere to be found. The signals were also relayed to the local sheriff's department and the secret service field office in Richmond.

A deputy sheriff was the first to arrive at President Andersen's farm. When the young officer, a veteran of almost four months, discovered the bloody parts of the beheaded former president hanging side-by-side from two separate saddle racks against the shiplap knotty pine tack room wall, he did an admirable job of contaminating the crime scene.

Chapter 38

Washington, D.C.
September 11
5:21am

Time had run out.

President Griffin sat at his desk in the Oval Office.

He'd arrived earlier than usual, and the impending dawn had yet to cast its first glow through the windows. His nerves were on fire waiting for the intelligence departments to complete more in-depth analyses of the data retrieved from the Al Qaeda training camp in Yemen.

Local and federal law enforcement officials across the entire nation had been placed on the highest alert levels. Thus far the preliminary intel confirmed that one or more arms of Al Qaeda, primarily AQAP, had major attacks scheduled to coincide with this year's anniversary of 9/11.

When the president glanced out the window, it surprised him to see that his helicopter had not yet set down on the South Lawn. He was scheduled to attend the 9/11 memorial in lower Manhattan to participate in reciting the names of the first responders who had lost their lives charging into the doomed twin towers on that Tuesday morning almost two decades ago.

As he poised to grab the phone, a sharp bleep sounded, indicating a priority visitor had entered the outer office. He punched the intercom button and said, "Who is it?"

He heard an urgent voice emerge from the speaker. "Agents Mike Finley and Steve Casella, Mr. President. They need to see you, immediately, sir."

Griffin gave his assent and rose from his seat as the door burst open and the two men rushed inside. When the door slammed shut, Finley started talking. "Mr. President. I've given orders for your helicopter to return to base."

Griffin turned to the sounds of the Sikorsky, which had abruptly pulled up from its approach and now hovered to the east of the White House grounds.

"They're awaiting your final approval to abort, sir."

The president glanced at his watch and looked up at Finley. "For the sake of taxpayer dollars and my carbon footprint, why don't we let them land on the South Lawn while you explain?"

* * * * * *

The brief meeting and the horrific news had rocked the president's world. He gave Finley his marching orders for the day. Griffin directed Finley and Casella to fly to Virginia and gather whatever evidence they could regarding the brutal slaying of Alice Andersen. In a gruff tone that allowed no room for argument, the president swore that the gruesome details of the beheading of the former president could never reach the light of day.

Finley's task force command center for investigating the threatened terrorist activities would be aboard an agency Gulfstream, with all breaking intelligence data funneled to and from the aircraft.

Slightly off schedule, Marine One took President Griffin to the 9/11 memorial in New York City. The flight gave him too much time to ponder the loss of his close friend and colleague. In the short time Alice Andersen had resided in the Oval Office, she did much to reverse the hypocrisy and corruption of the man she replaced. But Griffin knew he'd have little time in the coming hours to mourn for this woman. With the day starting out like this, he'd need every ounce of reserve to get the nation through whatever came next.

He reached the decision to attend the memorial in New York as planned but would make no announcement about the assassination of the former president until he returned to the South Lawn of the White House. The survivors of the September 11, 2001 heroes had seen enough grief.

Over and over in his head he could not fathom how anyone justified these horrific deeds carried out in the name of Allah. It seemed incomprehensible to imagine poor Alice slaughtered at her farm. The former president's chronic ailment had already taken its toll on her health. Her biggest wish: to spend the remaining years in peace. Who could so wantonly snuff out the life of this defenseless elderly woman? And for what reason?

Returning to D.C., Marine One circled the White House grounds and prepared its descent. The president gazed down at the crowd of reporters milling near the West Colonnade. When the chopper landed, he took a deep breath and said a prayer for Alice. The stairs lowered, but before he exited, a call came in from Finley. He gave the president a brief update and some interesting preliminary information discovered at Alice Andersen's Virginia farm.

The president stepped out of the aircraft and onto the South Lawn. Before heading to the podium, he paused and looked skyward. He said softly, "Well good for you, Alice. I should've known you wouldn't go down without a fight."

It appeared the blood found on a pitchfork and rubber matting in one of the stalls did not belong to the former president.

CHAPTER 39

Sonoma, California
September 11
5:27 am

Catori had agreed to join Edie and the kids on an excursion to Disneyland where Edie was scheduled to give a campaign speech. After stuffing the luggage into the car for their trip to the airport, Edie had just stepped back into the house when Steve called with the grim news of Alice Andersen's death. She had been close to the former president, and he didn't want her to hear the story via the media.

Edie stared at the phone long after ending the call.

When she looked up, she saw Rosa standing in the doorway. Catori, holding T.C., stood by her side. The little girl's eyes welled up with tears. "What happened to Aunt Alice, Mommy?"

Edie rushed to her daughter, dropped to her knees, and squeezed her tight.

"When Rosa heard you mention Alice's name," Catori whispered, "she ran to you before I could stop her." She shifted T.C. to one side of her hip and kneeled down next to Edie and Rosa. Placing an arm around the shaking mother and daughter, she said, "I'm so sorry, Edie."

Edie wanted to reply that those sick sonsofbitches were unconscionable cowards for targeting an old woman, crippled with Parkinson's, just trying to spend her remaining days on her farm. But for Rosa's sake, she said, "Alice has been suffering for a long time. Now she no longer has to live with the pain." She kissed Rosa and T.C. "She's at peace now, sweetheart."

"Daddy's gonna get those bad men who hurt Aunt Alice, won't he?"

Edie got to her feet and tweaked out a weak smile, trying to soften her appearance. "Honey, why don't you run across to the kennels and see if Sandy needs help before we drive to the airport. This will be the first time we're leaving her in charge."

Rosa straightened up and nodded. "Sure, Mommy." She started heading for the front door and then hesitated. "We're still going to Disneyland?"

Edie stood up, looking out the window with her back to Rosa as the tears replaced the smile. "Yes, Rosa. But then we're going to say goodbye to Aunt Alice and wish her a peaceful journey to Heaven."

"I'm gonna make a pretty card she can take with her," Rosa said, her words fading away as she charged out the door.

Edie swallowed hard and turned to Catori. Wiping the last tears with the back of her hand, she reached out to T.C. and took him into her arms. "Steve said it was bad, Catori—real bad."

Catori nodded but remained silent.

"And nobody saw it coming. The last-minute intel pointed to the president, but of course they believed Tyler was the target."

Edie's face transformed into a dark shroud and her shoulders heaved. "No. They found it more convenient to pursue an old woman. She had only two agents with her on the farm since early this morning. Alice insisted the others attend the memorial ceremonies at the Pentagon today. So far, the agents left to guard Alice haven't been found. They're dredging the pond on her property."

She paused and tried to stop herself from trembling. T.C. sensed his mother's distress and started to cry. She let out several cleansing breaths and stared at Catori.

Edie sat and cradled T.C., covering his ears. In a lower voice, masking her anxiety, she added, "They found a message. Dripping with Alice's blood. On the tack room wall—they spattered the words right under her... severed... head. The bastards wrote that it would be a very long but glorious day in the land of the Great Satan."

She closed her eyes and her body swayed as if witnessing the bloody scene at Alice's farm. "And that's not all. On a portable CD player in the tack room—they left a song playing in a continuous loop. *America the Beautiful.* And on the wall in between... Alice's... head... and... body. They wrote: *From sea to shining sea.*"

CHAPTER 40

Anaheim, California
September 11
8:54 am

The bright California sun greeted the short flight from the San Francisco Bay Area as it landed at John Wayne Airport. Edie, Catori, and the kids climbed into a cab. The ten-mile trip to nearby Disneyland seemed to take longer than the flight.

By the time the driver deposited their luggage in front of the main entrance to the Disneyland Hotel, Rosa's excitement had soared off the Richter scale. Edie checked in at the front desk. Without taking time to go to their suite and freshen up, they soon found themselves caught up in the swarms scurrying toward the fabled theme park.

Edie expected large crowds for today, but the numbers looked greater than she imagined. Catori reminded her that the Disney officials had approved a special event to coincide with this year's anniversary of the 9/11 attacks. Several diversity groups had lobbied long and hard to sponsor an affair for Muslim American families to commemorate their American citizenship and participate in the ceremonies at the iconic theme park— an integral part of the American culture in a diverse society.

Not all factions in the nation agreed with this scenario—especially on a day when the nation memorialized the Americans who died at the hands of Islamic terrorists. The same day that brought the United States into the heart of a holy war that many felt could determine the fate of Western civilization.

The administration had not looked the other way when Disney officials agreed to host this particular event. They expected thousands of Muslim families from across the nation to take part in this opportunity for inclusiveness. With the escalating divisiveness spreading across America's heartland, DHS feared it could represent another opportunity for people to take sides. As if the president's administration didn't have enough on its plate trying to get a handle on the intelligence data regarding potential terrorist threats from an Al Qaeda group in Yemen.

None of that dampened Rosa's exhilaration at the chance to live every child's dream. T.C. was too young to appreciate this fantastical world. The noise and alien environment disrupted his attempted naps and made him cranky.

Edie, while aware of the potential problems waiting in the wings like a cancer to cast a dark cloud over the day, gave in to Rosa's intoxication and let herself unwind amidst the many attractions, rides, and fast-food stands. As the day drew on and the time for her scheduled campaign speech approached, she knew the theme park adventures would soon end.

For much of the time Edie had noticed that Catori, although outwardly enthusiastic toward her and the kids, appeared more inwardly focused than usual. One particular episode instilled a sudden uneasiness in Edie.

While heading back to the hotel, Edie acquiesced to Rosa's begging to go on one last ride. Although the line looked lengthy, it moved fast. Before T.C.'s squirming reached DEFCON ONE, they were ushered into the next available boat and sailed into the darkened tunnel of the *it's A small world* attraction.

As the daylight behind them winked out, their ears were bombarded by the nonstop, mind-numbing tune, rendered again and again by animatronic creatures from around the globe. Rosa became swallowed up in the enchanted choruses bombarding her senses and remained oblivious to everything else. The trip, which lasted about ten minutes, encouraged T.C. to compete with the discourses of the Disney creations as they wound their way through the imaginary world.

But it wasn't T.C.'s outbursts that frazzled Edie.

Several minutes into the ride, Catori's face, reflected in the metamorphosing kaleidoscope of colors, exhibited a trance-like deportment at odds with the festive surroundings. At times, Catori's eyes opened wide but stared at nothing in particular. On occasion, her lips moved and Edie leaned in closer to catch a few of the words. Always the journalist, Edie reached for the small notepad and pencil tucked into a side pocket of T.C.'s diaper bag. Although she could've hit the recorder icon on her phone, pushing the familiar object across a tangible surface still gave her a larger degree of satisfaction than allowing the electronic ether to take notes for her.

She scrawled out as much as she could comprehend.

As the end of the ride neared—the journey winding through the western regions of America—their boat passed by a collage of Native American animatrons adding their own personal interpretation to the nonsensical tune. Catori's body stiffened and her eyes bulged open; the trance-like continence dissolved.

This time her mouth moved with a more frantic rhythm, but Edie detected no clearer message in the strange prose forming on Catori's lips. Again, Edie transcribed Catori's verbal gestures.

When the ride ended, daylight returned and they were ushered through the exit turnstiles. The real-world decibels of the song faded, but the mental manifestations of the music remained active in a recurring circlet known to thrive for indefinite periods of time.

Edie glanced at her watch, anxious to get back to the hotel and prepare for her speech. Steve had promised to join them tomorrow, and they'd have two additional days at the park. Due to the large crowds attending the special Muslim family function today, they spent most of the time waiting on long lines.

She didn't question Catori about her odd behavior on the *it's A small world* attraction until they'd gotten the kids settled down and parked in front of the hotel suite's TV, engrossed in an old Disney movie.

At first Catori looked confused and shrugged off Edie's description of what took place on the ride. When Edie yanked out her notebook and fed Catori the words uttered during her strange episodes, Catori whistled a few bars of the demonic theme song. She shook her head and raised both hands, looking more perplexed than before.

Catori attempted a brief smile. "I don't always have control over these visions—if that's what they were— sometimes the meaning escapes me until another trigger draws me back."

Edie thought she noticed Catori's eyes shift color, but the moment passed so quickly she decided to let it go.

Catori seemed to brighten, and she whispered to Edie, "Instead of tagging along with you to the ballroom, why don't I take the kids over to the *Downtown Disney District* for ice cream. I think after that they'll be ready for bed without too much of a fuss."

Edie hesitated, but then nodded. "Great idea. Rosa would be bored, and I don't need T.C.'s lungs added to the detractors that will be planted in the crowd. And if Steve can break away tomorrow and join us, Rosa will be rested and ready to drag him around the park like she did to us today."

She finished dressing and gathered up her briefcase. When she stopped to hug the kids, she felt an overwhelming darkness cloak the room, giving her the impression she'd never see them again.

Rosa complained and T.C. cried out as she involuntarily clutched them tighter. She told herself that the upsetting news about the death of Alice Andersen had at last hit home. Her eyes closed, and she said a prayer for Alice. She wished this magnificent person could've been a bigger part of her life. It made her sad that she had only recently discovered the role Alice had played in her father's younger days. When Nana confessed and told Edie, she had been stunned. How could they have kept such a secret from her? Her father never said a word about how Alice Andersen had been their neighbor when growing up in Hackensack. She had given him the guidance to change his life. He wound up joining the Navy, becoming a SEAL, and fighting for his country. Instead of the track he'd been heading on—fighting the system and winding up in prison.

Catori gave her a peck on the cheek, causing her to jump. "Give them hell, Edie. It's time you get back to helping the president clean up this mess."

As Edie eased the door to the hotel suite shut and stepped into the corridor, she heard Catori saying to the kids, "I've got a big surprise! Guess where we're going to go?"

Although the words put a smile on her face, Edie felt a shiver run down her back. She faltered for several steps before regaining her stride and headed for the elevator.

CHAPTER 41

Onboard agency Gulfstream somewhere over the United States
September 11

While Edie and the kids spent the day at Disneyland, Steve and Finley played catch-up with the spreading terrorist activities sweeping across the nation. Finley's team had barely started investigating the devastating scene at the former president's farm in Virginia when they received reports of an incident on Chicago's L train.

A small explosive device detonated on the tracks as an Orange Line train transitioned onto the Loop: the city's iconic symbol of its central business district. The timing of the explosion occurred several seconds early, but the train still derailed and slid into a nearby control tower causing it to collapse. Two people working in the tower sustained severe injuries. Passengers were badly shaken by the incident, with scores requiring medical attention.

Analysts worked around the clock since retrieving the data from the Al Qaeda camp in Yemen. While deciphering the information and verifying it through independent sources, they came up with imprecise regions of interest, but little proof of specific targets. Based on alleged threats aimed at the National Parks System, they were preparing to give the order to close all parks when a series of explosions tore away large chunks of granite from the presidential sculptures at Mount Rushmore. The blasts killed six tourists and sent at least three dozen others to nearby hospitals. Nine of those remained in critical condition.

This new intel data Corey Galloway brought back from the SEAL raid in Yemen remained difficult to interpret, and the clock worked against them as the sun journeyed across the nation's heartland. They needed more time to analyze the information. For most of the day, the terrorists stayed one step ahead.

The first concrete lead identified from the new Yemen data uncovered a plot to launch high-powered mortar rounds onto one of the nation's three sites which maintained and operated Minuteman III intercontinental ballistic missiles. DHS agents raided a thirty-five-foot Fleetwood motor coach parked at an RV campground adjacent to Malmstrom Air Force Base in Great Falls, Montana—home to the 341st Missile Wing. None of the six terrorists were taken alive, and the entire eastern section of the city had been evacuated while federal authorities inventoried and secured the stockpile of mortar rounds in the motorhome. While a successful attack would not have compromised the launch capabilities of the 150 ICBMs, which were scattered over more than 10,000 square miles, the potential loss of life at the local air base and the symbolic nature of the attack would have represented a significant victory for the jihadists.

Steve and Finley remained airborne for most of the day, pouring over data and reviewing reports coming into their mobile task force headquarters.

Steve pushed down the lid to his laptop. He stretched his arms and rubbed his eyes. "Damn, Mike. I can't grasp what the hell these guys are up to. What's their game plan?" He got up from his seat and paced the narrow aisle. He stopped next to the table in front of Finley. "I mean—first—why kill the former president? And then it seems like we're chasing our tails all day. Not to minimize the civilian casualties, but the attacks could've been a whole lot worse."

Finley nodded and pointed to his computer screen. "Yeah. When we first learned of the threats a few weeks ago it looked like an all-out effort to mastermind the biggest strike since the first 9/11. Those initial leaks discovered by the CIA convinced the president to send in the SEALs to the Al Qaeda camp in Yemen."

"In spite of a few lucky breaks, they seem no better organized than the usual lone-wolf terrorist plots we've dealt with before."

"Well… they're still making us look like a bunch of bumbling idiots. At least the data Galloway recovered is starting to give us something more reliable to work with."

They were flying at fifteen thousand feet, assessing the situation over Great Falls when Finley took the call from D.C. Steve had been keeping an eye on the squadron of deployed UH-1N helicopters circling the outer perimeters of Malmstrom AFB.

After relaying a new flight plan to the Gulfstream's pilot, Finley tapped Steve on the shoulder. "We're going to Vegas."

Chapter 42

Anaheim, California
September 11
3:30 pm

Edie squeezed into the elevator and descended to the lobby of the Disneyland Hotel where her campaign manager, Evelyn Gregory, waited with a scowl planted on her face.

Ms. Gregory pointed toward her watch.

Before Edie could open her mouth, Evelyn grabbed her arm and ushered her toward the escalators leading up to the Magic Kingdom Ballroom level. As they stepped off and turned left, Edie heard a commotion, as crowds shoved their way onto the up escalators. Those that got left behind charged up the down-escalators, pushing aside startled guests.

Evelyn pulled Edie into the entrance foyer to the Magic Kingdom Ballroom to avoid getting trampled. Edie noticed that most of the crowd carried media identification badges. She looked at Evelyn, who shook her head. "No, Edie. Those animals aren't at the hotel to confront you." She glanced at the closed doors to the ballroom and the four-man security team straddling the entry. "Nobody gets in without an invitation and a photo ID."

Just as Edie was turning back to Evelyn, a freight elevator at the far end of the service corridor opened and a half-dozen riders stepped out. The two in front raised their agency shields and ordered the mob to back off and return to the main lobby level of the hotel.

Edie recognized the lead agent on the left as Olivia Davenport. Most of the crowd complied with the demands, but a few hunkered down close to where she and Evelyn stood.

Evelyn said, "I checked this out earlier. An activist—Patty Basara—is speaking at a female Muslim rights rally across the street at the Grand Californian Hotel and Spa. I suppose they tried to keep her sequestered at this hotel, but it looks like word leaked out to the media. I hear this girl is nothing but trouble. But don't worry. Once they scoot her out the door, the mob will follow. Shouldn't disturb your campaign speech. Let's stay out of the way until they get her out of the hotel."

Evelyn's phone rang. "Got it. We're ready." She ended the brief call and grabbed Edie's elbow. "Ten minutes to showtime. We'll wait right in this spot until the chairman finishes introducing you. We're far enough away from the media to avoid any association with this fanatical Muslim nut."

As Evelyn finished speaking, the doors to the freight elevator again opened. Edie locked eyes with Patty Basara, known to her as Patas Ta'anari. After a slight hesitation, she shook free from Evelyn's grasp and strode toward Patas, smiling and waving her hand.

"Edie?" Evelyn stuttered. "What're you doing? Are you outta your mind?"

Looking over her shoulder, Edie winked and said, "Gimme a second, Evelyn. I want to say hello to an old friend."

Evelyn froze in place, her mouth wide open. She pulled out her phone and stared at the screen. She couldn't think of anybody to call.

Several agents started reaching under their jackets when they saw a lone woman purposefully walking straight toward Patas. Olivia Davenport recognized Edie Pauling and told everyone to stand down. Patas stepped forward and hugged Edie. Stray reporters lingering on the sidelines had captured this on video and began shouting questions at Patas and Edie. Evelyn dropped into a nearby chair and shut her eyes.

After Patas exchanged a few hushed words with Edie, the security team led her to the escalator. Edie headed over to Evelyn. As she helped her campaign manager to her feet, the door to the Magic Kingdom Ballroom opened, and one of the guards motioned for them to enter.

Edie glanced back in time to see Olivia Davenport pacing down the corridor with one arm waving while shouting into her cell phone, "You want me to go where? But—"

CHAPTER 43

Anaheim, California
September 11
4:30 pm

Once the protection detail delivered Patas to the Sequoia Ballroom in Disney's Grand Californian Hotel and Spa, the tight security kept the rally from getting out of hand. The invited guests, primarily Muslim females, contributed to the peaceful setting for delivering her agenda on the reformation of Islamic culture in America. While Muslim men were welcome, very few attended. Showing up for a female speaker would be tantamount to yielding to her equal stature.

The earlier task of getting Patas from the Disneyland hotel and across the pedestrian promenades to the site of this rally had been a far different story.

And Olivia Davenport was pissed. Somehow word leaked out regarding the planned route. Hordes of media representatives jammed the Disneyland Hotel lobby and main meeting room level as Olivia's team attempted to whisk Patas from the freight elevator, using the service corridors. While her team concentrated on the primary objective of finding Jalal Ta'anari, that didn't stop Olivia's impulse to empty her extended magazine on the closest cameraman when the media rushed the elevator.

Olivia had just gotten word that the authorities believed Patas's brother was leading a recently uncovered threat at a Chevron oil refinery site in the San Francisco Bay Area, about 350 miles north of Disneyland. Although this lessened her concern about any imminent reprisals against Patas, it did little to calm her nerves regarding the escalating terrorist activities that had spread across the nation.

Patas ended her presentation with an invitation for all the children in the audience to join her for refreshments at the picnic grove outside the Disneyland theme park entrance. Before Olivia boarded the waiting helicopter, she took a moment to inform Patas of her sudden change in plans and the new priority.

Patas glanced at the agent and her eyes wandered over the crowd exiting the ballroom. "When it comes to my brother, I don't have much faith in intelligence data."

Olivia placed a hand on Patas's shoulder. "My team will remain with you, Patas. The president asked me to check out the situation at the Chevron refinery in Richmond, where your brother has been spotted. Maybe this time they got it right. And we'll stop Jalal for good. If it turns out to be another dead end, I'll be back here as fast as I can."

Patas gave Olivia a quick hug and nodded. Olivia called over to her second in command. "I want everything cleared one more time. Ms. Basara doesn't go inside the picnic grove until all the guests have been checked. We need to verify that all passes are legitimate—no exceptions."

Patas started to protest, but Olivia held up a hand. "Don't worry. We have several agents dressed in Disney character costumes and the kids will think it's part of the show. Others will be covering the entrances and exits." She turned back to the other agent. "I want the outside perimeter to the picnic grove under constant surveillance. I understand no agents—costumes or not—will be allowed inside the area during the party, so make sure everybody stays alert. It's going to be hectic. A lot of folks are planning to attend the special 9/11 memorial fireworks display later this evening."

* * * * * *

Jalal Ta'anari stood alone on the sixth-floor balcony of the Grand Californian. He dropped the binoculars from his face and stepped back from the railing. His sister, accompanied by a large number of security personnel had just left the hotel lobby, heading toward the picnic grove adjacent to the main entrance to Disneyland.

Something caught his eye, and he raised the binoculars again. He smiled at the sight of Agent Davenport rushing to a waiting SUV. The moment she closed the door, it sped off. "Those fools are so predictable. Once again they have let their guard down." Lowering the binoculars, he turned and walked through the patio door into the hotel room.

Jalal's cell phone vibrated in his pocket.

"Yes?" Jalal listened. "Okay. Pauling can wait. For now, stay on her kids. When the opportunity arises, I want you to grab them. Yes, and make sure you bring me her Indian friend too. There is something I do not like about her. She has a habit of showing up whenever my plans go wrong. And as we discussed, do not make a scene. Use whatever props we have secured for this purpose."

Jalal listened while checking his watch. "Go. Get it done or you will pay the price. I must leave now. The window of opportunity is small, and I need to join the others. It is time for me to take care of my sister once and for all."

CHAPTER 44

Anaheim, California
September 11
5:05 pm

After letting Rosa finish watching one more Disney video, Catori gathered up the kids and left the hotel suite. She put on her happy face and teased Rosa while pushing T.C. in the foldable stroller. They'd exited the Disneyland Hotel lobby long after the media circus surrounding Patas had moved on. Catori had been following Patas's hectic schedule and knew she had earlier held a rally across the street at the Grand Californian. She glanced at the worked-up group of media, supporters, protesters, and counter-protesters milling about outside the Disney picnic grove. She avoided the crowds and led the kids down the more sedate path to the *Downtown Disney District.*

Catori started humming the *It's a Small World* song, coaxing Rosa to sing along. T.C. began clapping his hands and laughing as Catori zigzagged his stroller along the cobblestone pathway.

When they reached the opposite side of the pedestrian bridge, Rosa tugged on Catori's arm and whispered, "Daddy told Mommy that this song is evil. And if you listen to it for too long—it will make you crazy. Is that true?"

Catori laughed so hard that it at first startled Rosa. Then she decided to laugh along with Catori. T.C. chose this moment to turn his laughter into a series of escalating screams.

"Time for ice cream, guys," Catori spit out, stifling any further outbursts.

While Rosa and T.C. devoured their two-scoops Häagen-Dazs double-chocolate ice cream cones, most of which T.C. deposited in his lap and all over the stroller's fabric, Catori sat enjoying the innocence of the Casella children. She thought back to earlier in the day when she hadn't been completely honest in addressing Edie's concerns. She struggled with an underlying feeling of dread that stemmed from what little she could recall of the vision that slammed into her while riding on the *it's A small world* attraction. But she hadn't lied when telling Edie she didn't remember any details of the images—even when Edie read back Catori's own words she had uttered while in the boat.

Although the late afternoon sun washed its warmth across her face, a cold chill pierced her heart and took her breath away. In a panic, she refocused her attention on the kids, as if they might suddenly disappear—drawn into the vaporous nothingness of a black hole. But Rosa still held on to the stubby remains of her cone, her arm dripping with rivulets of melted ice cream, and T.C. continued to splatter gobs of chocolate over everything within his reach.

She rooted through the diaper bag, finding an almost full pack of wipes and scrubbed away the remnants of the kids' culinary artwork. Gathering up the soiled sheets, Catori backed several steps to a nearby trash container—finding it imperative to not take her eyes off the children.

After depositing the soiled towels, she felt the solid barrel of a handgun jammed against her spine. This was no internally manifested psychic phenomenon. The voice whispering in her ear sounded colder than the steel of the weapon. "My two friends are dressed like friendly rodents—but rest assured, if you attempt anything foolish, they are also armed and dangerous."

Catori looked on in horror as Mickey and Minnie Mouse kneeled in front of Rosa and T.C., bobbing their heads and pointing puffy, white-gloved appendages at them. T.C. clapped his hands and smiled. Rosa looked toward Catori.

The man's voice, still a hushed murmur, but reinforced by an added push of the handgun, hissed, "Smile. And nod your head at the little girl. Tell her we are going on a special adventure."

Catori did as told. Mickey and Minnie led them down a side alleyway and up to a fenced-in service yard. Mickey Mouse yanked off the glove on his right hand and punched in a code. He pushed open the gate and motioned for Catori and the kids to enter. Minnie Mouse continued rolling T.C.'s stroller forward and babbling to the kids about the secret adventure that would soon begin.

Catori detected a distinct foreign accent in the beloved wife of Mickey, and unless mistaken, Minnie's voice sounded male. With the continued urging of the man with the gun, Mickey and Minnie guided them all across the asphalt to a blocky-looking concrete structure and through an open door held in place by another Disney character. This one Catori didn't recognize. It spoke in a loud, but cheerful-sounding voice, prompting the group to move faster.

Rosa took one look at Catori's face and realized something was terribly wrong. As the heavy steel door slammed shut, Rosa's screams echoed about the stark chamber.

CHAPTER 45

Anaheim, California
September 11
5:15pm

Laughter sprang from the picnic grove. Patas was entertaining a large group of Muslim American children while their parents either wandered through the *Downtown Disney District* or waited in one of the many nearby food shops. Patas's security detail, under orders to stay outside the enclosed area, remained vigilant to prevent any potential adversarial incidents from hampering Patas's time with the children. As the event wound down, most of the media hounds lost interest and the agents prepared to escort Patas back to her hotel room. They fanned out along the route, hoping to avoid a repeat of the earlier problems encountered while getting Patas to the ballroom for her rally.

A wispy plume of black smoke rose from the rear of the structure housing the *La Brea Bakery* located near the southwest corner of the entrance pavilion to the two Disney theme parks. Patrons started fleeing the restaurant. Several loud popping noises near a side service door caused a quickening of the exodus. As the smoke thickened and billowed out of several ventilation stacks, and additional sharp bursts echoed in the background, people began shoving and screaming in an effort to get away from the building.

This drew the attention of Patas's security team, but they were disciplined enough to stick close to their assigned positions. Agents near the entrance to the picnic grove formed a barrier to make sure no one tried to enter. As the crowds rushed from the smoke-filled bakery, the agents widened the outside perimeter, keeping any large groups from congregating close by.

Several of the Disney monorail support beams stood within the picnic grove. A train had been passing overhead when the first signs of smoke escaped the *La Brea Bakery*. As per protocol, every in-service train operating on the monorail system halted. Including the one traversing above the picnic grove. The doors on the car centered over Patas and the children slid open. They faced away from the commotion and could not be seen by any of the agents.

Three braided rope ladders uncoiled. They dangled from the stopped train car and swayed in the slight breeze. Tall trees lining the monorail system shielded them from anyone outside the picnic grove. Three Disney characters stood in the open doorway. They waved to the children below and then twisted around to climb down the ladders.

The children, faces bright, eyes bulging, watched as the three colorful caricatures stepped onto the ground and bowed.

Patas stared at the prince from *Sleeping Beauty*. She stared at the prince from *Cinderella*. Neither looked familiar. Next, she focused on the beast from *Beauty and the Beast*. The character's real face was cloaked in a cartoonish rendition of the transformed prince from the story. But Patas had no trouble seeing the true face of evil beneath the mask. Both hands flew to her mouth at the recognition of her brother. Before a scream reached her lips, one of the beast's accomplices pulled a satiny pillow from an ornate leather sack, while the second one reached in and grabbed a sheer white blanket.

In a flash, they scooped up Patas.

The beast extended his arm toward her. From a tiny syringe gun hidden inside a gloved hand, a burst of tranquilizer shot into her neck. Patas's body slackened in the arms of the two princes. They eased her unconscious form onto the closest picnic table while wrapping her in the white blanket and setting her head onto the pillow.

The princes turned from the table and bowed once again to the smiling children who cheered them on. While the applause continued, the princes picked up Patas and, along with the beast, disappeared around the spiral path and through a half-hidden service door.

Chapter 46

Las Vegas, Nevada
September 11
5:29 pm

The sleek craft soared over desert landscape until barren wastelands yielded to the familiar, yet forever morphing skyline. In a few short hours the brilliant lights of the Las Vegas Strip would reign supreme over the darkening heavens.

Not surprisingly, this ultimate creation of Western culture's greed-driven salute to itself had always been on the nation's short-list for terrorist activity. Tonight, the pay-line on the one-armed-bandit was no longer a near-miss. The odds were stacked against the house.

Every airport facility in the wealthiest basin of the Nevada desert had been in lockdown for the last hour. As Mike Finley's Gulfstream approached the southern tip of Lake Mead, skimming over the top of Hoover Dam, the stark outline of the vast cityscape appeared more of a threat than its usual beacon to unsuspecting souls from around the world. After clearing the jagged peaks east of

Henderson, the pilot dropped the jet to a mere several meters above a spreading sea of tract houses and headed on a direct path to runway L25 at McCarron International Airport. It looked as if he needed to hit the casinos and drop a ten-dollar chip before the roulette wheel stopped its next spin.

Steve cringed at the closeness of the towering platforms supporting the high-voltage lines snaking out from the generating plant at Hoover Dam. He swore he could read the print on the red and black danger signs riveted to the steel monoliths. He turned to Finley, who held onto the seat's side arms like he'd been strapped into an electric chair on death row.

"You think this is bad," Steve said. "This guy flies jets." He pointed to a tiny speck at the end of the looming runway. "Wait till we get on the damn chopper. We both know helicopter pilots are certified insane before completing their flight training."

Finley nodded but didn't ease up on his death grip. "Should be used to this crap by now. But never expected to do this after I retired."

"Humph," Steve said. "By now someone should've debunked those rumors of your early retirement."

He smiled at Finley's expected retort of epithets.

The wheels bounced twice before the jet's gear hugged the hot tarmac, leaving clouds of acrid vapor as the pilot decelerated toward the helicopter waiting in the withered grass near the end of the runway.

Steve Casella and Mike Finley charged down the extended stairway. Amber followed close at their heels. They boarded the H-60 Blackhawk and the craft lifted off—veering onto an eastbound trajectory for the brief flight to Hoover Dam.

As they approached the site of reported explosive devices, Steve contemplated that once darkness arrived, the array of flashing emergency lights lining the dam's perimeter and access roads to the massive facility might dwarf the neon displays along the Vegas Strip.

The chopper pilot didn't disappoint Steve, and the H-60 plunged toward the concrete slab at the bottom of the monstrous arched structure. Steve felt close enough to grasp hold of the power lines spreading up and out of the cavernous pit.

Exiting the helicopter, Finley ran toward a group of men huddled near the base of the dam. Steve kept pace while glancing at Amber who tentatively stretched her front paws up the sloped concave-shaped walls. When her hind legs attempted to grip the concrete, she slid back, barking and whining.

As Steve slipped in next to Finley, he heard the agent-in-charge respond to a question. "Nothing to worry about, Mike. No real danger that a charge of this magnitude could've caused any significant structural damage."

Watching the man's features as he spoke, Steve got the impression the agent didn't agree with his own words.

Checking his notes, the agent continued, "We got a final tally—eight explosive devices at strategic points on the south penstocks. All neutralized. The intel data from D.C. gave us enough of a heads-up to stop these bastards—but not by a huge margin." He paused and inhaled a deep breath, exhaling slowly. "To be sure, we're still expanding the search perimeter. So far we've got four dead terrorists. Plus two in custody. They're not talking. Our guys shot three terrorists heading toward the north power generating plant." He hesitated and looked up, pointing to a spot about midway up the dam. "We were chasing the fourth terrorist along the top of the dam—right down the center of the access road. He climbed over the wire barriers and jumped onto the concrete wall—and over the side. Then slid down and detonated himself near the halfway point." He turned to Finley and shrugged. "As you can see, the explosives had little impact on the concrete, but the bloody body parts oozing down the side are gonna be a bitch to bleach out." He looked at Steve. "You might want to keep an eye on where your dog starts sniffing. We've cordoned off most of the pieces, but every so often more of the smaller fragments work loose and slide to the bottom."

Steve nodded while Finley checked his tablet, scanning through several pages. After finding what he was after, he tapped the screen. "Any update on this secondary threat at the Mirage?"

"According to the last report I got before you guys landed—all's quiet. The data forwarded from D.C. indicated the possibility of a disturbance at the hotel's zoo: *The Secret Garden and Dolphin Habitat.* If you recall, Mike, the information looked vague—references involving the tigers or the other large animals. We still got the Mirage under surveillance, but they've already transported the big white cats off premises for the night. We'll make sure nobody gets near the dolphins and—"

"Transported?" Steve interrupted. "What do you mean '*transported*'?"

The agent squinted at Steve. "The casino employees informed my men that every night the tigers are taken to Little Bavaria. It's a private—"

His cell phone rang in mid-sentence, and he raised a finger to Steve. He listened for several seconds, glanced at Steve, and then spoke into the phone, "So you didn't provide an escort for the transport van? Who reported the incident? Okay, your team needs to stay at the casino." He tapped Finley's shoulder after asking his man at the Mirage to hold on. "Your chopper available for a little detour?"

Finley nodded.

"We'll join the local first responders at the Little Bavaria location," the agent said into his phone.

He jotted down the coordinates on a notepad and ended the call. Finley raised his brows. The agent said, "Short flight. I'll explain on the way." Finley and Steve jogged toward the Blackhawk while the agent-in-charge gathered two other men and caught up. As the chopper lifted, they all donned headsets and listened to the agent relaying updates from the scene as they sped toward the disturbance in North Las Vegas.

"Just as the blue and white box van—the one transporting two adult white tigers—slowed to enter the private habitat, a truck sideswiped it. The truck stopped. Two guys got out and pulled open the driver's door on the van. They yanked him to the ground and shot him twice in the head. Before the private security personnel in the guard house could respond, the two men jumped into the van and drove away."

The Blackhawk now hovered above the site where the incident took place and began to slowly circle the area.

Steve jabbed a finger against the window and shouted into his headset. "Got it! A blue and white box van fitting your description. It's heading north—wait! It's turning into that casino's parking lot."

The pilot responded, "I've got him, agent."

He banked the chopper and descended at a forty-five-degree angle, heading for the casino situated just south of a nearby golf course. The front of the casino was packed with patrons rushing inside, balanced by an equal number of escaping customers whose credit limits more than likely had maxed out.

The adjacent parking lots and streets remained gridlocked following the suicidal tactics of the hijacked transport vehicle as it careened down the wide avenue and through the parking lot toward the casino.

Finley shouted into his headset and pointed to the golf course, indicating for the pilot to set down the chopper. When the pilot shook his head and pointed straight down, Steve predicted his next words, knowing they'd have a familiar ring.

"I can set us down closer. See those Humvees lined up in the valet parking zone next to the casino entrance?"

Steve played along and asked the obvious question. "So what do you think will happen when you drop this eight-ton flying anvil on those overpriced gas guzzlers?"

"That sounds like a challenge."

Steve listened to the pilot whistling into his mike while he prepared to land. Below, he saw people diving for cover as the transport van, which had temporarily stopped about twenty yards from the casino, started accelerating toward the glittering array of revolving glass doors.

Chapter 47

The heavy chopper jolted as the tail wheel pressed against the roof of one of the Humvees. Although he couldn't hear the screeching wails of collapsing steel, Steve felt the shuddering vibrations as the pilot planted the front wheel carriages dead center onto two more Humvees. The downdraft from the spinning blades sent debris gyrating in every direction. The heavy craft rocked and swayed until the pilot was satisfied his baby would hold a level attitude.

As they exited the craft, Steve witnessed the blue and white van crashing into the massive entryway to the casino, sending glass shards through the air. It looked like the rear left side panels of the van had been ripped apart from the collision. Gradually, the chopper blades slowed and quieted to the point where the screams of people near the scene overrode the waning engine throbs of the Blackhawk. Smoke and steam clouds spread out from the battered van. In the midst of anguished human cries, Steve detected guttural roars from inside the van. Climbing down, his feet had barely touched the asphalt when Amber sprang through the open door and onto the roof of an adjacent vehicle. She slid across the hood and leapt to the ground. Without waiting for any commands from Steve, she scrambled between rows of parked cars. Heading for the casino entrance, she disappeared into the panicked crowd of people in the large courtyard outside the casino.

Rapid gunshots, followed by a screaming howl, caused Steve's throat to clench. When he stared toward the sounds, he saw a huge white tiger jumping from the battered van. It twisted in midair before smacking onto the polished tiled courtyard and rolling to a stop in a mound of broken glass and mangled steel. Two men with drawn weapons staggered from the van and muscled their way through the broken doors after firing the rounds to stop the enraged beast. They vanished inside the casino as a second white tiger escaped from its damaged cage in the van. After a slight hesitation at the side of its fallen mate, it let out a thunderous roar and then lunged toward the fleeing men. Seconds later Amber materialized near the van, her barks almost as loud as the cries from the angry, charging tiger. She too stopped for a moment and sniffed the body of the unmoving beast and then joined the chase inside the casino.

Steve followed Amber as Finley shouted orders and secured the area next to the van and the prone white tiger. Additional back-up and medical first responders were experiencing major problems working through the congested traffic.

Leaving the other agents to handle the scene in front of the casino, Finley dashed inside and caught up to Steve, who had stopped in the huge atrium-shaped lobby.

With his weapon held at his side, Steve's eyes scanned the entire area but could see no signs of the terrorists, the angry white tiger, or the pursuing white German Shepherd. He glanced at the crowd milling about the eight-story cavernous chamber. While a few people looked guarded, the degree of concern appeared nowhere near the level of mayhem seen outside the casino.

Finley pulled out his handgun and stood next to Steve.

Steve shook his head. "Where the hell did they go?"

Finley nudged Steve's arm and pointed. "This place is one big dead end. To get anywhere else in the hotel you need to go through the main casino room."

Steve jogged forward before Finley finished. When they entered the gambling mecca, their senses ratcheted to extreme overload. The slots were at least ninety percent occupied; the card and roulette tables packed. Topless cocktail hostesses garnered more attention than the exposed semiautomatic handguns waved around by Steve and Finley.

Steve turned to Finley. "Maybe we're not as interesting as the bare-breasted women, but if the terrorists and two white roaring and barking beasts had zipped through, don't you think they'd make a lasting impression?"

As he said this, the bright lights above a nearby slot machine came to life and began rotating as a blaring siren uttered forth. An obese white-haired old man threw his arms in the air and knocked over his drink. Two topless hostesses joined in his celebration. Their enhanced breasts bobbed dangerously as the women jumped vigorously at the old man's side.

Finley shook his head. "Are you kidding me, Steve? This is Las Vegas. We're surrounded by pirates, volcanoes, the sinking continent of Atlantis, death-defying circus performers—to name a few—so you think a low-budget animal act running across the casino floor warrants a second look?"

Steve gazed at Finley and let out a long breath.

From behind, Steve felt something brush up against his shoulder. And then a voice whispered in his ear. "Care for a drink, mister? If you're playing, the house is paying."

Steve turned and stared.

"Ooohhh," the topless hostess purred, looking at Steve's handgun. "I like what you're carrying. It's really big. The guys usually don't take them out right here on the floor. Can I touch it?"

Finley pulled out his credentials and the woman's eyes widened. She stopped her antics and excused herself. Steve's mouth was still dropped open when he heard a sudden commotion erupt from an alcove on the left side of the casino floor. In one of the few dark and previously quiet areas in the bustling room, a set of steel doors slammed open and more than a dozen men spilled from the corridor on the other side, fighting each other to get through first. They all wore crisp white uniforms and tall, floppy chef hats. They screamed incoherently as they fled across the casino floor, pushing and shoving anyone in their path.

Chapter 48

Steve and Finley jumped into action and darted down the now vacant corridor marked with a sign that read: *Employees Only—Buffet Kitchen and Prep Area.* As they left the casino scene, they heard a few of the nearby patrons cheering at the scattering cooks. After showing their appreciation for another typically unique Las Vegas performance, the hardcore gamblers got back to work.

Moving away from the hubbub of the casino floor, Steve heard distinctive sounds echoing from the far end of the deserted corridor. Metal clanging and shattering china mingled with human and animal cries. Steve approached a pair of steel doors with windows set in the upper halves. He noticed tendrils of smoke unfurling through gaps at the top of the doorjamb and the narrow center rail separating the two doors. With it came the pungent smells of overheated cooking oil and blurry images of charring food in blackened pans as flames from abandoned cooktops continued unfettered.

When Steve got a closer look at the closed doors to the large commercial kitchen, he was momentarily relieved to see that one of the fleeing chefs had the wherewithal to jam several thick broomsticks through the center handholds, preventing the doors from being pushed open from the inside. He stared at the splintering sounds of the wooden broom handles and watched the sickening shudders as the doors prepared to give way to the incessant ramming from inside the kitchen. Steve started looking for a stronger object to replace the failing broomsticks when a familiar refrain sounded from the kitchen.

Amber.

Her barks and anguished howls caused Steve to abandon his previous task. He dove toward the doors and peered more closely through the glass. As the thickening clouds of smoke filled the room, a fire alarm sounded. Gas supply lines to the cooking appliances snapped off and powerful sprays from the overhead sprinklers and the chemical fire suppression system engulfed the kitchen.

At the moment, Steve didn't care about any fire danger. His eyes were glued to the scene playing out on the other side of the doors. Although the wooden broom handles looked badly splintered, they now prevented him from reaching Amber. An overturned steel food prep table inside the kitchen had fallen against the doors, jamming them in place.

Steve turned and saw Finley running to his side. "Come on, Mike. Help me push against these doors, we can free up the pressure that's wedging those sticks in the handholds." Grunting from their joint efforts, Steve kept one eye focused through the windows.

The action inside the kitchen had moved away from the exit doors. On the far right side, near the bank of wall ovens, a huge white, but bloodied tiger stood pawing at a terrified man trying to fend off the attack from behind a wheeled dish storage unit. Fragments of plates flew in every direction as the infuriated tiger snarled and threw itself toward its quarry. On the opposite side of the kitchen, a man stood with a gun in his hand, screaming in a language Steve could not comprehend. But he had no trouble understanding the guy's intentions.

Steve and Finley made one final push. This allowed them to shove the blocking broomsticks out of the way. They each grabbed a handle and yanked back both doors. Steve listened and watched in horror to Amber's out of control barking and the sight of her body launching off a stainless steel countertop.

Time slowed as he gaped at Amber's frame projecting through the smoke-filled room. He turned to see the man's finger squeezing the trigger at the same moment Amber's jaws latched hold of his arm. The impact forced him to his knees. This caused Amber to flip over and slide across the slippery floor as deluges of water spouting from the sprinklers mixed with the fire-suppressant chemicals.

The man screamed out in pain but scrambled to retrieve his handgun. He shouted again and took aim. This time he targeted Amber, who struggled to right herself and gain purchase on the slick surface. Steve was faster and placed three rounds into the man's chest before he got a bead on the dog.

After clambering to her feet, Amber gave a quick bark in Steve's direction but then turned her attention on the action across the room. She bounded away from him. Finley had cautiously approached with his gun trained on the tiger, making sure the man behind the steel unit had no weapons in sight. From Finley's hesitation, Steve could see he didn't want to shoot the tiger and was trying to figure out an alternative plan. Steve knew that their weapons, while lethal on human targets—would just make the tiger more agitated. The terrorists appeared to have been carrying superior firepower.

Steve inched closer to Amber. She started barking again as she approached the huge white tiger. To Steve, Amber's barking sounded different from the previous outbursts.

He looked on in disbelief at the sight of Amber striding up to the tiger. He trained his gun on the huge beast, while harboring the same concerns he knew Finley felt. To his amazement, the tiger took a step backwards as Amber nudged against its snout. Its roaring ceased and Amber bumped the tiger back another step. The man pushed out from underneath the steel unit, but Finley swung his weapon around. "Freeze, asshole. You make a move, it comes down to two choices. You or the tiger. And right now, I'm thinking of saving the taxpayers a few dollars."

As if on cue, the shrieks of the fire alarms silenced, and the sprinklers and fire suppression system hissed off.

For the next several seconds, no one—man or beast—moved.

Steve looked at Finley and shrugged. He racked his brain for an easy out but couldn't get himself to budge his feet.

The doors to the corridor swung open and he heard a stern, loud voice. A series of sharp commands boomed across the silent kitchen. Steve recognized the words— spoken not in English, but in German. He had used a few of the same commands in his own training with Amber.

Steve lowered his weapon, but Finley kept his trained on the one remaining live terrorist. They watched as the tiger padded across the kitchen and sat in front of the man standing in the doorway. In response to the man's directives, Amber started mimicking the tiger's movements until Steve called her, and she trotted over to his side.

With tremendous effort and determination, the man leaned forward and spoke to the tiger. Most likely for Steve's benefit, he spoke in English. The words, although articulated clearly, sounded as if they took a great effort to form. "Do not worry. Dr. Englebright is tending to our friend outside. She is going to be fine. Come. Let us go and join them."

Steve watched as man and beast walked away. He marveled how the tiger modulated its gait to keep pace with the struggling, elderly gentleman.

Chapter 49

Once the authorities secured the scenes at the entrance to the casino and the kitchen prep area, Steve took a few minutes and walked to the nearby golf course to let Amber frolic on the groomed lawns. In a matter of a few short seconds, he watched her select a tranquil pond and sand trap as temporary stomping grounds.

He'd left several messages for Edie. Apparently, she was still tied up at her campaign rally. He made the mistake of calling Edie's campaign manager, Evelyn Gregory, and got an earful about Edie's poor judgment to publicly speak with the young Muslim activist who in a short time had alienated just about everyone, including pro-Muslim supporters, Islamophobes, white nationalist groups, Antifa, Black Lives Matter, and a number of conservative *and* liberal talk show hosts across the nation.

Steve attempted to calm her down by asking if she'd seen President Griffin's latest tweet on the controversial Muslim female. He then listened to Evelyn meltdown faster than an ice cream sundae sitting on an Asbury Park boardwalk bench in August—one of Edie's favorite expressions—before he convinced her he was joking.

Steve realized he was only trying to calm his own nerves. He checked his watch. It had been a long and frustrating day, and he understood that the terrorists likely had not finished. Thirty minutes ago the analysts were closing in on what they believed could be the next target. That's what had Steve worried. He had no doubt California was still in the crosshairs. The news from Evelyn about Edie accidentally bumping into Patas at Disneyland served to heighten his uneasiness.

He called Amber and walked back to the casino to help Finley tie up any loose ends. If no further specific intel data materialized in the next ten minutes, he'd persuade Finley to head to Anaheim. Until the analysts finalized the exact location of the next potential target, that was as good a place as any to stage their resources. Besides, Steve recalled, Olivia Davenport was also in Anaheim guarding Patas. That should make convincing Finley a whole lot easier.

As he approached Finley, he noticed him speaking on his cell phone. And for the first time today Mike Finley looked as if the weight of the world had been lifted from his shoulders.

CHAPTER 50

Before Steve could learn any meaningful information, Finley directed the team to get into the waiting SUVs. They returned to Las Vegas International Airport and boarded the Gulfstream. As the jet taxied toward the runway, Finley started feeding Steve the latest updates on the unfolding terrorist activities in California.

"Olivia just touched down in Oakland, and a chopper's waiting to haul her ass up to the Chevron oil refinery. You know where that is?"

Steve nodded. "Sure. It's located in Richmond. Across the bay—northeast of San Francisco." He raised both arms toward Finley. "Why the hell did she leave Patas alone in Disneyland? It's the perfect opportunity for her brother to strike again. With the massive crowds—especially with the Muslim American activities taking place—nobody would spot him until it was too late." He pressed his neck against the headrest and rubbed his palms over his eyes. "Besides, Mike, I got a bad—"

Finley rested a hand on Steve's shoulder. "Relax, Steve. First, the president ordered Olivia to Richmond. The same for our team. That's where we're headed now. The local agents acted on an anonymous tip from a citizen who lives near the refinery. Looks like we finally got lucky. None of our intel, including the analyzed data from the Yemeni raid, pointed to any attacks on an oil refinery."

This news did nothing to curb Steve's anxiety. "I know. Until now, California has been a giant black hole regarding any specific terrorist actions. But I still got a bad feeling about Disneyland. What about—"

"I'm getting to it, Steve. Let me finish."

Steve stopped speaking; his body still tense. The jet turned onto the end of the runway and its engines throttled up. The sleek craft throbbed, and Steve got a whiff of jet fuel bleeding through the ventilation system. He tweaked the overhead nozzle, diverting the swift stream of air above his head. The jet started rolling and, in seconds, he felt the vibrations dissolve as the ground fell away. They banked hard to the left and quickly gained altitude.

Finley continued, "When the agents responded to the tip, they uncovered numerous timed explosive devices at key locations inside the refinery complex. They calculated that if the detonations had gone off on schedule—set for midnight—not only would the refinery have been leveled, but most of the petroleum storage tanks and the entire downtown neighborhood of the city would've been destroyed." He paused again and Steve caught an added excitement in his eyes. "But here's why the president wanted Olivia and us to go to Richmond. The authorities apprehended five suspected terrorists. And they tentatively identified one as Jalal Ta'anari. The president needs Olivia and us to make a positive ID." He sat back in his seat and folded his arms across his chest. "It's over, Steve. We had some setbacks today…." His voice cracked. "Those cowardly sonsofbitches killed the former president—a harmless, sick woman trying to spend her last years in peace."

He closed his eyes. "But it could've been a hell of a lot worse in terms of civilian deaths. Let's go get this Ta'anari bastard. This time he's not getting away."

Steve glanced out the window and for several seconds watched the Gulfstream level as it reached cruising altitude and headed to the San Francisco Bay Area. He bit his lip and turned toward Finley. Narrowing his eyes, he said, "I don't know, Mike. This all seems a little too convenient. So far Jalal Ta'anari has been a phantom; materializing only on his own terms."

He restated his earlier words. "I'm still getting bad vibes about this whole thing."

After hesitating, Finley's eyes fluttered open. He pursed his lips, but before he could speak, secure satellite phones up and down the aisle began chiming in the other agents' pockets. Both Steve's and Finley's did the same. The pilot's voice crackled over the intercom system. The Gulfstream banked sharply, making an abrupt change in course.

CHAPTER 51

Los Angeles, California
September 11
7:51 pm

The taxi sped through the exit at Los Angeles International Airport. Corey Galloway leaned back in the seat and closed his eyes. He'd been running on empty since waving goodbye to Nadheer and the prince while standing on the deck of the USS Oscar Austin and watching the prince's power boat grow smaller as it headed north on the Red Sea toward Saudi Arabia. That occurred two days ago. Getting the gathered intelligence data to the analysts had been the number one priority.

The Navy's plans to keep Corey under wraps and engrossed in multiple debriefing sessions had been overruled by the president. He'd undergone a medical evaluation at the US military base in Germany before they transported him to the National Naval Medical Center in Bethesda, Maryland. He'd spent time with his father after returning stateside. Although his dad downplayed how he discovered that Corey had survived the mission, Corey still found it mindboggling as to how he convinced the bureaucrats in Washington to listen.

It was better for all concerned that the methods remained obscure for the foreseeable future, but he understood that the initial findings brought to the president by his dad would most likely help the administration uncover those responsible for compromising the SEAL mission which had led to the massacre of Corey's platoon.

President Griffin made a brief appearance at the medical center to thank Corey for his efforts in getting the intel from the Al Qaeda camp back to the intelligence department analysts. He had told Corey to take an extended leave from duty. Corey was anxious to get redeployed, but he had one more thing to take care of first. He hoped to accomplish this mission before today ended. The butterflies in his stomach fluttered with a greater urgency than when his platoon had descended on the terrorist camp in Yemen.

When Corey's flight landed at LAX, he'd received a surprising phone call from Mike Finley. The president had advised Finley that Corey was headed to California to catch up with Patas Ta'anari. Finley filled Corey in on the close encounter Patas experienced with her brother but wanted to reassure him that Patas, while still a potential target for activists and extremists, was no longer in any danger from Jalal. Finley had just learned the authorities captured Jalal Ta'anari in the San Francisco Bay Area. He and his team were on their way to verify the story.

Corey had little time to process this news but beat himself up for failing to seek out Patas sooner. Even if she never wanted to see him again, he still felt compelled to shield her from any dangers. Since they'd parted ways at the White House three years ago, he'd had plenty of time to think about their differences. Regardless of how Patas may or may not feel toward him, he needed to set the record straight.

As the cab exited the freeway in Anaheim, he glanced at the time. He had planned on waiting for Patas at her hotel but now decided to catch her when she left the children's picnic party. He directed the cab driver to drop him off near the entrance to the Grand Californian Hotel and Spa. He'd walk over and wait for Patas outside the Disneyland picnic grove.

Corey paid the driver and strode toward the sprawling pavilion separating the two Disney theme parks. When he spotted the entrance to the picnic grove—he realized something looked wrong.

His eyes darted about, taking in the chaotic scene. A number of men he'd picked out as secret service agents, along with uniformed police officers, were pulling aside and interrogating people near the perimeter of the picnic grove. He watched other agents canvassing the area, speaking into handheld radios. Finley had assured him that Patas was still under federal protection. These had to be the agents responsible for guarding her. With a sinking feeling in his gut, Corey reached in his pocket for his phone, hoping Finley could shed some light on this troubling scene.

Through the confusion, he spotted a familiar face. One fixed with a terrified expression as she spoke into her cell phone. He dropped his own phone back in his pocket and rushed over to Edie Pauling.

CHAPTER 52

Anaheim, California
September 11
8:02 pm

Darkness ruled the western skies, but inside the Disneyland theme park the brilliant glow of lights afforded a familiar, welcoming backdrop. While many guests had spent the entire day in an unending state of fantasy, their enthusiasm didn't falter. The energy and momentum escalated as the crowds hustled into the best positions to gaze at the fireworks display almost set to begin. According to Disney officials, tonight promised to be an extravaganza to remember.

The building that housed the popular *Pirates of the Caribbean* attraction sat east of Royal Street, part of *New Orleans Square*. There was a little known and mostly off-limits venue tucked away on the upper level of the immense structure. Although not completed until more than forty years after the park's founder died, the *Walt Disney Dream Suite* aimed to live up to his visionary imagination.

Tonight, thanks to an influential figure in California politics—Daniel H. Chauncey—the suite played host to a cast of characters that had unlikely ever crossed Walt Disney's mind. Of course, the Disney organization could not link the current occupants to any corporation owned by Chauncey; or any individuals known to associate with the man.

Daniel H. Chauncey prided himself on keeping the path to his doorstep clean.

Jalal Ta'anari huddled with three other jihadists in the sitting area of the suite. It appeared his demeanor caused them more than a little concern by the way they struggled to assure him all preparations had been completed on schedule, without any hitches.

"Why did you cut it so close?" Jalal pressed.

"This was critical to our plan, Jalal," the more outspoken of the jihadists replied. The three men had worked as Disney employees for at least six months. The man speaking had worked as part of the fireworks crew for almost a year.

Jalal looked skeptical but let the man continue. "These nightly productions run on an exact schedule. We needed to coordinate the exchange of supplies from the contracted manufacturing sites according to the policies required by Disney management. They follow a rotating program with precise timetables that must be followed."

Jalal raised a hand to stop him. "Ahmad. Are you certain the fireworks containing the VX agent will be used this evening?"

Ahmad's head bobbed. "Of course, Jalal, of course. And remember, we have selected the five launch locations that provide the most extensive coverage. At the remaining sites, the normal devices will be utilized. But I assure you, this will not diminish our goal. The initial dispersion in its vapor state will blanket almost ninety percent of the park. The secondary contact zone will be much more far-reaching and, if the winds remain at their present speeds, a major portion of Orange County will be left contaminated. With no signs of rain in the next seven to ten days, we should achieve an even greater exposure timeframe."

He hesitated and then added, "As we discussed, my men are now clocked out at the end of our shift—this is nothing unusual—and will not cause suspicion. We have followed this work schedule for the past several months." Ahmad checked his watch. "To give ourselves sufficient time to escape, it is best to exit the park no later than fifteen minutes from now." He nodded at the other two men clustered next to him on the sofa. They appeared ready to bolt out the door.

Ahmad froze when he turned back to Jalal. A semi-automatic handgun with a silencer attached was aimed at Ahmad's forehead. The silencer, only a precaution. He knew the sounds could not be heard anywhere outside the suite. They were isolated from the external world, cloistered in a fantasy environment never meant for the likes of monsters like Jalal Ta'anari.

Three rapid shots, not unlike the sound of bursting balloons, came from Jalal's weapon and terminated the Disney employment status of the three jihadists.

For the sake of the other jihadists in the suite, Jalal spoke loudly over the dead bodies. "A small consolation, my friends, but the rest of us plan on staying until thirty minutes prior to showtime. This still gives us an adequate exit strategy." In reality, he hadn't counted on any of them leaving Disneyland alive, including himself.

He called out to the two remaining members of his team: the ones responsible for guarding Jalal's special guests.

When they approached Jalal and stared at the bodies of their dead comrades, he gave them a stern look. "Get rid of these cowards. They disgrace the meaning of jihadism. Toss the fools into the hall closet. When you're done, I want my sister separated from our other guests." He pointed to the master bedroom entry. "Bring her to me. I'll be waiting inside."

He listened to muffled screams arising from behind the locked door to the second bedroom. He then heard a hushed voice, followed by silence.

Jalal called out to his men. "Make sure you keep those kids quiet. I do not want to be disturbed. And a word of warning—the female who watches after them—I have run into her before. Be careful. She is trouble. For now, I need them all alive. But if she gives you any problems, do not hesitate to slit her throat. The female's only use is to keep Pauling's kids quiet. And having them alive may come in handy. Until we leave, make sure at least one of you stays in the room with them at all times."

The thought crossed his mind that Chauncey might frown on any members of Edie Pauling's family surviving unscathed. Jalal could understand the reasons Chauncey wished to be rid of President Tyler Griffin but could not comprehend his loathing of this woman.

CHAPTER 53

Jalal threw open the doors to the opulent master bedroom in the *Walt Disney Dream Suite*. He adjusted the lighting controls to cast a subdued glow over the satiny bedcoverings, leaving a muted portrait of the intricate floral-patterned carpet.

As he glanced at the scene, an upwelling of disdain crept through his body. He cursed his sister for the animalistic fever that consumed him. At last, she would pay for the base cravings he had so often succumbed to—generated by the lustful insinuations and carnal heat of her wicked flesh.

Impatient, he paced the quarters, his shoes sinking deep into the plush carpet, giving him a sensation of penetrating the vile womb of his sister. To his surprise, when he pulled open the doors of the carved Victorian armoire, he found himself staring at a well-stocked liquor cabinet with a small refrigerator unit tucked underneath an onyx granite countertop. Jalal peeked inside and checked the freezer.

He reached for a tumbler and stooped down to pluck a few ice cubes from the icemaker bin. His eyes scanned the various bottles, and after a brief hesitation, he selected the Absolut vodka. After pouring the clear liquid, he paused, listening to the crackling ice. When he brought the glass near his lips, the medicinal scents tickled his sinuses. He had not imbibed any alcoholic beverages for the three long years after fleeing America. That abstinence quickly changed with his recent return.

When Jalal closed his eyes, the unbidden image of his sister flashed in his head and consumed what little sanity he clung to. He threw back his head and gulped the astringent liquor and begged for the burning heat in his throat to quench the desire in his loins.

A tentative tap sounded on the bedroom door. He blinked open his eyes but stood frozen in place. A more forceful knock reverberated, followed by a shaky voice.

The scorching in his throat and gut gave way to a sense of calm. For the moment he again felt in control and ready to face his demons.

He placed the drained glass on the bar counter and swung the heavy doors to the armoire shut. In a quiet, yet commanding voice, he said, "Come in."

One of his fellow jihadists pushed open the door. A flood of glaring lights from the sitting room cast Patas Ta'anari in a harsh silhouette. Jalal snapped his fingers and waved a hand. The man standing next to Patas pushed her forward into the bedroom and closed the door, leaving Jalal and Patas alone.

Jalal's eyes readjusted to the dim lighting, and he stared at his sister.

In Patas's returning glare, Jalal detected an unfamiliar countenance. The darkness in her eyes left him cold. He saw no evidence of fear or shame—she appeared to exude a sense of profound pity, aimed directly at him.

Fighting the desire to snatch the vodka from inside the armoire and drink it straight from the bottle, he took several deep breaths. His right hand inched toward his holstered weapon.

He thought, *I should end this madness now.*

Chapter 54

Edie finished speaking to Steve as she reached the main plaza for the Disneyland theme park. After forwarding him the terrifying text message, she placed her cell phone back in her purse. This message confirmed that the uncovered terrorist plot at the Chevron oil refinery in Richmond was meant as a diversion and Jalal Ta'anari probably remained close by.

Once again, the arrogant bastard had played them. And now he taunted them. Jalal orchestrated the entire episode and now didn't care if they knew his real location. Whatever he had in mind, he had all the pieces in place. While relieved that Steve and the other agents were now on their way to Anaheim, she couldn't just stand around and wait.

Edie watched the charged activity buzzing around her. The agents from Patas's security team appeared on high alert and focused, scrutinizing the area adjacent to the picnic grove. As Steve advised, she began to look for the temporary agent-in-charge.

Before she could move, a familiar face emerged from the crowd.

Corey Galloway stopped several yards from Edie. The two stared at each other. The agitated mob looked determined to push them apart, but Edie fought her way forward. A mixture of emotions shot through her head. She bit her lip and the words poured out.

"Corey. Steve and I sat in the Situation Room—with the president—when he gave the go-ahead for the mission. Everybody thought you were dead. Then your dad showed up at the White House and—"

She stopped and searched his face before saying, "You must be here looking for Patas."

Corey's eyes raked over the hectic scene, looking like he didn't catch Edie's words. She took a few steps closer and touched his arm.

He turned toward her. "The president cut through the military protocol, and they released me this morning. Mike Finley gave me a quick rundown on the terrorist activities and what they've analyzed from the data taken out of Yemen. So far they've only deciphered small segments. He said by now they should have Patas's brother in custody. Part of an attack on an oil refinery near San Francisco." He looked around again, appearing puzzled by all the frantic activity. When his eyes rested on Edie, she saw his confusion turn to alarm.

"Wh—what's going on, Edie?"

She met his gaze, shaking her head. "The incident at the refinery was another distraction. Jalal is nowhere near the San Francisco Bay Area. H—he's somewhere close by." She pulled out her cell phone, scrolled to the last text message, and handed him the phone.

He cocked his head and then read the message:

I have your children and the female who was with them.

I know the real identity of the activist who calls herself Patty Basara. Your government tried to hide the fact that Patas did not die three years ago.

My sister, your children, and the female have front row seats to tonight's show. If things do not go as planned, their presence should prove far more useful.

I believe it is unnecessary for me to leave a signature.

Edie watched Corey's hands start to shake as he read the words.

"I received this text as I left my campaign rally. I tried to contact Catori—she doesn't answer. Catori took Rosa and T.C. for ice cream across the street at the *Downtown Disney District*, but there's no sign of them. After getting this text from Jalal Ta'anari—I called Steve. He told me to show it to Patas's security team. From the looks of things, they already know she's missing."

"When I spoke to Finley, he was on his way to San Francisco."

Edie shook her head. "Not anymore. They've changed course and should be getting here soon. Olivia realized the guy in custody wasn't Jalal Ta'anari. This text confirms it."

They weaved through the mob and fought their way toward the cordoned-off zone outside the picnic grove. Corey spoke in short bursts. "Doesn't make sense—I should have seen this coming with Patas—but—why the hell did he take your kids? That complicates things. Jalal's a terrorist. And terrorists like to keep things simple."

Corey's eyes checked over the area. He looked toward Edie and swallowed hard; his face ashen. "Besides, why didn't he just kill Patas? According to Finley, that's been his plan all along."

As they burst free from the crowd, a uniformed officer ordered them to stop. The look on Corey's face told Edie he was out of questions and didn't want to hear any of the answers. Her hand grasped his arm as she turned to the cop blocking their way.

Edie demanded to speak directly to one of the secret service agents on site. That got her nowhere as the officer stood his ground. His attempts to move Edie and Corey away from the perimeter raised Edie's ire, and she ratcheted up her efforts. Corey looked ready to wrestle the man to the ground. But compared to the way Edie felt, he appeared calm.

Exasperated, Edie suddenly remembered her White House security clearance ID. She cursed out loud and thrust her hand into the purse hanging from her shoulder.

The officer mistook her actions. He grabbed for Edie's arm while starting to call for back-up.

Corey lunged forward to interrupt the escalating confrontation.

Chapter 55

After dumping Patas Ta'anari in the *Walt Disney Dream Suite's* master bedroom with Jalal, the man headed back to join the second jihadist who stood guard over the woman and the two children. Earlier today they had reworked the locking mechanisms on the door and switched the hinge pins so it could be secured from outside the room. They rendered the room's sole window impenetrable by padlocking the heavy exterior shutters. Still, when he unlocked the door and entered the room, he was relieved to find his friend still in command of the situation. He had not needed Jalal's warning to make him wary of the woman.

Although he could not pinpoint the source of his concern, he got an uneasy feeling whenever she looked in his direction. This made him feel like a fool. Catori Torrence stood less than five feet tall and couldn't have weighed much more than a hundred pounds.

What kind of trouble could this tiny creature possibly cause?

She was a stunning beauty—and this also made him edgy—stirring in him a growing lust.

Perhaps… if we had more time....

After closing the door and double-checking the interior keyed deadbolt, he realized Catori had ignored his entry, her energy focused on the two infidel children. She sat relaxed on the embroidered sofa. The toddler slept in her arms, and the girl rested with her head on Catori's lap.

He hadn't caught it at first, but now he watched her lips moving and heard a soothing, lyrical voice singing to the children. The little girl was awake and from time to time sang along with her. While the sweetness of Catori's voice at first lulled his senses, the words and the tune soon grated inside his head.

He walked over and nudged the other terrorist. "How long has she been doing this?"

Startled, the man pulled wads of tissue from his ears and stared at him.

He repeated the question.

The man answered while patting the handgun resting on his lap. He shook his head. "She has been uttering these cursed words since you took Jalal's sister from the room. I am tempted to shoot her. It is as if the devil has entered her body. May Allah intervene. These chants are driving me insane." He shrugged. "At least she is keeping the children quiet."

Catori looked unmindful of her surroundings. Her eyes open, but not focused on anything either man could see.

She continued droning the reprise:

…Though the mountains divide,

And the oceans are wide,

It's a small world after all.

It's a small world after all.

It's a small world after all.

It's a small world after all.

It's a small, small world...

The two jihadists turned from Catori and stared at each other while her lips kept moving; the lyrics and melody squeezing the oxygen from the room.

CHAPTER 56

Patas wore a red plaid cotton shirt and tan slacks. Dark russet sandals covered bare feet. Her honey blond hair—not her natural color nor covered by a headscarf—cascaded to her shoulders.

When her deep brown eyes took in the form of her fugitive brother, it surprised her to no longer feel threatened or intimidated by him.

"Jalal. Hello, *brother*." Her head swayed from side to side, and she couldn't stop the tight smile from forming. She did everything in her power to keep her head high and push back the lingering tears shed for her mother—and even her father.

She glanced at the bed and shrugged. "After three years, you're still predictable."

He closed the gap in several quick strides and slapped an open palm across her cheek.

Rivulets of blood streamed down her chin. She lifted her head higher, shutting out the pain.

His hand shook and he stared at the blood smeared on his fingers. His other hand clasped the grip of his holstered weapon. "I could kill you right now, Patas."

"I don't think so, Jalal. I see now you're much too weak. Is this what your hatred is all about?" She spread both arms to her sides and took a half step closer to him. She pressed a hand to his chest.

Back in the picnic grove when Jalal and the other two men had seized hold of her, she thought her life had ended. She mourned for the fate of Islam. Now she felt in her heart that the rebirth of Islam would not end with her death. But she still regretted the lost opportunity with Corey Galloway.

She recalled waking up in Catori's arms. Although guarded by Jalal's accomplices in a locked room, a feeling of strength soared through her body. They did not get a chance to speak, but Catori conveyed to her a sense of resolve.

It was clear that Jalal had already coordinated several terrorist attacks on this 9/11 anniversary and now prepared to execute far more horrific acts. If she remained strong and could keep him focused on her, it may give others a chance to unravel his plans.

She took a deep breath and slowly exhaled. "I can see it in your eyes, Jalal. You pretend to carry the sword of the ancient Prophet. But the three years spent in Yemen were a waste of time. You continue to hide behind the Koran. You use the radical ideology of the past to disguise an inner loathing."

Pausing, Patas shrugged. "But on the surface... I noticed how you speak to your men. You seem to have lost your California charm... and now sound like a caricature in a Hollywood movie about terrorists. Very convincing, *brother*." Her voice lowered and her eyes widened. "I can see right through your little act though."

Jalal's one hand remained fixed on his holstered weapon. He dropped his other hand—still trembling—to his side but did not respond.

It took every ounce of her strength for what she did next.

"I take no pleasure in the realization that you despise me for what I am and how I make you suffer." Her feet felt as if heavy anchors held them in place, but she summoned the courage and walked to the opposite side of the room. The plush king-size bed loomed between them. She reached out her arm and raked a hand across the satiny bedcovers. The scratching of her nails sounded like the tempting hisses of a serpent.

Jalal pulled the gun from his holster and aimed it at his sister. Breathing hard, a grunt expelled from his lips as spittles of saliva sprayed out his mouth.

"All the other times—I hid my face in shame. The tears stung my eyes while you drove yourself, purging your lust. The room was always dark, but it failed to mask the pathetic urges you forced my body to endure."

Patas watched as Jalal's finger slipped onto the trigger. She refused to close her eyes.

His voice cracked as his finger tightened. "You should have died in that river three years ago. It is you who shamed our family. Father told me what needed to be done." He paused and a shallow laugh escaped. "But he was a coward. I could see his weakness back then." His face turned rigid, taking on a granite-like quality in the dim light.

From across the room, Patas absorbed the dankness of the sweat running down his neck. In spots, his shirt dampened and clung to his chest. He no longer appeared human. Although, she considered, he had long ago shed any veneer of humanity.

His jaw moved in stark contrast to his stone façade. "When I visited Father several days ago, I observed that the longer he spent in this country of infidels, the weaker he became. That made it easier to make him a martyr for the cause."

He smirked. "And Mother, of course, got what she deserved."

Patas saw a gradual change in Jalal. His disguise draped back over him, and his anemic smile transitioned into a gut-wrenching laugh. "They served our jihad. Just as you will. You think grandiose words from a female can change time-honored traditions? Look what you have accomplished. We have taken advantage of your movement and have inflamed the division in America. All sides now fight against one another. And once we unleash today's last event, the entire nation will implode. The infidels will self-destruct. The bleeding hearts on the left and the staunch opponents on the right shall finish the job for Islam."

Her eyes narrowed; her heart pounded through her chest. "What do you have planned?"

Jalal nodded. Taking his finger off the trigger, he turned the gun from Patas and returned it to his holster.

"How many Muslims do you think are gathered tonight in America's greatest theme park?" He struck his hands together. "Very soon they will all die. And in case you are wondering—so will we." A finger went to his lips. "But do not tell the two fools watching your friends in the other room. They still think we have an escape plan." His head shook and his features cast a maniacal shadow.

"And by tomorrow, the world will blame one of your finest hate groups for the deed. They do not know it yet, but they will soon make an announcement—claiming credit for getting rid of a bunch of peaceful Muslim American families. Or as they will state, Islamic terrorists. Of course, we have helped today's cause by unleashing actual terrorist attacks across this land of infidels."

He shook a finger at his sister. "To the average American, it looks like we failed. But as you will see, those staged attacks were only diversions for our main event: The release of a deadly chemical agent as part of tonight's fireworks display. Our little episode near San Francisco helped give me these last moments with you, *dear sister*. Did those fool federal agents believe a concerned citizen discovered our actions at the oil refinery? That phone call was just another part of the distraction."

Patas knew what was coming next and braced herself as Jalal, once again in complete control, strode toward her. His hand darted up and grabbed the front of her shirt. The popping buttons and ripping fabric echoed across the bedroom.

He pulled her close and whispered in a voice that reminded Patas of his former self. "We've got lots of time, *sis*, and I'm in no fucking rush."

This caused her legs to weaken, and she almost lost all hope as his tone brought her back to those long, dark nights, waiting for the creaking of her bedroom door and the raspy breathing coming from deep within his demented soul.

CHAPTER 57

Onboard agency Gulfstream—final approach to John Wayne Airport

September 11

8:10 pm

The Gulfstream's pressurized cabin closed in around Steve. Although traveling close to the speed of sound, he felt stuck in a time warp where the whole world zoomed by while he remained trapped in this flying prison.

He needed to get to his family.

He couldn't believe everything had changed so quickly. One minute they were heading to the San Francisco Bay Area, ready to wrap-up the day's long battle with terrorism and end the search for Jalal Ta'anari. Then a frenzied stream of communications bombarded their team.

Agent Olivia Davenport had arrived at the scene of the thwarted terrorist attack on the Chevron oil refinery in Richmond. She immediately assessed the situation and determined the suspect claiming to be Jalal Ta'anari was definitely not the man they sought.

Within minutes of that revelation, Steve received a frantic call from Edie regarding the disappearance of Catori, Rosa, and T.C. She had forwarded him a text— from Jalal Ta'anari. He claimed to have kidnapped them along with Patas. Before he could digest that news, the temporary agent-in-charge for Patas's security team had called Finley to confirm that Patas had disappeared from the picnic grove near the main gate to Disneyland.

As the jet's speed crashed the sound barrier diving toward an unorthodox final approach to John Wayne Airport in Orange County, Finley received a follow-up message from Olivia Davenport. The local agents in the San Francisco Bay Area had given her ten minutes alone with the incarcerated terrorist claiming to be Jalal Ta'anari. She persuaded him to be more forthcoming and learned of additional activities at a laboratory located only blocks from the refinery. She fed the information to analysts back in D.C. who were struggling with a portion of the Yemeni data pertaining to shipping schedules from three fireworks production sites in California.

The final pieces of the puzzle fell together.

Their jet hit the tarmac and smoke billowed from the wheels, filling the air with a biting haze. Almost before the Gulfstream skidded to a stop, the stairway dropped down and all onboard agents, with Steve Casella in the lead, sprinted toward a waiting helicopter. This time Steve prayed the pilot was even crazier than the one in Vegas.

The chopper lifted off, maintaining a low altitude. It skimmed above the trees and structures. They would arrive at their destination in a matter of minutes.

Donning headsets, Steve and Finley argued about how to proceed. They found no good options, and a quick glance at his watch confirmed to Steve that they were almost out of time.

After Finley got confirmation from agents already inside Disneyland, he looked at Steve and nodded. "This is the best we can do. I'm sorry." He placed a hand on Steve's shoulder. "You know how many people could die. Not only in the park, but a good portion of Anaheim and the surrounding county. We still don't know the number of bastards we're dealing with. But if we pull this off, we can save lives and buy time to find out where the sonsofbitches took the hostages."

Steve shot Finley a brief look and turned toward the window. At this low altitude the ground swept by at an alarming rate, but it still seemed way too slow. He focused his attention on the surreal, glowing brightness spreading out from Disneyland—the park appeared light-years away. Instead of proffering images of fantastical adventures and delighted children, the radiance from the theme park reared ominous and deadly.

He considered his commitment to the job as a firefighter and working with the federal government's task forces on fighting terrorists important, but what did it all mean if he failed to keep his own family safe when things got rough?

Amber nudged Steve's arm. He reached down and scratched her ears. Though he knew she couldn't hear his voice above the throbbing sounds from the helicopter, he said, "We can't afford to get this one wrong, girl."

Chapter 58

Anaheim, California
September 11
8:20 pm

To avoid alerting the terrorists that their plans might be compromised, Finley directed the pilot to land on the far side of the Disneyland Hotel. He found a small grassy area in the courtyard near *Trader Sam's Enchanted Tiki bar*. Agents on the ground evacuated the patrons seconds before the chopper swooped out of the sky.

As they exited the helicopter and ran toward the plaza entrance to the park, the crowds thickened, making progress more difficult. Amber tried forging ahead, weaving about the legs of startled individuals, but Steve succeeded in reining her in before someone got hurt.

Oblivious to the unfolding drama, the festive mood of the near-capacity Disney crowd intensified as people scrambled to find the best spots to view this evening's fireworks display. Some filed inside the theme park while others took up strategic positions at various locations throughout the vast domain of Disney properties. The pushing sea of guests ended at the line of armed officers forming a tight security boundary at the site where Patas Ta'anari had been last seen.

Up to this point, Patas's security detail, with the exception of Olivia Davenport, had been kept in the dark regarding the true identity of the young Muslim woman they had known by the name, Patty Basara. The latest events prompted Finley to reveal her real name to the temporary agent-in-charge during his most recent update as the Gulfstream switched course and headed to Anaheim.

The ongoing investigation near the picnic grove delayed Edie and Corey from speaking to Patas's security team. Having spent precious minutes failing to convince the police officer guarding the perimeter that she had key information about Patas's disappearance, brought Edie close to the breaking point.

Corey had intervened as the harried officer attempted to stop Edie from getting what he thought was a weapon from her purse. When Edie's hand reemerged with a plastic ID card embossed with the seal of the US presidency, the officer relaxed. Soon after, they'd been directed to the temporary agent-in-charge of Patas's security team.

With Jalal Ta'anari's text for proof, Edie persuaded him that the abduction of two kids and a young woman somewhere between the Disneyland Hotel and the *Downtown Disney District* was related to Patas's disappearance.

In the midst of this heated debate, a sudden outburst of barks caused the agent speaking with Edie and Corey to look up in surprise.

While Steve gave Edie a quick hug, Finley grabbed the agent and led him several steps away. He made it clear what he needed done and pointed to Steve. The man glared for a second and then nodded with a resigned look. The agent pulled several of his men aside and gave them a quick rundown.

Before leaving, Finley stepped back to Steve. "Work with these guys. Concentrate on finding those kids. My guys in the park tell me they can get it done without Jalal figuring it out until it's too late. I'm going inside to check on things." Pausing, he extended his arm and gripped Steve's shoulder. "You understand—there's no room for error. I have to think about the thousands of people in the park. And a population of more than a quarter-million within the potential kill zone." His other hand reached out and pulled Steve closer. He stared hard into his eyes. "I know it's your family, but if we get this wrong—we're *all* dead." As he turned and started toward the park entrance, he made a point of looking back at Steve. "Even if we get this right, you got little time before Jalal catches on. Once he does—"

Steve watched Finley sprint toward the gate, waving his credentials and yelling orders at any nearby Disney personnel. Several of Patas's security team led Corey inside the picnic grove. Steve didn't need Finley to finish his sentence to know they were running out of time and options. Although neither he nor Finley had discussed it, Steve understood that no matter what went down, Jalal Ta'anari had no plans of walking out of Disneyland tonight. And that made him far more dangerous.

The look he gave Edie said there's no time to discuss the details. He watched as her eyes widened and her body went slack. To keep her from falling, he latched an arm around her shoulder. He guided her through the entrance and joined the others.

Steve focused on the agent's words to Corey.

"Look, son. I understand your concern, but it's unlikely she—" The agent looked at Steve and Edie. "Or your kids—are anywhere in the immediate vicinity. We've gone over every inch of this place. When we interviewed the kids who attended the party, they told us about a little skit, and how these costumed princes and a cartoonish beast dropped down from the sky and carried her away. They all applauded the act. Then the characters disappeared inside a service door around the corner...." He paused, glancing over his shoulder before continuing, "The door leads to a gardening utility room. And it's a dead end. They could've disguised her or stuffed her in a garden cart and—" He lowered his head, setting his jaw. "And slipped past my men. They got distracted by the smoke billowing from the restaurant and the mob running away from the supposed fire."

He shook his head, muttering almost to himself. "She didn't want any security inside the picnic grove to scare the kids. Davenport got word the brother was no longer a threat, and they sent her up north. But we still shouldn't have broken protocol."

Collecting himself, he looked up at Steve, Edie, and Corey. "I think the terrorists are long gone." He addressed the next words to Edie. "The same goes for your kids and friends, ma'am. That text you showed us confirms the two incidents are related, so...." He stopped when he saw the odd expression on Edie's face and turned to Steve. "Is she okay?"

Not knowing the answer, Steve riveted his eyes on her, lifting her chin.

She blinked several times and shook her head. "They're inside the park."

The agent said, "What the hell are you talking about?"

Edie ignored the agent and stared at Steve. She uttered a single word.

"Catori."

Before Steve responded, a fleeting smile touched her lips. "She's waiting for Coyott."

Steve and Edie glanced down at Amber who jumped up from her haunches and barked. Although Steve considered himself a simple man, not one to ponder the mystical corners of the universe, he'd witnessed more than his share of unnerving experiences involving Catori. He needed no further confirmation for Edie's sudden revelations. A chill surged through his body as he remembered Catori's reference to the legend of Coyott made last week, minutes before the devastating storm swept across Lake Coeur d'Alene.

A look of horror distorted Edie's face. She grabbed Steve's arm. "We need to hurry. The kids must be terrified."

Chapter 59

The bright lights and boisterous crowds shrunk from his consciousness. Steve charged down the spiral pathway in the northeast section of the picnic grove. He headed toward the service door close to Disneyland's main entrance. The rest of the group struggled to keep up.

"This is the best lead we got." In contrast, his gut screamed to check out where his kids had disappeared when Catori had taken them for ice cream. Even with no witnesses, Amber might dig up a scent. But Edie was right. There's no way these two events weren't perpetrated by Jalal Ta'anari. They'd be wasting time circling back to search the area between the Disney Hotel and the *Downtown Disney District*. Any trail to find Patas would also take them to his family.

When they reached the service door, one of the agents handed him a large canvass bag. "Can you use this?" he said to Steve while looking at the dog. "It belongs to Ms. Basara... or as Finley finally informed us... Patas Ta'anari—Jalal's sister. She asked me to hold it when she went inside the picnic grove."

Steve kneeled in front of Amber and held open the bag. She sniffed, pawed it, and whined. He nodded to the agent who checked a notepad and punched numbers on the keypad next to the door. "Disney security gave us this emergency access code. It overrides the normal entry procedures used by the staff." He glanced over his shoulder at Steve. "But don't get your hopes up. We've already cleared the room. It's small; no place to hide. And there's no other exit."

He pulled open the spring-loaded door and held it in position. An inside ceiling light blinked on. The interior walls and ceiling were wrapped with brushed stainless steel panels. The room was approximately fifteen feet square. Wide cedar boards covered the floor.

Amber charged past the agent and padded around the room. Steve held up a hand to keep everyone else out and followed Amber inside. She stuck her nose in every corner, sniffing the garden tools hanging on the back wall and the supplies stacked on narrow gray steel shelving units bolted to the side walls. A lone garden cart sat in the far corner. Amber circled the space two additional times and then barked at Steve as she downed in the center of the floor. She placed her head between her front paws and kept a fixed gaze on Steve.

Edie peeked inside. "What do you think, Steve?"

"Amber says Patas was in this room." His eyes scanned the empty space and he frowned. He looked at the agent still holding the door and nodded. "But I'd have to agree with your assessment—don't see any other exits."

He bent down and attached a lead on the dog. "Let's go, girl." Amber barked and pulled back on her haunches, her nails digging into the wood planks. He gave a gentle tug on the lead and said, "Good girl, Amber. Let's go." With a sharp high-pitched bark, Amber sprang to her feet and followed Steve outside. As she crossed the threshold, her head turned toward the room, and she let out a final whine before catching up to Steve. The agent released the door, and it slammed shut with such a loud noise that Edie jumped.

"Sorry, ma'am." The agent faced Steve, Edie, and Corey. "Like I said, they used smoke bombs in the restaurant as a distraction. Then either disguised Patas or hid her in a cart like the one we saw in the utility room and wheeled her out."

Not waiting for him to finish, Steve got Amber busy again. This time he started near the picnic table where Patas had earlier entertained the Muslim American children. In practiced moves, Amber switched between air scenting and tracking the ground. Steve had trained Amber to discern the correct direction her quarry moved by following specific scent trails. She never ventured far from the service door they'd just checked out.

Steve let out a long breath and gave the agent a hard look. "Amber's indications tell me Patas was definitely inside that chamber. But if they got her out, they did so without leaving any scent patterns."

He recognized that while a dog's nose is far superior to humans—in some cases, they don't always get it right. This made him hesitate before continuing in a more tentative voice, "Even if they hid her in a cart and wheeled her out, Amber can usually pick up airborne traces clinging to shrubbery or nearby structures. And this area is isolated; not a lot of people stampeding through to contaminate it."

Corey said, "I've learned to trust one of her offspring. I've seen my dad's dog, Kobe, do it—so I'd put my money on Amber too."

Steve and Edie nodded. To the closest agent, Steve said, "Can one of you guys grab a Disney security employee and see if he can tell us anything about hidden doors or passageways? There's got to be another way out of that utility room."

Corey's eyes lit up. "Yeah. They must have tunnels running everywhere beneath the park. That's how they move all the characters and staff around without being observed by the guests."

The agent shook his head. "You're talking about Walt Disney World—in Florida. Everybody thinks they got the same set-up in California, but it's just a myth. They learned from their mistakes from this park and designed a complex tunnel system when they built—"

Before he could finish, the heavy steel service door made a loud creaking noise and swung open. They all turned at the sight of a tall, lithesome girl, with long golden hair woven into a tight single braid cascading over the short, puffed sleeve on her left shoulder. She worked one end of the braided locks, hastily securing it to the shorter strands of hair about her neck.

She wore a flowing satiny gown with a laced bodice in fused hues of lavender. Silhouetted in the doorway, as if posing for a photo op, a smile spread below her rouged cheek,s and a ray of sunshine twinkled from her emerald-green eyes.

No one spoke.

The young girl curtsied and said, "Hello. I'm Rapunzel." As an afterthought, she added, "Woo-hoo... Woo-hoo... Woo-hoo."

Rapunzel took a step forward, allowing the steel door to slam shut behind her.

Amber tilted her head and turned toward Steve, as if to say, *I told you so.*

CHAPTER 60

Steve and Corey edged closer to the radiant caricature. Steve noticed that the girl—woman—now appeared older than he'd first guessed. Late thirties to early forties.

Steve flashed his fed creds and told her they were investigating the disappearance of several people in the vicinity.

Rapunzel sighed and leaned back against the doorframe. "Oh. I thought you were guests. I shouldn't have opened the door before checking out my costume."

Edie leaned forward. "Where'd you come from?"

Rapunzel's eyes darted around. "You sure you're not testing me? When caught like this, I'm supposed to say that after escaping the tower—blah, blah, blah—I've been hiding out and waiting for my prince to come—blah, blah, blah—and sweep me away. Last week I got in trouble when two little kids asked where the prince was, and I said *'waiting for bail money'*...."

She stopped rambling when Edie shot her a look.

Steve stepped in. "We know you didn't enter the room using this door." He glanced at the agent who had discredited the tunnel stories, and asked Rapunzel, "So is this like a stage door giving Disney characters hidden routes to move around the park?"

"Well… first off… despite this costume, I'm not a real Disney character. I'm—"

Edie broke in. "Please! My babies and two women are missing—and in a little while something very bad is going to happen."

Steve checked his watch and placed a hand on Edie's shoulder, feeling the tension shoot up his own arm. He stared at Rapunzel. "If there are tunnels, we need you to show us how to access them. Now."

"But I could lose my job!"

"We're working under direct orders of the president of the United States. Any problems, he'll fix them later. Right now, we're almost out of time." He pointed at Amber. "This dog is trained to follow scent trails. She tells me one of our victims entered this utility room and never came out."

After a brief hesitation, Rapunzel nodded. "Follow me." She spun around, yanked open the door, and disappeared inside.

Steve turned to the agent-in-charge. "Can one of your guys go with us?"

"You got it, Casella. According to Finley, you're calling the shots." He shouted to one of his men. "Hey, Denzel. Team up with Casella." He looked at Steve. "It might be worthwhile checking out the route from your wife's hotel room to the *Downtown Disney District*. See if we can shake out somebody who might've seen the kids. I can bring my other men with me to canvass the area while you check this out. Maybe we'll get lucky."

"Good thinking." Steve's phone buzzed. He listened to Finley for several seconds and updated him on their current plans. After ending the call, he turned back to the agent. "Finley is going to call you in a couple minutes with the details of what he's up to. Once the fireworks start, he wants teams staged around the park and needs as many men as you can spare."

Edie reached into her purse and grabbed her phone. After punching a few icons, she handed it to the agent. "These are pictures of Catori and the kids you can show around."

When Steve and Edie dashed through the door, Corey and Denzel were standing inside next to Rapunzel. The door slammed shut. He glanced around expecting a secret opening to materialize. Rapunzel stepped to the right side of the room near the front and placed her left hand against an area on the side wall.

"Please stand away from the front wall."

The section where she pressed her hand looked no different from the rest of the stainless steel panels lining the room, except for two lightly stenciled Mickey Mouse ear outlines barely detectable on either side of her spread-out palm.

A hissing sound preceded the slow movement of panels sliding out from both side walls, forming an additional wall that hid the door leading to the exterior. Once the panels clicked into place, Rapunzel removed her left hand and pressed her right hand on the same spot. The entire room shuddered and began to descend.

"Well I'll be damned. It's an elevator," Corey commented. "The tunnels are real." He shook his head.

"My dad is not going to believe this. He always told me Walt Disney was the one person you could trust."

Rapunzel smiled. "Technically, this is considered 'backstage'. While a small number of underground passages exist—such as the one we're headed for—during the last two years we've been reconfiguring many of the park's structures and attractions. I'm the head engineer for the project. I'm in costume because my job requires me to spend time in public areas where guests are present. Many of the routes are not yet linked to the new centralized production studio."

Steve asked Rapunzel, "You got any maps of this set-up?"

She tapped the side of her head. "I got a few passageways digitized on my tablet, but most of it's up here. The system's not in general use and won't be for at least six months. I'm still tweaking the newest links to make sure we get the most efficient routes in place."

With a slight thud, the utility room/elevator came to a stop. An instant after Rapunzel placed her left hand on the side wall, the front panels glided back into the walls. A door identical to the one on the upper level stood in front of them. Before opening it, Steve checked Amber's collar and made sure he had the lead properly fastened. He nodded to Corey, who pushed back the door and stepped aside. Amber barked and yanked Steve across the threshold and into a narrow corridor.

CHAPTER 61

Amber scrambled over the gravel surface. Steve had trouble keeping his balance as his feet dug into the rough grade of the unfinished floor. The walls and ceiling blended into a barrel-shaped canopy with a Gunite-like texture still emitting a wet concrete fragrance. A single string of bare utility lights hung from the highest point along the tunnel. He didn't dare look over his shoulder to check the progress of the others for fear of tripping. About to call Amber back to unhook the lead, he noticed a sudden loss of tension as the section they approached doubled in width.

Several seconds later, Amber stopped.

The passage split into three different tunnels. Amber sat in front of the one that dog-legged to the left. Steve gave her the command to wait and turned in time to see the others draw up to his side.

Amber barked, pawing the loose gravel. Her head stayed trained on the narrow corridor. Steve looked at Rapunzel. "Where does this lead?"

She groaned and bent down to rub her ankles. "You should try running over this crap wearing these damn princess slippers." Using two fingers, she pointed in the same direction of the dog's nose. "This takes us to a new backstage pathway behind the west side of the *Main Street* buildings. As you can see, the tunnel makes a sharp turn after about twenty feet. Then it angles up and ends in the basement of the *Emporium*."

Rapunzel paused, gulping in a sizeable breath. "This is the shortest of the three tunnels we're looking at—*Thank Jesus*."

Steve kept Amber's lead attached and signaled for her to resume the search. A few minutes later, after reaching a level plateau in the tunnel, the path ended. Rapunzel punched in the access code on a keypad and opened a steel door framed into the concrete wall. They all scrambled inside a large, empty cubicle-shaped chamber.

Rapunzel then followed Amber's cue and double-timed it to another door. Amber scratched on the lower panel. This door was made of wood and not locked. Rapunzel turned the doorknob and yanked it back. Amber padded across an immense storage room. On either side of where Amber passed, Steve saw rows of heavy-duty steel shelving units. Unimaginable varieties of merchandise and supplies filled every shelf. The room measured at least fifty feet long, and the lines of shelves extended thirty feet on both sides of the central walkway.

Amber paused at the far end of the space and checked out what looked like a freight elevator. Adjacent to this stood a paneled door fitted with a large glass pane in the upper half. It led to a set of stairs. She whined in front of the closed door, choosing the stairs over the elevator.

Rapunzel needed to enter another access code to open this door. "The freight elevator would take us to the main stockroom for the various storefronts. These stairs are a continuation of what you call our tunnel system. They'll take us to the largest and newest staging area for the cast. It's all concealed as part of the *Main Street* structure complex. There are dressing rooms, a small workout room, dining facilities, and a sleeping area."

When they exited the upper level of the stairwell, Amber charged down the main corridor, ignoring the numerous alcoves and doors that led to the activity centers described by Rapunzel. They traversed the full length of the walkway without running into a single cast member. Amber fidgeted by the exit while Steve turned to Rapunzel. "Where are we—and what's on the other side of this door?"

She gave him a quick rundown. "I mentioned that this new system is still under construction and not in general use. The area we just passed through, however, is fully functional."

Edie stepped forward. "So... where is everybody?"

"We're approaching zero hour. Showtime." Her hand waved at a large digital clock above the door. "In one minute the fireworks display starts. And more than ever, for this evening's special event, it's all hands on deck. For the duration of the show, every cast member is required to maintain—*maximum guest contact*—as I like to call it." She paused. "That door leads to an outdoor service area, but this one's not off-limits to the public. And depending on where your dog picks up the scent—we're sure to run into a substantial number of guests. Especially today with the Muslim American event still in progress. Not to mention the special memorial fireworks planned to honor the casualties of 9/11."

As they opened the door, Steve heard the escalating sounds of the crowds reacting to the musical notes that signaled the start of the fireworks. Emerging from the backstage catacomb, he almost drew his weapon as a reflex to the sudden pyrotechnics that lit up the entire sky above them. They all stood mesmerized for several seconds.

Steve had unconsciously held his breath, even though Finley's latest update had been optimistic. When he inhaled, it surprised him to not detect any untoward aromas. He knew the VX gas was odorless, but he thought the air would be charged with the usual sulfurous acridity of gunpowder from the massive launchings. Then he recalled that Disney had switched over to the newer compressed air propelled fireworks, which resulted in a significant reduction in the amount of gunpowder detonated and a much quieter experience. Under normal circumstances that was environmentally prudent, but for tonight he considered it a negative since the elimination of the initial gunpowder ignition made the final fusion step for the VX gas all the more potent and reliable.

With Amber chafing at the bit to get going, Steve had no time to worry about the consequences. After a brief circling and checking out several routes, she homed in on her targeted scent and pulled hard on the lead. All Steve could do at this point was to follow Amber's track and pray that Mike Finley and the other agents had accomplished their goal of switching out the VX-laced fireworks with the regular back-up supplies. If not— they'd all be dead in a matter of minutes anyway.

By not aborting this evening's fireworks display, Finley hoped to give Steve precious minutes to locate the hostages before the terrorists realized their plan had been discovered.

CHAPTER 62

Steve felt it first as another slight loss in tension on the lead. Then Amber's head swung up and she started loping in random patterns but sticking close to Steve. She whined, completed a wider circle, and checked an outdoor dining patio across from Disneyland's *Central Plaza*. Other than distracting guests from watching the fireworks display, she came up empty. After taking a few tentative steps toward the nearby bronzed images of Walt and Mickey, she whined again and sat in front of Steve.

Edie rushed to Steve's side and grasped his arm. "What happened?"

The changing colors from the fireworks cast an eerie reflection from her eyes.

"She lost the scent. This spot looks far more contaminated than the previous places." As he said this, he finally got a whiff of gunpowder-tainted air and wondered how much this could also interfere with Amber's nosework.

Edie's head twitched, turning in all directions. "I keep hearing Catori's words from her vision earlier today. They don't make sense, but feeling her presence while we stood outside the park, I got the impression her vision might still hold the key." She ran her fingers through her hair. "Rosa and T.C. must be scared out of their minds. Where could they be? And what the hell does that bastard want with them?"

Steve put an arm around her shoulder and pulled her closer. The cell phone buzzed in his pocket.

"This is Casella." With the background music and the ongoing bursts of the overhead fireworks grating his sanity, Steve found it difficult to hear. He strained for a few seconds and his body came alert. "Good work, agent. Can you give Finley an update? Thanks."

Ending the call, he turned to Edie.

"We've got witnesses who saw Catori and the kids eating ice cream on a bench outside Häagen-Dazs in the *Downtown Disney District*. They remembered it because Mickey and Minnie Mouse appeared, and they all left together. They headed toward—" Steve stopped and looked at Rapunzel. Before he could ask the question, she handed him her tablet with the screen displaying a tourist map of that particular section. He stared at the screen and pointed. "According to the agent, the Disney characters took them through a locked service area, and they entered a door behind the *Naples Ristorante*."

Rapunzel nodded and grabbed the tablet. "When Disney constructed that concession area, they built an underground passageway to connect with an existing utility shaft in the park. I've been working on upgrading the interior to include an electric tram for the cast members to ride to the satellite parking zones. At the moment, it's not in use, and there's only one exit inside the park."

She scrolled through several pages on the screen and pointed. "For now, it ends at this location. A steel access panel hidden in the ground and surrounded by dense foliage. This is the area of the park known as *New Orleans Square*." She looked up at Steve. "Very few people know the tunnel exists and, according to our security procedures, it's locked."

"Are there any surveillance cameras or alarms?"

"Well, security cameras are located throughout the entire Disney properties, but none specific for these access points. And as yet, no security alarms."

The noise from the fireworks continued, but Steve pushed the distractions aside. Since everyone remained alive and breathing, he'd concluded that Finley had done his job and successfully replaced the VX-laden projectiles with the correct fireworks from the reserve supplies.

But he also assumed that if Jalal Ta'anari remained in the vicinity—as Edie insisted—he'd soon come to the same conclusion. The question was what he planned to do about his failed efforts. "Which way to New Orleans?"

"Ordinarily, we'd take the *Adventureland* roadway, but with the fireworks in progress that route will be packed with guests—we'd never get through until the show's over and the crowds have thinned out."

Steve worried that by the time the show ended, Jalal may have already acted out his rage on the hostages. He shook his head. "That's not going to work, Rapunzel."

"Come on," she shouted over her shoulder as she cut away from the crowds near the *Central Plaza* and darted behind the *Enchanted Tiki Room*. "I've been working on this passage for the last two weeks. It'll take us on an almost direct route to *New Orleans Square*." She pressed her palm against a smoothed-out section on the back panel of an interactive park map. Five feet to her left, a section of a simulated stone wall slid sideways, exposing a cobblestone walkway illuminated by the soft glow of ground-level solar-powered lamps.

Rapunzel jogged through the opening, waving them all through. After activating the locking mechanism, she turned and hurried ahead. Above the noise, she yelled to Steve, "Make sure you got a tight hold on Amber."

"What?" Steve shouted back, trying to catch up.

Before Rapunzel answered, Amber's lead wrenched hard. He grabbed on tighter while stumbling off the path. Almost losing his balance steps from a flowing river, he gaped at Amber. She sat frozen at the sight of a half-dozen elephants framed in the dark waters. Like Amber, they remained uncannily still.

"We're backstage in *The Jungle Cruise*. I thought it clever to use the attraction's existing stage settings to hide this cast route without going underground or making more structural changes. But I didn't plan on bringing a real animal into this fake jungle."

Steve convinced Amber that she'd had her daily safari quota filled back in Las Vegas and coaxed her back to work. The group pushed forward, surrounded by realistic-looking animatronic jungle creatures and amazing varieties of vegetation from the far corners of the world.

As Rapunzel promised, in a short time the path took them through a complicated series of rivers, tundras, waterfalls, hosts of wild jungle creatures, and several primitive native villages. They exited through a similar hidden opening in the wall.

She pointed across the street to the promenade and garden area where the exit to the future tram tunnel from the *Downtown Disney District* was hidden. Unfortunately, the entire area surrounding the site remained crammed with people. It appeared to be one of the more popular venues to view the fireworks display.

Edie pulled a small stuffed pink poodle from her bag. To Steve's embarrassment, one of T.C.'s favorite toys. She presented it to Amber, who barked and stomped a paw on the pavement, but otherwise showed no indication of picking up T.C.'s scent. And she'd already lost Patas's trail.

Steve turned his head skyward and realized the grand finale of the show had already started. Once the crowd started moving, it could make a bad situation worse. Amber, although one of the best scent dogs in the country, appeared stymied by the scope of the heavily trodden ground and possibly the drifting smells from the fireworks show.

They all stood in the shadow of *Tarzan's Treehouse*, which afforded them a relatively quiet space from the throngs of guests. Edie couldn't stand still and paced in an erratic fashion, staring aimlessly in every direction. She covered her eyes, rubbing her palms against the lids.

Steve figured she was still looking to Catori's vision for answers.

All of a sudden, she reached into her purse and pulled out her notepad. She skimmed through the pages, looking desperately through the jotted-down notes from Catori's earlier mumblings during the *it's A small world* ride. She stared at her scribblings until Steve thought she'd burn a hole through the paper. He moved closer and gently rubbed her neck. "Close your eyes. Listen. Catori got through to you before. You two can do it again."

She looked at him, eyes pleading, head shaking. "But she said she didn't know what it meant."

He continued rubbing her neck. His voice softened to a whisper. "Close your eyes, Edie. And listen."

She remained so still that Steve feared moving his hand. Terrified she'd collapse. Then he felt as if a lightning bolt shot up his arm.

Her eyes popped open, and she again flipped through the notepad. Her eyes stopped on the last page. She read the words out loud. Slow, barely audible. Then her voice became energized.

She repeated the same lines over and over.

"Take a wench for a bride... We wants the redhead... Take a wench for a bride... We wants the redhead... Take a wench for a bride... We wants the redhead."

As if those words drained every ounce of strength from her body, her legs turned to rubber and she sunk. Prepared, Steve held her tight to his chest, feeling her sobs.

"Oh my God!" Rapunzel screamed. "That's from the original version."

Steve felt Edie's body regain some degree of rigidity. They both stared at Rapunzel.

"I've watched it at least a hundred times on YouTube. So cool. Then a couple years ago the social justice warriors started clamoring for a fight. And Disney caved to all the politically correct garbage and modified the whole scene."

"What the hell are you talking about?" Steve and Edie said in unison.

"The original *Pirates of the Caribbean* attraction. The old auction scene. It involved horny pirates and women as sex slaves. Now the damn redhead is a pirate, and her male counterparts are chasing around women to steal their food. How lame is that?"

Steve's eyes followed where Rapunzel's head had turned.

She said, "The *Pirates of the Caribbean* building. Come on."

Chapter 63

After Jalal had tossed the torn piece from Patas's shirt on the floor, he leered at the sight of the smooth olive flesh on her exposed abdomen. The remnants of her bra still hung over her chest. With both hands he yanked the front of the silky undergarment. The elastic snapped and the metal clasps cut the skin on her back and shoulders as his fingernails grazed against her breasts.

Patas refused to flinch.

Trying to keep composed, she pulled the shredded material of the flannel shirt over her breasts. She held her head high and stared at her brother. Eyes wide open, not hiding the revulsion she felt for him.

He grunted and glanced at his watch. Part of the sick urges contorting his face appeared to recede to a deeper level. His voice sounded calmer. "Now. Get on the bed. Sit up against the brass headrail."

Without a word, she complied.

"Extend both arms across the top of the rails."

She hesitated and then did as told, watching him grab several heavy nylon zip ties from a tool bag on top of the nightstand. He fastened one to each of her wrists, making sure her arms stretched as far as possible as he secured them to the rails. With her torn shirt dangling apart, she could do nothing to conceal the bare flesh. It surprised her that instead of tugging the blue jeans from her hips, he stood back to admire his handiwork and spoke in a controlled tone.

"I had hoped that after all these years the sight of your body would no longer feed the lust. And gazing at your nakedness would repulse me."

His finger tapped the face of his wristwatch and he smiled. "We still have a few minutes, and I must make one final check on our hostages. While I am gone, you should contemplate what comes next."

He strode out of the master bedroom and slammed the door. She heard the sharp clanking of the locking mechanisms.

Patas feared it was far more than her life at stake and prayed to Allah for the strength to make things right.

＊ ＊ ＊ ＊ ＊ ＊

Jalal hurried through the sitting area of the suite. Instead of using his own key, he knocked on the door to the second bedroom, calling out to the last two members of his team. After listening to the sound of a key inserted and the inside deadbolt turned back, he watched as the door opened and one of the men stuck his head out. Jalal noticed the man had been sweating profusely, his face tense; but at the sight of their leader, his expression brightened.

"Jalal. Have you noted the time? We must leave now to escape the deadly gas. It may already be too late—the show is about to start."

With a brief smile, Jalal nodded. He motioned to the second man who still held a weapon aimed at the woman and the two children. "Yes, it is time. Come quickly."

Both men bolted through the door.

Jalal peered inside and glared at Catori. "Do not move or I will shoot the children." He pulled the door partway shut and stepped close to his men. He pointed to a wooden crate on the far side of the sitting room. "Hurry. Lift that box. We are taking it with us." He nodded to the man with the automatic assault rifle, signaling for him to hand it over. "I will hold this and get the door for you."

When the men stooped to grab the metal handles on the crate, Jalal positioned the weapon against his waist and pulled the trigger, fanning the silenced rounds across the unsuspecting jihadists and filling the room with a pungent smoke.

Satisfied, he dropped the weapon on the coffee table, cracking the glass top. This sounded louder than the popping from the rifle firing.

He turned back to reopen the bedroom door and stepped inside to check on the hostages.

On the sofa near the shuttered window, Catori clutched both kids to her breast. Jalal could hear their uncontrollable sobs. She cooed into their ears while her eyes thrust daggers at him.

Jalal barely noticed the beauty of this young woman. He had other demons to tame. And, at the moment, those vile thoughts masked most of his outside world.

Before leaving the room, he said, "It is a pity you cannot see or hear the fireworks display that Disney has planned for tonight. But the deadly VX gas will still penetrate the ventilation system."

Catori kissed the tops of the kids' heads. She looked at Jalal. "Please, Jalal. Let the children go."

Jalal swallowed and took a breath. Shaking his head, he shrugged. "It is too late for any of us to leave this land of fantasy. Tonight, we will instill our jihad with a vigor that has not been seen in centuries. Along with the infidels, many Muslims will die. This chemical weapon of mass destruction does not discriminate. The VX gas is odorless and persistent. If the initial vapors do not kill you, the residual particles left on every surface will complete the task."

He sighed. "This is such a hateful country. They despise the thought of a different culture interfering with their majority privileges. So much so that a lunatic right wing hate group took it upon itself to release this deadly agent and kill thousands of innocent Muslim families whose only crimes were wanting a small part of the American dream and celebrating their good fortune at Disneyland."

"You're a sick son of a bitch, Jalal."

Rosa's eyes popped open at her words.

Catori shook her head and mumbled, "Nobody is going to listen to your damn lies."

She spoke with little conviction and Jalal understood that Catori feared today would ignite a fire sufficient to destroy America from within.

"But now I must comfort my little sister. She is waiting for me. I have a different plan for her demise."

He abruptly left the room, slamming the door shut and locking it from the outside. He paused before heading back to Patas, and in a trancelike manner stopped to gaze out the window in the sitting room.

Jalal was not aware of the amount of time that had passed. When his senses returned, he realized the fireworks display was already in progress.

And the stark realization hit him.

The crowds remained cheering—and alive. This could not be happening. Something had gone wrong.

The rage inside him soared, but lust once again consumed his sanity and overshadowed his demented religious fervor. He ran across the sitting room and unlocked the master bedroom door. His heart thundered in his chest, and his breaths erupted in raspy gushes.

No longer could he silence his hunger for Patas.

CHAPTER 64

With Steve taking the lead, they raced toward the *Pirates of the Caribbean*, one of the most popular attractions in the park. As they got closer, Amber's behavior shifted, her nose channeling in vast quantities of familiar and unfamiliar odors.

Steve knew they were back in business.

He motioned to the others as Edie reached his side. Her face still reflecting the desperation they both felt. Denzel and Corey helped guide Rapunzel along in her struggle to keep up with Steve.

High above Disneyland, the sound and light show had just concluded. Steve dreaded the sudden silence more than the airborne bombardments from the fireworks display.

His thoughts flashed to recent events at the Jewett House in Coeur d'Alene. Once again, time had run out. And now, he couldn't predict how Jalal Ta'anari would react to another failed mission. This time the lives of his two kids were at stake.

Without warning, Amber barked, whined, and bayed. She skirted the entrance ramps, away from the guests crisscrossing the promenades of *New Orleans Square* and found an isolated walkway to the side of the structure housing the *Pirates of the Caribbean.*

She left the main attraction behind and weaved around the *Indiana Jones Adventure,* down a darkened pathway. Confronted by another barrier, Amber leapt up and thrust her paws against the wrought-iron gate. Steve reached her side a split second before she erupted into another string of barks. Amber sat and stared at the building on the opposite side of the locked entrance.

When Rapunzel stumbled up beside Steve, he asked, "Does this take us to the pirate ride?"

She gazed at the building while catching her breath; then shook her head. "No. And it's not a backstage area for the cast. This leads to a special place. Walt Disney conceived of the idea, but it never got built until years after he died. It's one of the most coveted dedications to his memory."

Once again using two fingers, Rapunzel pointed to a row of ornate windows and balconies. "That's the *Walt Disney Dream Suite.*"

After Rapunzel unlocked the gate, they huddled in a circle and focused on her tablet's ten-inch screen. She gave a detailed narrative describing the layouts of the different rooms comprising the little-known Disney memorial located in the heart of the theme park and hidden above the *Pirates of the Caribbean.*

"Any more questions before we go inside?" Rapunzel asked.

Steve looked at Denzel and then back to Rapunzel. "I need the access codes. And please don't tell me it requires a handprint. You're going to wait outside."

She shook her head. "No handprint—but let me help. I'm familiar with the design and—"

"You've been great. We wouldn't have gotten this far without you, but I can't let you go in."

She started to protest, but Steve continued, "Denzel's reporting the situation to our boss. More agents are on their way. I need you to let them in and brief them on the layout upstairs. Besides, I'm going to leave Amber with you."

"Why don't you wait for the other agents?"

Edie said, "There's no time."

Rapunzel wrote down the access codes. As Steve unlocked the lower door to the building, Denzel grabbed him by the shoulder. "Casella. Don't you think your wife should stay with Rapunzel? Based on my briefing, this Ta'anari character is a real asshole, things might get a bit dicey upstairs."

Edie shot him a look and walked ahead of them.

Steve followed while whispering to Denzel, "First, as you can see, that's not going to happen. And second, my sweet bride taught me how to handle a gun. And third, she's a hell of a lot better shot than me—and probably you and Corey."

Corey checked the handgun he'd borrowed from Finley. He shrugged and squeezed in front of Denzel. Steve watched as Corey's hand tapped his chest in what looked like a reflex action.

Once inside the building, sounds from the outside world disappeared. They stopped talking and switched to hand signals. Steve bypassed the elevator and took the first step on the narrow staircase leading to the upper floor and the *Walt Disney Dream Suite*.

Before his other foot hit the tread, faint popping sounds echoed from above.

Then an outburst of screams mingled with the muted reports from the silenced weapon.

Chapter 65

As soon as Jalal had left the master bedroom to check on the hostages, Patas started twisting the lower half of her body. She extended her right leg up toward the headrail, where her outstretched hand was secured to the top rail.

Failing to bring her ankle close enough to her fingertips, she grunted and shifted her torso, wiggling it into positions she didn't think possible. Pain shot up her spine. After taking several cleansing breaths, the threatening muscle spasms receded. She repeated these moves over and over with little success, expecting her brother to return at any moment.

Through the windows of the master bedroom, the start of the fireworks show bombarded the chamber with a startling display of light. She ignored what it meant and doubled her efforts. The scope of her brother's madness had grown beyond comparison.

After what seemed like an eternity, she got the leg close enough for her thumb and forefinger to snag the cuff of the blue jeans and slide the stiff fabric up her calf.

When Jalal had left without stripping off Patas's jeans and finishing the job right then and there, she had offered a silent prayer to Allah. Of course, she had been thankful for the temporary reprieve from enduring another brutal and defiling act. And now she held the other reason firmly in her hand.

Without wasting time, Patas maneuvered the cutting edge of the knife she'd pulled from a nylon sheath under the leg of her jeans and jammed the point into the zip tie holding her wrist to the brass headrail. She whispered another hasty prayer to Allah for her not dropping the knife during this awkward manipulation.

Blood dripped from the blade slicing into the flesh of her wrist as the nylon restraint popped open. Ignoring the pain, she made quick work of freeing the other wrist.

As she used the knife to cut a strip of fabric from the pillowcase and wrap it around her wrist to staunch the flow of blood—the chilling sound of a key sliding into the locking mechanism and the turning of the deadbolt screeched in her ears.

Patas tumbled off the bed and scrambled across the room, making almost no noise on the thick carpet. She pulled herself up and plastered her back against the wall on the hinged side of the door jamb.

The door burst open, and Jalal stomped into the room. He stopped short, still holding onto the edge of the door. Patas could see her brother's face reflected in the dresser mirror on the opposite side of the room. His mouth froze open, and a confused look spread over his face. She leapt forward, slamming the door shut and thrusting the knife at him before he could react.

Her arm, wielding the four-inch blade, flailed wildly.

Again and again she pummeled him. Aside from the first strike which landed a serious hit to his left thigh, he deflected almost every jab. Grabbing her by the shoulders, he flung her around and pinned her body to the wall. She felt a sharp poke in her back from the lighting control switch. The room blackened as the broken dimmer knob fell to the floor. A weak glow from the overhead fixture in the master bath cast the faintest of shadows to parts of the bedroom. The farthest corners remained black and hidden since the earlier bursts of light from the fireworks had now ceased.

The hastily applied bandage did little to slow the oozing from her cut wrist, and the knife slipped away from her bloodied fingers. She sensed, more than saw Jalal, reaching for his holstered weapon and crawled off on all fours to seek cover. Her head banged into an end table. With an anguished cry she pulled herself to the side of a tall chest as silenced shots from Jalal's Sig pinged and splintered the heavy mahogany piece. One more pop, and a sharp sting seared through the fleshy upper part of her left arm. She sucked in a breath and bit her tongue. Knowing it was a desperate move, she dropped to the floor and rolled under the king-size bed.

A rapid buzzing sound caused Jalal's frantic motions to stop. Patas had no clue as to what it meant, but Jalal reacted with a string of epithets. He pulled the offending phone from his pocket and threw it against the wall. His fury, more than the dark shadows in the bedroom, appeared to blind him. He let out a guttural scream. She listened to his breaths coming in rapid heaves. She thought she could smell the sickness oozing from his pores.

"The bastards have not only stopped the attack, but now our little hideaway has been discovered."

She no longer recognized the sound of his voice. His next words sent a chill through her bosom and speared her heart.

"Well, it's not over yet, little sister. But, at the moment, I think those two little kids are a more fitting equalizer than you."

With a grisly shriek, Jalal shot off two more rounds in her direction. Both slugs struck harmlessly into the wall above the headrail. She heard the door pull open and, in the harsh light from the corridor, the grotesque image of her brother momentarily appeared silhouetted in the doorway, before he sped out of sight. In the distance, cries from inside the other bedroom filled the air.

Ignoring her injuries, Patas crawled out from under the bed and dashed toward the open doorway. Like the twinkling of a distant star, she caught the tiniest glimpse of light reflecting off metal. With all the blood shrouding the knife, she didn't know how that was possible. Her hand grasped the weapon she'd dropped near the door.

Patas charged out of the room.

Chapter 66

All thoughts of stealth abandoned, Steve rushed up the stairs. Edie, Corey, and Denzel remained a step or two behind. A steel door bordering the top landing blocked their way. Steve punched the keypad and unlocked the door. For the moment, no more sounds escaped from inside the *Walt Disney Dream Suite*. The faint, muffled sounds of Amber's barks drifted up the stairwell, and he wondered how long Rapunzel could keep her tethered.

He opened the door and crossed the threshold. It felt as if he'd entered an alternate universe. Gone were the dull, commercial grays from the blank walls and ceiling behind him. Replaced by inviting pastel murals of unimaginable landscapes that seemed not of this world. Fantastical painted creatures peered out from lush vegetation that radiated lucent shades of greens and golden browns. Tapestries displaying vivid colors of deep crimson, breathtaking whites, and bold blues contrasted with hushed earthtones. He listened to a lulling serenade of an enchanted forest—emanating from hidden speakers—and drew in the imaginary bouquets from a childlike conjuring of the Garden of Eden.

He blinked again and again until his breathing returned. Straight ahead on the opposite wall stood the last barrier to the inner sanctum of the fabled suite. This impediment was different than the others. Large double French doors crafted from African mahogany and stained a dark umber framed small panes of cut glass etched with frosted profiles of Disney characters.

From the opposite side, an animal-like scream breached the glass. It resounded down the long corridor he observed through the doors.

More popping sounds followed.

From inside the suite, near the far end of the hallway, a door opened and Jalal Ta'anari toppled into view. A semi-automatic pistol gripped in one hand. The other hand clasped against his left thigh. Blood oozed between his fingers and the flaps of torn fabric already stained a dark red. Jalal shot a quick glance in Steve's direction, revealing a monstrous visage. A dark purplish unmasking of hatred.

A second later, he disappeared around the corner.

From the same doorway, Patas emerged and followed close on Jalal's heels.

A flannel shirt hung in shreds from her shoulders. Splotches of blood covered exposed flesh. It looked like she held a knife in her hand.

Then, like her brother, she was gone.

The translucent, glass-like finish of the white marble floor gave Steve the impression that the running siblings had been spiraling through space. Only the crimson puddles left in their wake anchored the scene to the harsh reality of what they faced.

As Steve fumbled for the hidden keypad beneath the swath of velvet that framed the ornate door casing, he felt an arm shoving hard against his shoulder. Corey Galloway's body slammed through the French doors. Shards of glass Disney characters shot from the delicate grills. The center styles gave way when the locking mechanisms—squealing in protest—burst free.

Propelled forward, Corey slip-slided on the broken glass and fell hard to the floor. Steve could sense the pain radiating from Corey's body as his bandaged arm took the brunt of the impact. When Corey rolled over and pushed down with both hands, Steve grabbed his shoulders and yanked him to his feet. The two men bolted down the corridor, their footsteps echoing off the marble floor. Both held semi-automatic pistols in their hands.

They slowed at the end of the hallway and peered into a large sitting room. Bulky furniture crowded the carpeted space. Crystal chandeliers hung from the coffered ceiling. Two bloodied bodies were heaped in the corner.

Steve thought he detected a familiar sound. When he glanced back, he saw only Edie and Denzel closing in. He listened again but couldn't pinpoint or identify what he'd sensed. Then all his energy focused on the screams coming from an unseen alcove on the far side of the room.

Guns raised, Steve and Corey darted around the elaborate furnishings blocking their path. They heard, then saw, the bedlam as they turned the last corner.

With the key bent and stuck in the lock, Jalal kicked repeatedly at the closed door. Neither Steve nor Corey had a clean shot. Patas hung onto her brother's back, struggling to stop him from breaking open the door. The knife she'd been wielding lay useless on the floor.

Before Steve or Corey could move forward, Jalal freed one hand and fired a shot in their direction. As they dove behind the corner, chunks of plaster slammed into Steve's eyes, momentarily blocking his vision. When he blinked out the debris he peered around a heavy wood cabinet. He saw Corey crouched behind the far wall.

Steve motioned to him, signaling with his hands how they could rush Jalal. If they kept far enough apart by hugging opposite walls, Jalal might not get both of them. Steve felt a hand on his shoulder and glanced back at Edie. He saw movement from behind a nearby sofa and caught a glint of steel from Denzel's gun. With the lives of the kidnapped victims at stake, including his own two kids, Steve felt helpless. Whatever they chose to do next could get them all killed. Jalal had nothing left to lose.

He detected a definite clatter, more distinct than before. It seemed to originate, not from behind him, but from somewhere else in the suite. He tried to visualize the floorplan Rapunzel had shown them.

With a splintering crunch, Jalal's boot broke the last vestiges of the cracked stile, and the bedroom door flew open. The kids belched out gut-wrenching screams. Catori appeared at the other side of the doorway with a bronze table lamp held in both hands above her head. Although armed with a formidable weapon, the tiny creature proved no match for the enraged terrorist. In a quick series of moves, Jalal thrust Patas aside. Her body slammed against the closest wall with a sickening thud as her head bounced hard.

Jalal swatted the lamp from Catori's grip, letting it crash to the floor. He lifted her to his chest as if she weighed no more than a feather. He faced his challengers, with Catori serving as a shield. His gun kept swinging between Catori's head and the inert form of his sister slumped on the floor about fifteen feet away.

More anguished gasps spilled from the bedroom. Steve grabbed Edie, jerking her back behind the wall as she attempted to lunge toward her babies.

"Make a move and I will kill them all." Jalal's arm cinched tighter around Catori. "This little bitch goes first." He took a step back toward the bedroom door. Rosa and T.C. continued to cry out from inside the room.

Suddenly Rosa's voice changed.

Then it sounded like T.C. had clapped his hands.

Edie screamed at Jalal, "You son of a bitch. Leave 'em alone. You pathetic—"

The rest of her words stopped as a shadowy form from inside the bedroom launched itself at Jalal's back. The force of the impact caused him to lose balance. Catori pulled away but got tangled up in Jalal's flailing legs as he toppled to the floor—fighting off the white German Shepherd.

Amber had tempered her attack as if fearful of hurting Catori.

Denzel joined Steve, Corey, and Edie as they charged toward the bedroom.

Jalal reached out and grabbed the back of Catori's collar, trying to keep her as a shield. He dove for the Sig, which he'd dropped when Amber's jaws bit into his arm. With Catori held in front, he fired a shot at Amber, whose teeth had now sunk deep into his leg.

Uttering a loud yelp, Amber's grip slackened and Jalal shook free. He turned the weapon on his sister, still motionless on the floor. His finger squeezed back on the trigger, getting off a shot before Catori twisted away and planted a quick kick to his groin.

Jalal's screams were cut off when a volley of rounds hit its mark.

Edie dropped her gun and ran into the bedroom, scooping up her babies.

The instant Jalal fired the kill shot at his sister, Corey had thrown himself on top of Patas and took the bullet meant for her.

Steve kicked Jalal's weapon across the room.

Denzel squatted down and pulled Corey's body off Patas. Steve fell to his knees at Amber's side.

Finley and a team of agents charged into the suite.

Against all odds, Jalal was still alive.

His breathing came in shallow, rapid spurts while blood oozed from his nose and lips. All evidence of rage had drained from his face. His lips twitched in an attempt to smile as his final words spilled out. He spoke to no one in particular.

"You are all fools… You think you have beaten me… But you are wrong… The final jihad is underway… This…." He raised a shaking hand and made a weak waving motion. "Is only a small setback… and the infidels lose again… in this great holy war." His chest gave a final heave, and his head dropped to the side.

At first Steve ignored Jalal's words while frantically tending to Amber, but when he caught the expression on Mike Finley's face, a sudden fear tightened his chest.

CHAPTER 67

Denzel eased Corey's body to the floor, placing him face down on his stomach. He peeled up Corey's jacket and stared at the spot where Jalal's bullet struck. He shook his head.

Patas, who had regained consciousness in time to see her brother's gun pointed at her head, began sobbing at the sight of Corey's body. Tears filled her eyes and a wail built in her throat.

Corey shuddered and groaned. "Damn—hurts like hell."

Denzel smiled. "I know you SEAL wusses always gotta wear those vests. But for chrissakes—this is Disneyland."

Amber whimpered and shook her body. Steve dabbed his handkerchief against the upper part of her left front leg. The wound oozed blood, but the bullet had only grazed the skin. "You're okay, girl."

Amber whined again and placed her head on Steve's lap as Rosa ran to his side. Tears streamed down her face. Steve put an arm around her. "She's gonna be fine, sweetie." He looked up to see Edie and Catori standing in the doorway. Edie held T.C., who appeared to have fallen asleep.

"It was like a magic show, Daddy. I heard this scratching noise and then Amber burst through a small door," Rosa said.

Steve gave Rosa a confused look. Finley walked over and squatted at his side. "A set of service stairs ends in a utility closet in the bedroom. Your friend downstairs— Rapunzel? Really?—showed us the floorplan. Amber took the lead before we could stop her."

* * * * * *

Corey pulled himself to a sitting position and ignored Denzel's chides. He stared at Patas, worried about the extent of her injuries.

Denzel stepped in and covered Patas with a blanket. He informed her that the paramedics were on their way up the stairs. While keeping her eyes on Corey, she said to Denzel, "I'm okay. It's just a graze and some minor cuts."

Denzel faded into the background.

Patas threw her arms around Corey's neck and clutched onto him as hard as she could. He stiffened while stifling a gasp as the pain shot out from at least one broken rib—more likely two or three.

Patas pulled back and bit her lip, probably thinking he didn't want to see her. Her face clouded. "Sorry. I suppose I've changed since the last time you saw me." She shrugged and wrung her hands together. "Maybe you don't even remember what I looked like before."

His heart beat faster as he gazed at her new appearance. An unbidden image flashed into his head. He saw the dripping Champagne bottle. The hijab and the long silky garment dropping to the floor. The delicate blush of her cheeks and her probing, deep brown eyes. Jet black hair caressing her shoulders and framing a chiseled jawline.

Corey felt his face flush but never took his eyes off this lovely creature before him. He had waited three years to see her and to tell her how much she meant to him. All he could say was, "I'd never forget those eyes." His hand reached out and touched her chin, raising it up. He couldn't stop the smile from forming. He moved his hand behind her neck but didn't have to coax her. Together they leaned closer. Lips coming together in a passionate exchange. When they separated, Corey mumbled, "You look damn good with blond hair too."

She playfully punched his arm. When he winced, she whispered in his ear. Corey wondered how he'd accomplish that without massive doses of painkillers. But as a Navy SEAL, he'd give it a shot.

Chapter 68

Washington, D.C.
September 12
1:56 am

President Griffin hung up the phone and glanced around the Oval Office. Mike Finley had given him the final rundown on the events in Anaheim, reassuring him that Jalal Ta'anari had died at the scene.

To the president, his voice sounded restrained. When questioned, Finley said before Jalal died, he'd made additional threats. He listened to Finley's concerns and gave him the authority to further interrogate all surviving terrorists apprehended from any of the attack sites across the country. He ended the call after brief chats with Steve, Edie, Patas, and Corey, thanking them for their assistance.

Olivia Davenport remained in the San Francisco Bay Area where the president had ordered her to go. Once again, Griffin thought, he'd gotten it wrong. Jalal Ta'anari had played him, and he'd taken the bait. For most of the day the terrorists had maintained the upper hand. They blindsided him before the day had dawned by cutting down his close friend and mentor, Alice Andersen. He'd never forgive himself for not beefing up her security in light of the warnings received prior to this year's 9/11 anniversary.

The latest reports from the intelligence chiefs pointed to Jalal Ta'anari as one of the major orchestrators for the wave of attacks across the nation. The president leafed through a dossier on Ta'anari and shook his head.

"For all the good this did us—I could've thrown it into the fireplace. How the hell did we let that son of a bitch back into the country?" He'd already vowed that heads would roll for that mistake but knew the responsibility for security failures rested with him.

Not for the first time, he chastised himself.

I must be getting soft.

Letting those self-righteous social justice fanatics interfere with the safety of this nation.

He rubbed his hands over his eyes and then stared out the window at the waiting helicopter.

Seven years.

What the hell have I accomplished?

His thoughts turned to Edie Pauling. He'd been pushing her hard. She's back in politics and hopefully heading to Washington.

In a loud voice, he spoke out, aiming his words at the portrait of George Washington over the fireplace. "Well, that's one politician ready to stand her ground."

The president jumped when the private door to the Oval Office opened.

"Sir? Did you call for us?" the agent asked.

Shaken back to reality, Griffin checked the time and nodded. "Later than I thought. Yes, it's time to go." He hesitated and asked, "The media?"

The agent shook his head. "As ordered, sir, this flight is blacked out. And only one chopper. Outside of your security team, no one has the details of the schedule unless you personally informed someone of your destination. Once you're in the air we'll apprise the three agents on duty at your retreat of our impending arrival time." The agent paused and cleared his throat. "Mr. President? It's not too late to alert the squad at Base Andrews to scramble additional aircraft and security personnel. Policy dictates—"

The president shook his head and smiled. "It's been a long day for everyone, son. Sorry you guys drew the short straws."

"Then if you don't mind a little more company, Mr. President, we'll make sure all other seats on Marine One are occupied by your security detail."

Griffin nodded once. With a smile, he added, "The first lady has plans to cook breakfast for everyone at the house tomorrow… so we might need to make a quick detour to the Newton Shoprite. You guys eat almost as much as my son Sean."

The young agent relaxed and spoke into his lapel mike.

The president stood, collected the files on his desk, and stuffed them into an already bulging briefcase—the same one he'd carried for years. His escorts walked with him through the West Wing and onto the South Lawn. A few minutes later, Marine One lifted off and headed toward Stillwater, New Jersey, taking the leader of the free world back home.

From inside the lavish cabin, the president looked out the window as the lights of the White House grounds and Capitol Hill faded. A haunted expression crossed his face. A cold shiver shot through his body. Shrugging it off, he sat back, closed his eyes, and pictured Alison, Brianna, and Sean asleep in their Stillwater retreat. His two older boys would be joining them tomorrow evening.

He patted the plush armrest on his seat. The aging VH-3 Sea Kings would be mothballed before the end of his final term. They had served as presidential transports for the White House for almost sixty years. But a lack of parts, extensive hours, and poor efficiency by today's standards dictated the change. At the moment, President Griffin felt a deep kinship with the Sea Kings.

Chapter 69

Green Township, New Jersey
September 12
2:59 am

Trinca Airport is located approximately seven air miles southeast of the president's personal retreat in Stillwater, New Jersey. The private grass airstrip in Green Township is owned by a well-seasoned Korean War vet. He is the manager, mechanic, groundkeeper, flight instructor, and fuel attendant. He prefers the locally endowed title of '*crusty old bastard*'.

When the mood hits him, he's also the part-time air traffic controller. He can be seen wearing his worn leather flight jacket and holding a portable handheld radio, staring into the sky. On occasion he'll stick a moistened index finger into the wind and begrudgingly respond to an incoming private pilot's request for landing instructions.

Much of his time is spent tinkering with his baby, a Piper J-3 Cub; circa 1946. Rumor has it he had piloted its maiden flight. He claims to have still been in diapers at the time and had to stand on the seat to get a clear view of the horizon.

Air traffic in and out of this quiet airstrip had increased significantly this week as pilots flew vintage aircraft into the rural community in preparation for next weekend's Sussex County Air Show. For the moment, under the supposed keen eye of the airport manager, a small fleet of biplanes from WWI and WWII sat on the apron, keeping the J-3 Cub company.

At this late hour, the crusty old bastard was usually sound asleep in front of the TV inside the small residence on the east side of the airfield.

Tonight—that didn't happen. His body rested in a pool of blood underneath an old tool bench in the far corner of the rusting Quonset hut which served as the airport's original hanger when it first opened sometime in the mid-twentieth century.

A half-dozen men sat in the cramped office next to the runway. Earlier today, while the sun was still high, one of the biplanes had been rolled into the hanger. Two of the men worked on the engine, fitting it with a cam disk, cam follower, and control yoke to synchronize the firing of the fuselage-mounted Colt-Browning 7.62mm machine gun they brought with them.

After waiting the remainder of the day and most of the night, the jihadists feared the operation had been scrubbed. When the call came in well after midnight, they scrambled to prep the planes. At the designated time, five biplanes and a single Piper J-3 Cub taxied down the dark grass strip and, one by one, took off for the short flight.

Speed was not an issue, but early detection could be a problem. They hugged the fields and treetops, flying near stall speeds. Maneuvering under such conditions could be suicidal, but that was the purpose of tonight's mission.

None of the men expected to see the light of the next day.

Chapter 70

Stillwater, New Jersey
September 12
3:26 am

The president blinked open his eyes, feeling the gradual shift in airspeed and the vibrations accompanying the landing gear deployment as Marine One approached his Stillwater retreat. The craft started its near-vertical descent. This maneuver helped with noise abatement control to avoid shaking his closest neighbors from their beds.

Griffin shrugged off any remnants of sleep and glanced at his untouched briefcase. He had intended to catch up on the reports from other cabinet members which he'd ignored during this latest crisis. The overwhelming fatigue of the horrific day had taken its toll, so he'd try to get to it tomorrow—actually later today. The sun would be rising in a few hours.

He looked down at the large colonial estate, and the day's tensions melted away.

Two agents stood to the side of the landing zone, each holding a shoulder-mounted surface-to-air missile launcher at his side. He knew the third man remained in the secret service's on-site command center—a small cottage on the eastern edge of the landscaped plateau where the Griffin estate sat.

Anxious to see his family, he unclasped the seat restraint on the captain's chair and crossed the cabin. He knelt near the doorway and peered through the closest window. One of the agents sitting in the side bench seat gave the president a quick smile but didn't question the chief executive's actions. As surreptitiously as possible he turned from Griffin and whispered something in his communicator to the pilot.

When Marine One's landing gear hovered several feet from the ground, an urgent message blared over the cabin's speaker system. The screens on the newly installed low altitude enhanced radar system in the command center at the president's estate had lit up. At the same time, Marine One's collision avoidance warning alarms screeched.

Several small aircraft had appeared out of nowhere, seemingly springing from the branches of the huge oak trees lining the western perimeter of the property. Griffin looked on in disbelief as one of the single engine planes climbed for several seconds and then dove straight at his house.

The scene unfolded in such a bizarre series of events that at first the grim realization of the attack had escaped the president's rational thinking. The vintage biplane had flown into the roof of the south-facing sunroom, the main feature spanning the entire front of the two-story stone colonial residence. The most vulnerable point of the structure. The wall and ceiling glass panels disintegrated on impact.

A huge fireball erupted and flames mushroomed upward.

The voice of the agent in the service's command center boomed from the speakers in the chopper. "Three more bogeys approaching on collision course. Abort landing. Repeat. Abort landing."

The pilot ordered the president back to his seat and began to throttle up the engines. With his eyes fixed on the burning house and the thoughts of his family trapped inside, Griffin pulled the emergency lever on the door. A small charge ejected the door/stair ramp unit, catapulting it away from the fuselage and into the ground. The noise of the revving engines rushing in blasted the previous quiet of the insulated cabin.

Before anyone from his detail could act, President Griffin jumped from the aircraft and hit the ground as the craft started to climb. He rolled away from the downdraft of the rotating blades. When he reached the abrupt edge of the landscaped plateau, his body tumbled into a deep ravine as three converging biplanes collided with the helicopter. The explosion shook the ground and lit up the sky. The smell of high-octane aviation fuel replaced the usual scents of the late-summer blossoms that had hung in the nighttime dews.

Griffin shook himself off and clawed back up the hill, toward the house. From over his shoulder he heard the growing drone of another approaching aircraft. The two agents were lining up shots with their anti-aircraft armaments as the *rat-a-tat-tat—rat-a-tat-tat* of the fuselage-mounted machine gun on the vintage biplane cut them both down.

One of the agents had managed to launch a missile before being hit. Instead of the biplane's original path of nose-diving into the house, it exploded and dropped onto the command center. A secondary blast disintegrated the cottage, killing the last agent inside.

Griffin charged forward as the proliferating flames engulfed his house. It appeared the sole biplane which crashed into it had no additional explosives on board. But the highly flammable aviation fuel was doing its job. The intensity of the heat and flames made entry through the front foyer impossible. Running around the outside of the attached three-car garage, Griffin found the rear service door approachable. He yanked it open and called out to his family.

He headed inside and crossed through the laundry room and kitchen. When he entered the large family room, he noticed that the massive concrete and stone structure comprising the interior rear wall of the sunroom had kept the plane from penetrating the rooms on the main level. But the fire continued to grow and spread to the upper floor. The escalating smoke was already making the air difficult to breathe. He heard voices coming from Sean's bedroom. Thank God the kids' rooms were located on the north side—far from the point of impact in the sunroom. He ran down the hall and saw his daughter, Brianna, trying to coax Sean out the door. He snatched Sean up in his arms and grabbed Brianna's hand. As fast as he could, he guided her through the smoke-filled first floor and out the service door.

After stopping a safe distance from the burning inferno, he lowered Sean next to Brianna.

"Where's your mother?"

Brianna clasped her cheeks with both hands. "After she got me and Sean out of the house, she told us to wait down by the pond. Then she ran back inside—I think Slugger is stuck in one of the guest rooms upstairs. We heard him barking when Mom was getting us out." She glanced at her brother. "Before I could grab him, Sean followed Mom back into the house. I caught up with him in his room."

As Brianna finished speaking, Griffin heard Slugger's barks coming from inside the house. He knew Alison would never leave their Irish Wolfhound behind. He pointed the kids toward the pond at the western edge of the lawn. "Do like your mother said and wait near the water. You understand that, Sean? I'll go get her."

"But Dad!" Brianna cried out. "Let me—"

"Go! Now!" He pointed again. "Take care of Sean."

He turned and ran back inside the house. Stomping through the family room, he headed toward the staircase and the sounds of Slugger's barks. He crouched close to the floor as he reached the second story. The barking came from down the hallway on the right. As he crawled into the guest bedroom in the east wing, the smoke thickened and flames licked across the ceiling. Slugger jumped at him and continued barking. He saw Alison's body slumped beside the bed. He sprinted forward and heaved her over his shoulder and dove out of the room as a section of the ceiling came crashing down. The flames intensified as it devoured the added oxygen.

Carrying Alison down the steps, Griffin burst out one of the patio doors on the east side of the family room. Slugger ran at his side, and they joined Brianna and Sean by the pond. He placed the first lady gently down on the lawn. She coughed and gasped for air. He tore off what remained of his shirt and directed Brianna to soak it in the cool pond water.

After he wiped the sweat and grime from her face, the first lady looked more alert. With the president's help, she sat up—her eyes darting wildly about. She reached out to Sean and Brianna and pulled them to her breast.

"We're fine, Mom," Brianna squeaked out.

Alison looked at Tyler. "What about the guys?"

He shook his head. "They didn't make it."

She shut her eyes, shaking her head.

Griffin stood up and scanned the sky. It showed the first signs of graying as dawn approached.

"More terrorists could be on the way. We need to leave—now." He spotted the government's Suburban parked in a carport near the security gate. Alison tried to get to her feet but lost her balance and plopped back to the ground.

"Stay. I'll bring it around."

As he jogged toward the carport he checked the sky for signs of more planes. Circling past what remained of Marine One, his anger ratcheted up, thinking of the fallen agents who'd accompanied him from the White House, and the dead agents scattered on his front lawn and inside the command center. The air remained thick from the burning house and the acrid fumes of the aviation fuel.

Climbing in the Suburban, he started the engine and backed it out of the carport. He cued up the emergency radio and gave the watch commander a quick rundown of the situation as he drove toward his family. They'd already dispatched a team within seconds of receiving the automated distress signals from Marine One.

The president's brain churned into overdrive as he ran down the short list of people who knew his planned itinerary. His eyes widened in amazement as he realized it could only be one person.

"That two-timing sonofabitch." His head fumed with the potential fallout if they made this implication public.

He'd gotten about halfway to the pond when a yellow single-engine plane popped above the nearby tree line. In the emerging light, he recognized it as a vintage Piper Cub. He looked toward the pond. Alison and Brianna were waving their arms wildly and pointing skyward. He spun the wheel hard and accelerated, trying to distance himself from Alison and the kids.

An instant later the small plane crashed into the Suburban. The president never heard the screams as his family ran toward the fiery wreck.

CHAPTER 71

A small suburb south of Chicago
(approximately 55 years ago)

Every event has consequences. In most cases, at the time of the occurrence, it is not possible to predict potential long-range impacts on the course of history.

In the greater scheme of racial tensions and the violent uprisings that swept across America in the mid-1960s, the brief conflict that occurred on a hot summer night in Dixmoor, Illinois, was considered a minor blip on the radar screen.

Dixmoor is a suburb of Chicago. The attempted shoplifting at a local liquor store sparked the incident, dubbed the Gin Bottle Riot. When the shopkeeper wrestled with the young African American female perpetrator from Chicago, he was accused of brutally beating the woman. This triggered several nights of protests and rioting on the streets of the small community. Dozens were injured and a number of arrests ensued before the brief firestorm ended.

Another visitor from Chicago during that same time period, seventeen-year-old Rebecca Patterson, got caught up in the heat of the moment. Four police officers grabbed the frightened African American teenager and flung her in the back of a squad car after she refused to remove herself from the middle of the street.

Earlier in the day Rebecca Patterson had scraped up her last few dollars and boarded a bus for Dixmoor, trying to track down her drug-addicted ex-boyfriend to beg him for money. He'd disappeared almost seven months ago—the very next morning after Rebecca informed him she was pregnant. She'd recently discovered him shacked up with another woman in Dixmoor. That reunion hadn't gone well, and Rebecca left empty handed. She wandered aimlessly until she walked into the midst of the brewing riots.

On the way to the local precinct, Rebecca went into labor in the back of the squad car. The terrified young police officer pulled over and helped deliver a baby boy. Shaken, he dropped the young mother and newborn infant off at the emergency room of a nearby community hospital, never reporting the incident to his superiors. No one ever linked the name, Rebecca Patterson, to the Gin Bottle Riot, until years later when a budding politician embellished his own version of the story to rally potential voters to his platform.

While resting in the emergency room, Rebecca Patterson looked down at the tiny creature swaddled in her arms. Transfixed, she sucked in a deep breath, her senses fusing with a tangy scent of sugared milk, softened by a delicate floral bouquet. Her heart almost burst when she grasped the enormity of this new responsibility.

She whispered, "Hi, Evander." And gently placed a moist kiss on his shiny bare head. Evander had been her grandfather's name.

Baby Evander's eyes blinked open and besieged his mother. His first smile spread across a wrinkled face and took Rebecca's breath away. Years later, Evander Patterson had honed that particular skill until it never failed him while on the campaign trail. And by that time, he'd developed a number of such tricks in his repertoire.

Evander had a gift for influencing people. His mother had been the first, but certainly not the last. That helpless bundle in Rebecca's arms changed her life. From that moment on, she swore Evander would never wind up like his father. She struggled to find work and eventually got a job as a live-in housekeeper for a wealthy but childless couple in Chicago. They too were mesmerized by Evander and gave him every opportunity to make something out of himself.

The tenacity and will to survive came from Rebecca. The refinement, education, and a guaranteed place in society were gifts from Rebecca's employer.

The natural-born confidence, oratory skills, and political savvy were his.

* * * * * *

In a somber ceremony on the morning of September 12th, Chief Justice Austin Gildebrand swore in Vice President Evander Patterson as the forty-seventh president of the United States.

Four days later the world looked on as America buried two presidents. In less than twenty-four hours after learning of former President Alice Andersen's assassination, the nation was struck a second blow when

President Tyler Griffin died as part of the same ongoing series of terrorist attacks.

Not knowing the extent of the evil that had occurred on the anniversary of 9/11 and avoiding the emotional turmoil she felt from the deaths of two of her closest friends, Edie Pauling threw herself into her US senatorial campaign.

Steve remained supportive but kept his own feelings to himself. When he thought about the hatred and violence driven by the growing divisiveness from opposing political discourses, he considered the consequences from the coming election. And how the results would impact the well-being of his family.

He and Edie had been thrown together by the fallout of a corrupt leadership in Washington.

Where would this next step take them?

CHAPTER 72

Southern California Coast
November 15

The nation experienced a low voter turnout for last week's elections. In general, off-year campaigns don't generate a lot of interest, and this year proved no different.

The insidious terrorist plot coinciding with the 9/11 anniversary, while leaving Americans stunned at the targeting of both the former president and the current leader of the free world, had once again taken its usual backseat to the everyday lives of ordinary citizens.

From the time Evander Patterson had been sworn in as the forty-seventh president of the United States following the ruthless slaying of Tyler Griffin, the explosive political environment that had escalated during the Griffin administration appeared, at least for the moment, to have run out of fuel.

One particular special election in California did, however, hold the interest of the former chairman of the California democrat party, Daniel H. Chauncey. At this juncture in Chauncey's life, party affiliations were meaningless. Democrat—republican—independent: it didn't matter. What mattered to him was the propensity of the individual to succumb to his demands. After the unbridled success of getting his man into the White House—without the fuss of running a campaign—he had looked ahead and chose to tie up a few loose ends.

And he considered Edie Pauling to be one of those loose ends.

Pauling, a staunch advocate for Griffin and the Restraint in Government Alliance, had fought her way to the top of the polls. She was considered an outsider, only a contender in the race due to the recent change in the state's constitution regarding the rules for primary elections. Prospective US senatorial candidates competed in non-party affiliated fields, and the top two vote-getters advanced to the general election.

As election day drew near, most polls had the candidates in a dead heat.

Almost a year ago, when Daniel Chauncey learned of his old colleague Senator Mahorney's ill health and inability to complete his term, he had already selected a suitable replacement. Chauncey now chided himself for not acting with more force against Edie Pauling from the start of the special election primary for Mahorney's California US senate seat.

He had made a brief attempt at dissuading Pauling from getting into the national political spotlight by orchestrating a veiled threat against her family on the same day her campaign shifted into high gear. The apparent terrorist-inspired kidnapping of her two kids and a close family friend had gone unheeded. Perhaps Chauncey's techniques were too subtle. She had not gotten the message. And the assassination of two presidents on that same 9/11 anniversary seemed to have the opposite effect. Pauling dove into the campaign and dialed up the rhetoric faster than her opponent could hope to deter.

Ten days before election day, Daniel Chauncey stepped in. He garnered the power and might of the nation's largest and richest political machines. He unleashed a smear campaign that hit with the sudden force of a major earthquake and spread faster than the most devastating wildfire in California's history.

Chauncey's advocacy groups launched a massive attack on Edie Pauling, bombarding the local and national airwaves with a series of political ads aimed at gunning down not only her qualifications, but her character. Chauncey's internet campaign pulled out all the stops and denigrated the aspiring young politician.

Still, on election day, Edie Pauling held on. For most of the day and a good part of the evening hours, exit polls gave Pauling a slight edge. The race was so close that voters didn't learn of her defeat until the next morning.

Today, Daniel H. Chauncey sat on the deck of his estate, perched high on the cliffs overlooking the vast Pacific Ocean. After folding a copy of the Santa Barbara News-Press, he stared south through the clear glass railing panels at the distant images of the Channel Islands and the lesser land masses lined up in a westerly arc. He took a final sip of his coffee and considered where he'd dine this evening. More important, whom he'd invite to join him.

Not one to dwell on recent victories, he still considered himself a patient man. But not so patient as to have allowed Tyler Griffin to finish out his second term.

Late last summer, Chauncey learned that Griffin had chosen not to lend support to his vice president, Evander Patterson, for the next presidential election. And that could present a problem.

This information, not yet made public, had come from Chauncey's top source in the White House.

The same man who disclosed that story had also leaked key information regarding the SEAL raid in Yemen and Griffin's secret itinerary to his New Jersey estate on the last anniversary of 9/11. Plus dozens of other key reports on the inner workings of the Griffin administration.

And now that same man sat in the Oval Office. Chauncey looked forward to, if things went his way, nine years of manipulating President Evander Patterson.

That led him to another potential loose end that needed fixing. Butch Carlisle, the new senior senator from California, needed to go away. Chauncey considered him an inconsequential simpleton with an overblown ego, but that made him potentially more dangerous. This last thought had just solidified Chauncey's dinner guest list. He'd make reservations for two at 8:00 pm at his favorite California French restaurant, bouchon Santa Barbara.

And if Edie Pauling threw her hat into another California jungle primary to replace the soon to be deceased Senator Carlisle—well—that might make for another fine Santa Barbara dining experience in the near future.

CHAPTER 73

Davis, California
New Year's Eve

Patas held tight to one end of the nylon pull toy as Kobe's teeth dug in and whipped his head back and forth. Her hair had almost returned to its natural dark luster as the lightened strands grew out. From the sofa, Corey watched her struggle to keep his dad's German Shepherd from yanking her prone form across the living room carpet.

The Christmas tree stood in the corner, lights twinkling through glistening strands of silvery garland. Corey couldn't remember the last time his father's house had been adorned with any type of Christmas decorations. Certainly not since his mother had died.

"I don't know what's wrong with you kids," Ethan Galloway said. His old leather recliner creaked as he shifted his body. "It's New Year's Eve—you should be out having a good time—not babysitting an old man and his dog. There're plenty of parties in downtown Davis. I should've worked the night shift as usual. This is one of the quieter times for the university's security staff. Most of the parties are off campus."

Patas let go of her end of the pull toy and Kobe turned his attention to Corey by planting it in his lap. She propped herself up with both hands and got to her feet. Standing behind Ethan's chair, Patas reached her arms around his neck and kissed the top of his head.

"Daa—dd," she said in a lyrical tone and playfully tussled his hair.

Corey saw that his dad couldn't stop grinning.

Patas had been given a new identity—Patty Basara—by the president, over three years ago. She had burst into the somber and lonely lives of the Galloways on a fateful Halloween night in Sacramento where she had been the prime suspect in the attempted assassination of the California governor.

This year on Halloween, Corey gave Patas another new name—Patas Galloway. They'd gotten married in Las Vegas. All government records still showed that Patas Ta'anari had died more than three years ago.

"We told you. Corey wants to get an early start tomorrow, Dad." Patas scooted over and sat next to Corey while plucking Kobe's toy from his lap and tossing it into the kitchen.

She nestled her head against Corey's shoulder. The injuries Patas and Corey sustained leading up to and including the 9/11 anniversary had healed. Corey was scheduled to report to Naval Base Coronado for a quick two-week refresher stint before his next overseas deployment in February.

Patas had not lost her passion for reforming her religion. In light of the violence witnessed by opposing factions exemplified during her rallies for Islam, Corey and Patas struggled with a suitable compromise to her approach. She transferred to San Diego State University and agreed to focus her attention on local projects while working toward a bachelor's degree. At least for the next several months.

"We got a ton of things to do in our apartment before I ship out." Corey winked at Patas and rose from the sofa. He headed into the kitchen.

Ethan looked at Patas. She smiled and remained silent.

From the kitchen, a loud popping noise caused Kobe's ears to perk up. A few seconds later, Corey returned holding a tray with two glasses of Champagne and one glass of water.

Ethan checked his watch and raised his eyebrows. "It's not even 8:30. Don't you think it's a bit early to ring in the new year?"

Corey passed the glasses out and stood between Patas and his father. He held up his glass as Patas got up from the sofa and joined him.

Beaming, Corey said, "We've got something else to celebrate—Grandpa. It was a big disappointment to find out Edie had lost the election, but at least something good came from that night."

CHAPTER 74

Sonoma, California
New Year's Day

Edie couldn't remember the last time this happened. Steve jolted awake so fast that Amber, who had been sound asleep against the footboard, raised her head and barked twice before letting out a loud groan and settling back down with her head resting on the oak rail.

Steve sat up and slapped both hands against his temples. Edie watched the dim light reflect off his blue eyes as the dawn gained traction against the darkness. She turned, arching her head and rubbing a hand across his shoulder. Feeling the tension throbbing from his clammy neck muscles, she said, "What's wrong, babe?" She pushed up higher, bringing herself closer to him and pressed her body tight to his back. "You're shivering, Steve. And your skin's soaking wet."

Steve took a deep breath and rubbed his eyes. He shook his head, letting out another mouthful of air. He reached his arm around Edie's waist. She could still feel the cool dampness as his hand embraced the warm flesh of her abdomen. As she coddled his hand and brought it to her lips, the tremors evaporated.

He made a clumsy attempt to stroke her neck, and said, "Just trying to get your attention. We gotta couple minutes before Rosa and the baby wake up. Thought we'd fool around a bit."

Edie caught the hitch in his voice and knew he was avoiding whatever had startled him awake. "Nice try, Mr. Macho Firefighter, but talking about your dream is a much better way to release the tension." Her hand tugged on his chin, turning his head toward her. She stared at him until she sensed that every smartass answer got washed out of his head.

Steve sighed and twisted his legs over the side of the bed, feeling along the floor for his shorts. He slipped them on and walked to the window. He pulled back the drapes, letting in a rush of the swelling brightness. After a few seconds, he swung back around. Edie felt his eyes grow hungry and caress her naked body. She waved a finger at him and, in one smooth motion, jumped up and swept the bulky black and red sweatshirt from the bedpost, shimmying into it. Next, she plopped back on top of the bedcovers and motioned with her hand, patting the pillow for Steve to join her.

When she saw a familiar look spring from his eyes, she added, "You're going talk to me, Steve."

With a resigned expression, he snuggled next to her.

"It's been years, I can't even recall the last time." He gave her a light jab. "And you've gotten me to fess up about all this before."

"Your dad? You dreamed about your dad?" At first Edie felt herself relax—but a sudden rumination constricted her gut. She kept her face neutral.

Steve nodded and then shrugged. "Right. Back in the day—before you came into my life—I had this constant nightmare—could never understand what my dad was trying to tell me. In the dreams—like in real life—he always wound up dead before he could spit it out. I'd wake up from the same never-ending story."

He smiled at Edie. "After our little trip up north to see what Dad had been up to for those last years, the nightmares shifted into pleasant dreams as I began remembering the good times before—" He stopped and leaned over to kiss Edie's forehead.

She sensed this wasn't another attempt to end the talking and segue into a more physical mode, so she enjoyed the tender sentiment and remained quiet as he gathered his thoughts.

He swallowed hard. "But this was different than those old nightmares. It was as if Dad was calling out to me from the grave. He looked so desperate. Pleading to me. He wanted me to know the truth. And forgive him."

Steve exhaled and once again slapped his hands to his temples. "Jesus! What an idiot I am."

Edie understood where he was heading, but Steve's sudden change in demeanor still startled her. She hesitated before asking, "What're you talking about, Steve?"

"Damn. It's Uncle Vinnie. Don't you see?"

Not long after Edie's loss in the senatorial race, Steve got a call from his cousin Dominick. He informed Steve that Uncle Vinnie, recently paroled from the federal penitentiary in New Jersey, had suddenly taken ill. The doctors gave him only days to live. At the time, Edie had been in New Jersey with the kids visiting her brothers. She got to spend a few hours with Uncle Vinnie before Steve arrived. By the time he flew in from California to see Vinnie, it was near the end, but at least he had the chance to say goodbye.

Steve shook his head. Edie could see him fighting back the tears. "Guess I'll never know what Dad tried to tell me." He sighed. "And then at Uncle Vinnie's bedside, when I leaned in closer to hear him better, I still couldn't make any sense of what he said about my dad. His words sounded incoherent. And now he's dead too. I suppose that's what's haunting me. I'll just never know."

Before Steve finished talking, Edie had gotten up and stood at the foot of the bed, stroking Amber's belly. For several moments she let her eyes drift across the room as if she were a stranger in her own home. She shut her eyes and hesitated even longer before making up her mind. When they opened, she locked onto Steve's puzzled gaze and said, "Steve, I think I can answer some of your questions."

Edie made her decision—there would be no going back.

She felt a sudden chill run down her spine.

Until now, their life together had been an open book. She now feared how Steve would react. No matter how well she knew him, this was something she couldn't fix. And with the fragile relationship that had once existed between Steve and his father, she dreaded his response. And what this could do to their own relationship.

As she opened her mouth to speak, Rosa called out from the hallway, banging on the door. "T.C.'s awake—aagghh—he didn't make it to the potty. And I'm hungry."

THE END

Afterword

While I was working on the final edit for *Amber Waves of Grain*, our beloved German Shepherd, Greta, passed away. After sharing ten and a half memorable years with this magnificent creature, she will be forever missed. My wife Addie and I were blessed to bring Greta into our lives and are eternally grateful for the joy she gave to us.

As you may have guessed, Amber, the lead canine character in *The Amber Restrained Series* is patterned after Greta. Not so much her physical characteristics; but most of Amber's temperament, personality, and intelligence are clearly borrowed from Greta. Amber's looks come from our second dog, Sophie, a pure white German Shepherd whose image appears on several book covers in the series. In all honesty though, quite a bit of Sophie's quirky disposition is also woven into Amber's distinctive nature.

While taking an undeniable measure of literary license in the details describing training techniques, nosework activities, search and rescue work, and the K9 practices that Amber and several other canine characters in the series carry out, I believe I may have still grossly underestimated the remarkable abilities of these special animals.

As expected, Sophie—two years younger than Greta—was also devastated by the sudden disappearance of her lifelong friend. She is, however, not alone as a third canine companion joined our family slightly more than a year ago. If you've finished reading *Amber Waves of Grain*, you will have already gotten a brief glance at this youngest member of the family: Reckless.

The venues for the opening scenes of *Amber Waves of Grain* were inspired by the several trips made to select and adopt Reckless into our family. At this point I must remind the reader to review the disclaimer which appears on the copyright page of this current work of fiction. And let your own imagination filter out truth from fabrication.

Never far from our thoughts, Greta will live forever in the hearts and minds of our family. I hope that the inspiration she provided has in some small way been immortalized in the deeds and actions of a white German Shepherd called Amber.

In loving memory of Greta,

Ron Vergona

Author's Notes

Amber Waves of Grain is the seventh book in *The Amber Restrained Series*. The series chronicles the escapades of two disparate individuals, Steve Casella and Edie Pauling, who surmount their differences and form an interminable bond that takes them on a journey to fight the injustices assailing the American dream. Together they challenge the seemingly unending barrage of incompetence and corruption that is ignored, facilitated, or orchestrated by the almost invincible power structure of an encroaching government. Along for the ride is Amber, a dog Steve has rescued from a fatal house fire. The sometimes disobedient canine companion is a constant source of frustration and amusement, but as part of their team, no one is more capable to assist when times get rough. As the nation and the world gather at the brink of extinction, Steve and Edie desperately try to gain traction against the slippery slope toward ultimate destruction.

<<ronvergona.net>>

Books by Ron Vergona

Opposition Reflex

Terrible Swift Sword

The Guarding State

Targeted Validation

Amber Alert

Justice Matters

Amber Waves of Grain

www.ingramcontent.com/pod-product-compliance
Lightning Source LLC
Chambersburg PA
CBHW050915250626
47155CB00001B/241